03/03/09

P9-DVI-375

6

The
Blood Ballad

**Center Point
Large Print**

**This Large Print Book carries the
Seal of Approval of N.A.V.H.**

The
Blood Ballad

A Torie O'Shea Mystery

RETT MACPHERSON

CENTER POINT PUBLISHING
THORNDIKE, MAINE

This Center Point Large Print edition
is published in the year 2008 by arrangement with
St. Martin's Press.

The text of this Large Print edition is unabridged. In other
aspects, this book may vary from the original edition.
Printed in the United States of America.
Set in 16-point Times New Roman type.

ISBN: 978-1-60285-219-8

Library of Congress Cataloging-in-Publication Data

MacPherson, Rett.
    The blood ballad : a Torie O'Shea mystery / Rett MacPherson.--Center Point large print ed.
    p. cm.
    ISBN: 978-1-60285-219-8 (lib. bdg. : alk. paper)
    1. O'Shea, Torie (Fictitious character)--Fiction. 2. Women genealogists--Fiction.
  3. Missouri--Fiction. 4. Large type books. I. Title.

PS3563.A3257B57 2008b
813'.54--dc22

2008006150

IN LOVING MEMORY OF MY GRANDFATHER,
Lawrence Allen (1892-1976),
who gave the gift of music to his children,
and whom I adored unconditionally

Acknowledgments

The author would like to thank the following people:

My agent, Merrilee Heifetz; her assistant, Claire Reilly Shapiro; and all the people at Writers House. Also, my editor, Kelley Ragland, and her assistant, Matt Martz, for all of their hard work.

My writing group: Tom Drennan, Martha Kneib, Laurell K. Hamilton, Debbie Millitello, Sharon Shinn, and Mark Sumner. Also, a big thank you to Jonathan Green and Darla Cook.

And to all of my uncles who played music with my father and helped to make all of those special childhood memories of "the boys playing." Music is a spiritual experience, an expression of life and the history of a people.

Thank you, as usual, to my husband, Joe, and my kids for not kicking me out of the house, for not getting too angry when I racked up all of those overdue charges at the library, and for allowing me to listen to the most obscure music at all times of the day without a revolution.

One

Eighty-two years ago, Isabelle Mercer was a girl like many other girls of the day. She was about to be married. Her father had just become mayor of New Kassel and she read the St. Louis society pages every day. Faithfully," Rachel said. She stood in my living room, wrapped in a shower curtain and wearing her hair piled on top of her head in a big loose bun. "Her fiancé came from the glitzy world of Westmoreland and Portland in St. Louis, and Isabelle Mercer wanted to fit in terribly. Then one night after she had spent the evening at her friend Verna's house, Isabelle disappeared into the night, never to be seen again."

When my daughter had finished her little spiel, she looked at me with a mixture of triumph and hope. That is until her younger sister, Mary, rolled her eyes and said, "Loser."

"Mom!" Rachel screeched. "Don't listen to her."

"I'm not listening to her," I said.

"You know as well as I that I did good. I did good, didn't I? Say it?"

"Yes, you did good."

"Good enough to get the job?" she asked. If possible, she made her big brown eyes even bigger. That works on her dad, but since my mom has the same brown eyes, I've been immune for a while.

I was in the middle of trying to find somebody to give tours of the historical homes of our native New

Kassel, Missouri. It's a nice, very small tourist town located on the Mississippi River, and people come from miles around for our festivals, food, and antiques. I am the owner of two historical landmarks, the Gaheimer House and the Kendall House, and I'm also head of the historical society. It's my job to hire people for this sort of thing, and Rachel desperately wanted to be hired.

"So do I get the job?" she asked. "You know I can do it. I even did all that research on my own."

"What?" Mary screeched. "You liar. I helped!"

"Did you even know about Isabelle Mercer?" Rachel asked, ignoring Mary's indignant cries. "Huh?"

"No, actually," I admitted. Rachel acted as if I knew the name of every single person who had ever lived in this town. It was nice to know that she still thought of me as being nearly supernatural. I had thought of my mother as having supernatural powers until I was about twenty.

Another look of triumph swept across Rachel's face.

"Rachel," I said. "You're wearing my shower curtain."

"It was the only thing I could find that was long."

"You are the biggest loser," Mary said again. Mary, however, had never thought I possessed those "secret" superpowers that parents seem to have. She'd pretty much realized on the way out of the birth canal that I was just human.

"I needed something that looked like a long dress. You know, like the costumes that you use when you give tours," Rachel said to me.

"You never thought of a sheet?" I asked.

"Oh," she said. "Well, you can't hold that against me."

"Rachel—" I began.

"No, no, no. Anytime you start a sentence with my name in that tone of voice, it means I'm about to be disappointed," she said, holding up one of her hands, while the other one clutched at the curtain. "I can do this job. It'll be like I'm following in your footsteps. Come on. I graduate in May, and I need some extra cash for college."

This would be the exact reason I didn't want her to have the job. I didn't want her to have *any* job. I didn't want her to be seventeen and ready to leave the nest. I mean, I did want her to grow up and leave the nest and get married and have babies and become like, I don't know, a leading scientist in the search for cures of horrible diseases, but . . . Not. Yet. Not yet, not yet, not yet! She may have been ready, but I wasn't.

Where had the time gone? I still needed to be her mom. I know, I was being selfish. I realized that. I figured I earned brownie points for at least admitting it— but I still felt it.

"Mom?" she asked.

"You're not seriously going to give her this job," Mary said. Mary, my second child, who was in that horrible age of not being a child anymore but not quite comfortable in her newfound skin and her C cup, could be quite a challenge to her siblings—and her parents. And, well, anybody, really. She was at that age

11

of not being able to drive, work, vote, or do anything, but yet physiologically and intellectually she was so beyond Barbie and cartoons that it was nearly painful to watch. I always thought Rachel was like seventeen going on thirty. With Mary, it was like she was four-teen going on four, some days, and twenty-five the next—then back to four. It was enough to give me a nosebleed. "You can't give her this job."

"Why not?" I asked.

"Because, she'll, like, embarrass us all. Not to men-tion I helped her with that research and she didn't give me any credit!"

"She won't embarrass us," I said.

"She's a doofus. You're wearing a shower curtain, you doofus," Mary pointed out.

"Well, at least I care about *something*," Rachel coun-tered.

Oh, here we go, I thought. An all-out catfight. Teenagers do not need reasons to be hateful to one another or have a big knock-down-drag-out fight. I've seen my daughters fight over who sits on what side of the car, who got more mashed potatoes, and even who would be least likely to eat a cockroach. I kid you not. They'd argue for three hours over a hypothetical situ-ation that would never happen. But then, there were times they fought over real things, too. Mary had recently become more withdrawn and full of angst—I write that off as hormones, and please don't tell me any different, because I'm all right with it being hor-mones, because that means that someday she'll grow out of it—and she resented her older sister's perfectness with a passion, not that I could blame her.

I stood up, trying to stop this fight before it started. "Okay, stop. Mary, go brush down the horses."

"I just did it!"

"That was yesterday. Go do it again."

"Ugh," she said, and threw the couch pillow at Rachel, catching her square in the face.

"God, I hate her," Rachel said as Mary stormed past her and out of the house.

"Rachel," I said.

"Fine, I'll take off the shower curtain and go see if Pierre is hiring at the bakery," she said with a crestfallen expression.

"No," I said. "You can have the job."

"Really?"

"Really, but you have to listen to me better at work than you do at home, or I'll fire you within the first week."

"Whatever," she said, rolling her eyes. "You won't be disappointed." Then she headed upstairs to her room.

"And hang the shower curtain back up!" I yelled after her.

My son, Matthew, came in then with my binoculars in one hand and a dead squirrel in the other. "Look what Fritz brought me!" Fritz, our wiener dog, likes to bring us dead rodents. And he won't drop the rodent on the ground. No, he must place it in our hands. I was about ready to have a panic attack then and there, since there was a dead and oozing rodent in my house. More so, because there was a dead and oozing rodent in *my son's hand*! Matthew must have noticed that the blood had drained from my face, because he said, "You don't look very good." He's a very observant six-year-old.

"Outside!"

"Oh, okay. I just wanted you to see what Fritz caught!" And off he ran.

"Get back in here. No, wait. Take that squirrel outside, then get back in here so I can disinfect your hands!"

There were days I wasn't sure how I got anything else done. As I was looking for the bleach to disinfect Matthew, the phone rang. It was one of my good friends, Helen Wickland. Helen served on the events committee of New Kassel, helping me schedule festivals and the like, and she was on the board of officers at the historical society, too. If that weren't enough, she was a chocolatier and gave me free chocolate.

"Hi, Helen," I said.

"Torie," she said. "I just wanted to nail down the dates for the Christmas stuff. We're having the Santa parade the weekend before Christmas and the choir festival the first weekend of December, right?"

"Right," I said. "And don't forget, we need to get bell ringers."

"Bell ringers?"

"Yeah, you know. Those people who stand on the corner and ring bells in different pitches, so that they play a song."

"Oh, bell ringers," she said.

"Isn't that what I said?"

"All right, what about the bird Olympics?" she asked.

Yes, you heard right. Eleanore Murdoch had somehow convinced the events committee to allow her to host a birding Olympics. "It's this coming weekend, isn't it?"

"Oh, I haven't done any advertising for it," she said with a worried tone.

"I don't think you have to," I said. "Eleanore sent out word via her bird people. We've got like fifty-something people coming, and I really don't want any more than that, so don't worry that you didn't get it out on the wire."

"I hear you're participating," she said.

I could hear the laughter in her voice, even though she wasn't actually laughing. "Do you value our friendship?"

She couldn't hold it in any longer, and she began to laugh. "How did you ever get roped into such a thing?"

"We needed at least five people from the events committee to participate. Sort of like chaperones, and she kept coming up short. So, I . . ."

"You what?" she asked.

"I have a stepfather who volunteered me. Hey, don't laugh. I didn't see you volunteering to help on this event. You weren't even there for the vote!"

"Sorry, I was in Vegas. You can hardly hold that

against me. So, what exactly will you be doing?" she asked.

"I'm not really sure."

"Will the birds be doing backflips and the butterfly stroke?" She was laughing again.

"No," I said. "I think the birders split up into groups and everybody identifies all the species they see in a twenty-four-hour period. The group with the most species wins. Or something like that. I honestly don't know the details."

"I thought we agreed not to let Eleanore host anything else to do with birds."

"I know, I know, but the events committee voted. How was I supposed to know that three-fourths of the events committee members were birders? I figured, Oh, hell, they'll shoot this down right off the bat. But they didn't. I could have used your vote. You're not allowed to leave town again."

"Is there anything I need to do to prepare the town?" she asked.

"Oh, well, Daisy Rickard might need some help with the coffee and cocoa runs. And the Porta Potti—"

"I am not doing anything that involves portable bodily secretions. I'll just tell you that right now. I love you, Torie, but not that much."

"Well, considering you skipped town and weren't there to help nip this in the bud, I oughta put you in charge of Porta Potti duty and make you clean them!"

"Ooooh, vindictive, aren't we?"

"Desperate," I said.

"Okay, so coffee and cocoa runs?"

"Yeah. I'll tell you more after I talk with Eleanore later."

"You know, Torie, you manage to get yourself into more trouble than anybody I know."

"Trouble? How is this trouble?"

"You're going to be in the woods with fifty birders. Something will happen."

"Maybe I'll fall in a sinkhole."

"There ya go. You can always hope," she said.

I hung up with Helen and tried to find the bleach, but couldn't. So I found a big bottle of alcohol and went outside to find my son. When he was completely disinfected, I made dinner for my family. I had dinner on the table by six o'clock, and it wasn't even macaroni and cheese! I actually made chicken and dumplings. I had called my grandmother and asked her how to make them because I didn't want my mother to know that I was forty and didn't know how to make chicken and dumplings. It would have made her feel as though she'd failed as a parent. Believe me. It would. I know my mother.

When my husband, Rudy, came in and sat down, he was stunned at the spread of food on the table. "Wow, what's the occasion?" he asked. For the record, I like my husband. I don't just love him, and I don't just think he's sexy. I actually like him. He's one of the few people who can keep me laughing even when there's very little to laugh about, and he's probably the only person aside from my mother who can tell me when

17

I'm overreacting and live to tell the tale. Now, I don't necessarily listen to him when he tells me I'm overreacting, but it sinks in eventually, and I don't behead him, like I would anybody else.

He cautiously sniffed the food and looked around the table to see if anybody else was going to take a bite first. I can't complain. I'm a lousy cook, and they've learned to be wary. When nobody else volunteered—they were waiting for big brave daddy to do the taste test—he took a very small bite. "Hey," he said, "this is actually good."

He smiled, and the kids dug in and ate.

"Fritz brought me a squirrel!" Matthew said.

"He's disgusting," Mary said.

"Can we discuss dead things at a different time?" Rachel asked.

Rudy smiled. "Yeah, save the dead rodent stories for later, okay?"

"Okay," Matthew said, and shrugged.

"Mom gave me the job!" Rachel said, exuding happiness.

"She did?" Rudy said. "Well . . . that was . . ."

"Yes?" I said.

"What were you thinking?" he asked.

"Hey! I can do this job."

"She can do the job," I said. "Leave it."

"So, Mary, what's new with you?" Rudy asked.

"Don't ask," she said from behind a mound of dumplings.

"Why not?" Rudy asked. It was an innocent-enough

18

question. Rudy hadn't quite learned that you don't ask innocent questions of fourteen-year-olds whose angst level is higher than their hormones.

"Because there's either nothing to tell you, or the stuff I do have to tell you, you don't want to hear anyway, so just drop it," Mary replied.

"You are such a crabby witch!" Rachel spat at her sister.

"Yeah, well, being a crabby witch is part of my charm."

"'Charm'? Oh, I'm sorry, was that charming?" Rachel asked in the most condescending tone I'd ever heard. I mean, I couldn't have done it better myself.

"Stop!" I said. "Not now."

"Whatever," Mary said. She had recently taken to wearing as much hair as she could over one eye. I think she thought it was some sort of statement, and it was. It stated that she was a grouchy, hormonal teenager who had absolutely nothing to be unhappy about and was pissed off about it. I was actually more concerned that she'd run into something one of these days from lack of depth perception than I was about any statement that she was trying to make.

"There's a guy living in the woods," Matthew said.

"Where?" I asked.

"Back there," he said, and pointed in the direction of our back lot.

"It's probably a hunter," Rudy said. "It's deer season, you know."

"Oh, yeah, it's the let's-go-show-how-testosterone-can-make-us-act-like-idiots season," Mary said.

"We've had this discussion before, Mary," Rudy said. "Without the existence of any natural predators anymore, hunting is necessary, or else the deer will eat the forest down to the ground."

"It's barbaric. It's lame. Guys just like to kill things."

"No they don't," Matthew said with big worried eyes. "Daddy, do you like to kill things?"

"Yes, he does," Mary said. "He likes to kill nosy little brat boys like you!"

"Stop!" I said, and found myself standing. "Just stop. Now, I had to call my grandmother and admit to her that I was forty years old and didn't know how to make stupid chicken and dumplings, just so I could make this dinner for you guys and you wouldn't have to eat out of a box, or a take-out bag, or at a restaurant or what have you! And you guys *will* shut up and you *will eat*!"

Everybody just stared at me.

"Quietly. Pleasantly. End of discussion!" I added.

Everyone shut up, probably because I was waving my fork around like a madwoman, and I sat down and ate my dinner as quickly as I could. When I was finished, I said, "Rachel you've got dish duty. I'm going to my office."

That's where I stayed until it was time for Matthew to do his homework. After I helped him, I went to bed and dreamed about a world where the only things I had to worry about were what type of massage oil I wanted and when my next infusion of chocolate would be.

Two

I sat in my office at the Kendall home, wondering who in the world ever told me that I should be a parent. As I recall, I wanted the job badly, but why hadn't anybody ever said to me, "Torie, there is no way in hell you can *do* this job"? Why were changing diapers, juggling feeding times, and getting through potty training easier than getting two teenagers to make it through a day without shaking open the entrance to hell? Well, regardless, it was too late now. It wasn't as if I could just stop the process and say, "Sorry, everybody out of the boat. I can't do this."

I was deep in thought when my sister Stephanie knocked on my door. Stephanie is my half sister and we don't look that much alike, but we have the same eyes. We got those from our dad. But we're much more alike on the inside, and I can't express how scary that is. My father's genetics are not only overbearing but they're skewed beyond comprehension. Aside from that, I like Stephanie. She's the only person I know who will let me eat brownies for breakfast and not tell anyone.

"Okay, so what's going on?" she asked.

Telepathy. That's another cool thing about her.

"I have to participate in this birding Olympics tomorrow and I really don't want to."

"That's causing all of this running around and being at the wrong office on the wrong day?"

"What?" I asked. "What are you talking about?"

"You're supposed to be at your office at the Gaheimer House today, not here at the Kendall home."

"What day is it?"

"It's Friday."

"It's not Thursday?"

"If it were Thursday, would you be participating in a birding Olympics tomorrow?"

"Oh," I said. "So it's not Thursday."

"I'm assuming you're on autopilot and your autopilot thinks you're at the Gaheimer house, and that's why you keep bumping into walls."

"Oh."

"Yeah, oh. Look, Torie, is there something you want to talk about?" Stephanie asked.

"I'm having a midlife crisis and there's not enough chocolate in the world."

"You're having a midlife crisis because there's not enough chocolate in the world, or was that last part just an observation?" Stephanie asked, trying desperately to keep up with me.

"Both."

"Look . . ."

"No, I'm being serious," I said. I glanced around my office. The Kendall home was a new acquisition to my holdings in town. I'd inherited the Gaheimer House from Sylvia and Wilma Pershing when they passed away; it houses the historical society. I had worked for Sylvia for over ten years and had grown up in her shadow, wanting to be just like her. Well, except for the lonely, hateful, spiteful part. She had lived in New Kassel her entire life, and it had meant everything to her. She and her sister had established the Gaheimer House as a tourist attraction and had founded the historical society. She was sort of a big sister to me, what Rachel is to Mary. A big shadow that, although I loved, I sort of wanted out from under.

Enter the Kendall home. I bought it last year and have gone about turning it into a museum for women's textile arts. I actually get more traffic from the World War I enthusiasts, because one of the upstairs bedrooms has a painfully horrific mural, sketched by a talented—albeit disturbed—hand, depicting the trenches during the war. It's been photographed and studied, and you can even find details of it online, but I refuse to paint over it. I'd never ruin the original.

"I'm having a real midlife crisis," I said.

"As opposed to . . . ?"

"People throw that phrase around, and I think I've thrown it around myself in the past. It's like when people say they're depressed, only they really aren't. Then one day when they really are depressed, they're like, 'Oh, hey, so this is what depression feels like.' "

Stephanie's hazel eyes were sort of blank.

"Well, that's what's happening here. I'm like, 'Oh, hey, so this is what a midlife crisis really feels like.' "

My sister tucked her hair behind her ears and sat on the edge of my desk. "What gives?"

"My daughter graduates this year."

"So? Isn't that a good thing? I mean, the alternative

23

would be that she didn't graduate. Which would mean that she had either flunked, quit, or . . . worse. In which case, you'd have a lot more to worry about than the world's shortage of chocolate."

"Oh my gosh," I said. "What if the world did run out of chocolate?"

"Torie. Focus. What is going on?"

"Well, I knew when I had my kids that they were going to grow up."

"So?"

"So, I just didn't think they were going to grow up." Stephanie laughed at me then.

"No, I mean, in my mind's eye it was going to happen. Like a long time down the road. I just didn't think that I'd be . . ."

"You'd be what?"

"I don't know. I feel the same as I did seventeen years ago. I thought I'd be old, or feel old, or that I'd just naturally be ready for her to graduate and leave home—and I'm not. Mentally, on the inside, I'm still that twenty-three-year-old girl who struggled for sixteen hours to bring Rachel into the world. I'm just not ready."

"Well, she is ready," Stephanie said. "So you're going to have to deal with it."

It was the exact same thing I would have said to her or anybody else, but I didn't want to hear it. I shrugged. "I dunno, there's more to it than that. I can't put it in words."

"Torie, the world doesn't end when she graduates."

24

"No, hers is just beginning. But it changes everything. Everything I've ever wanted and everything I've ever been just changes."

"Oh boy," she said, and reached for the phone.

"What are you doing?"

"I'm calling Helen. We need serious chocolate."

"Joke all you want."

She hung the phone up and then she reached over and squeezed my hand. "You've got the Olympics to get ready for."

"Right, I know. What do I need?"

"Binoculars."

"Yeah, I've got those. Do I need bug spray? Because I hate mosquitoes."

"It's December. We may not have actual deep-freeze winters here anymore, but we don't have any mosquitoes in December. At least I hope not, because that would be . . . well, it would have to mean something globally bad."

"I'm taking some just in case," I said.

"Good," she said, and laughed. "You do that."

"So what else?"

"Comfy shoes, warm socks, and dress in layers, because it will get cold at night. Sleeping bag—are you allowed to sleep?" she asked. "Oh, and you have to have a notebook and pencil to write down all the birds you see."

"What am I supposed to write down? The only birds I know when I see them are a cardinal and a blue jay. All of those brown birds just sort of look alike. So, what am I supposed to write down? 'Three brown birds with stripes'? 'One brown bird with a white belly'? I have no clue what I'm doing."

"Then I suggest you go and purchase a bird-identification book. They've got them in the visitors center."

"How do you know?" I asked.

"Because we're right on the river, and evidently this is a hot spot for birds. I'm told that we have one of the few groups of Eurasian tree sparrows in the country."

I just stared at her. "Why aren't you going on the birding Olympics?"

"Because I don't have a stepfather who hates me," she said and smiled. "Now, you really need to be at the Gaheimer House, because I'm supposed to be covering this house."

"Oh," I said. "Okay." I grabbed my purse and jacket and headed for the door. "By the way, Rachel starts giving tours at the Gaheimer House next week."

"I know," she said. "She called and told me."

"Okay, then. I'm off to buy a bird book."

"Oh, wait, one more thing. Somebody named . . ." she began, stammering. She thunked her forehead with her finger and then smiled. "Glen Morgan called."

"Glen Morgan? Should I know him?"

"Maybe." She shrugged. "He said he needed to speak to you about our grandpa's music. Or something to that effect. He wouldn't tell me anything. He said he could only speak to you. Even after I told him that he was my grandpa, too."

Our grandpa had been one of the premier fiddle

players of southeast Missouri in his day. His day would have been a long time ago—like during the twenties. There were few people left alive who remembered him unless they were related or a musicologist. Since I knew everyone who was related to him within three generations, I figured Mr. Morgan had to be a musicologist.

"You look clueless," Stephanie said.

"I'll call him Sunday, after the Olympics."

"He didn't leave a number. He said he'd call back."

I thought about it a moment and wondered what he could possibly want. I was always on the lookout for new photographs of my family or any new tidbit of information, so, mostly, my interest was piqued and I couldn't wait to hear what he had to say. There was a part of me, though, that kept thinking I ought to know the name Glen Morgan. It nudged and tickled at the back of my brain, but my poor brain was either too tired or too stubborn to turn loose any knowledge of one Glen Morgan. So I'd just have to wait until he called back.

"If he calls tomorrow, tell him to try me on my cell phone."

"You're taking your cell phone to the birding Olympics? If Eleanore finds out, she will have a cow."

"Well then, call the *National Enquirer*, because Eleanore can just have a cow. Maybe she'll have a two-headed cow, but there is no way in hell I'm going to be out in the woods for twenty-four hours without a way to contact the outside world. Besides, it's not like

Eleanore's going to be right beside me the whole time."

"All right, I'll give him the message."

I gave her a quick hug and left.

Tobias Thorley was working at the visitors center when I entered it at just a few minutes past eleven. Tobias was a skinny, wiry man with a hook nose, and he could play an accordion better than anybody for a hundred miles. Okay, well, he was probably the only accordion player within a hundred miles, but still. He was very good and had been entertaining the tourists of New Kassel since the 1970s. He was also a plant expert and an amazing gardener. "Hi, Tobias. How are you? Ready for Christmas?"

He rolled his eyes. "Don't feel like Christmas. It's too warm."

"I know." It had been unseasonably warm for the past few winters. Even though we might get a cold spell and snow now and then, the overall winter was nearly nonexistent. Not like when I was a kid, or even ten years ago. A person used to be able to ice-skate on ponds or lakes in this area in the winter, but not in the past few years. Very sad, when you think about it. "Look, I'm here to get a bird-identification book."

"Sure thing," he said and handed me two of them. "I'd get this one."

I looked at both of them and went with his suggestion, because, well, he was Tobias and knew all sorts of things that I didn't. I trusted his judgment. "Are there really this many kinds of birds in eastern Missouri?"

"Sure. Not all at the same time, though. You need to look at the map; it will tell you their winter range."

"Oh, I gotcha." About that time, a bird landed on the patio outside the door. "What kind of bird is that?"

"Starling. Female."

"You mean you can tell the difference between male and female?"

"Some birds," he said. "So, you're participating in the Olympics, I'm taking it."

"Yeah," I said. "And you?"

"Yup. I'll be there."

"Should I take a sleeping bag and a tent?"

"There's no sleeping," he said. "Otherwise, you'd miss all the owls. And bats."

"Bats? Bats are birds? We have bats?"

"Of course we have bats, and no, bats aren't birds, but I think they're nifty to watch anyway."

"Well, for my sake, I hope we don't see any bats."

He laughed at me and then said, "So, you ready to put in that garden this spring?"

Smiling, I tucked the bird book in my purse. "If you will help me, I'm up for it."

"Good," he said. I'm not a plant person at all. I loved my grandparents' farm, and I could spend hours in their orchard. I used to eat Grandma's strawberries right out of the patch. Either the green thumb gene passed me up or I never gave it a full chance. Well, after last year's successful rose show, I decided I wanted to plant things at my new house. Tobias was my most obvious choice for help, because the man could get anything to grow in the worst conditions.

I headed for the Gaheimer House, which was just down a few blocks on the main road in town, called River Pointe Road. Most of the townsfolk and shop owners were busy getting the Christmas decorations up because this weekend was our big holiday kickoff. Many people disagree with me, but I've made it a point not to decorate until the first weekend in December because I believe that Thanksgiving should be its own separate holiday. We all took a vote one year and the majority—surprisingly—agreed with me. So the big New Kassel decorating frenzy doesn't happen until the first Thursday and Friday of December. Saturday would be the beginning of our choir festival, while I would be out in the surrounding woods, hunched down with binoculars, looking for birds.

My stepfather, Colin Brooke, was walking down the street just as I reached the Gaheimer House. Colin used to be the sheriff in town, and now he was the mayor. Which was sort of good and sort of bad. It was good that the old mayor was gone and it was good that Colin was no longer in my hair as acting sheriff. That meant that he could no longer arrest me, which has happened more times than you would think. If you think being arrested by the man who will eventually become your stepfather doesn't put a strain on your relationship, it does. At any rate, it was good that he was no longer in a position to arrest me. It was bad because he was absolutely bored at being mayor and he had to be mayor for another two years. If Colin is bored, he makes everybody else miserable. But I had news for him. The townspeople—myself included— really liked the new sheriff, and so if he thought when his term as mayor was over that he'd just waltz back into his old job of sheriff, he just might get surprised.

"Hello, Torie."

"Just keep walking. I'm not speaking to you today."

"What did I do?"

"You got me into this birding Olympics," I said.

He laughed, and I wanted to hit him. Colin was a big guy— ridiculously tall and casting shadows all about all the time. My mother fed him way too well, and as if he hadn't been big enough before, he'd now "filled out" to his capacity. Any more "filling out" and I could officially call him overweight, but he just hovered on the edge. On one hand, I felt sorry for him. My mother was the greatest cook in the world, and anybody would expand their normal boundaries while living with her.

"Hey, I'm going to be there, too," he said.

"You are?"

"Yeah," he said.

"Oh, great. So, how exactly does this work?"

"We split up into groups of two. One looks for the birds; the other one writes down the birds they see. Simple as that."

"Do we move around, or stay in one place?"

"That's up to the birders. Everybody has their own secret way of doing things. I've even been told that Eleanore brings a bag of sunflower seeds to entice the birds."

"Is that cheating?"

He shrugged. "I dunno."

"Who's my partner?"

"Call Eleanore and ask her."

"Who are you with?" I asked.

"I'm with Elmer," he said and rubbed his hands together. Elmer Kolbe, our semiretired fire chief, is a renowned outdoorsman. "I smell victory."

Victory was actually my real first name. There was a joke in there somewhere, but I was entirely too irritated to find it. "Great," I said. "May the best birder win."

With that, I entered the Gaheimer House and shut the door behind me. Colin and I actually had more in common than one would think. We both loved my mother, we both hated bad guys, and we both thought the other was the most irritating person on the planet. It was enough to keep the family get-togethers civil. And besides, my kids were crazy about him, and it's difficult to dislike somebody entirely if your kids like him. Basically, we'd given up on all-out animosity and settled in a precarious relationship based on annoyance.

I kept myself busy for the next few hours. I called my local costume maker and ordered two dresses for Rachel to give the tours in. One was a Civil War-era costume. Since discovering that the Gaheimer House was part of the Underground Railroad, we had focused a little more on the Civil War era when giving the tours of the house. I also had a dress commissioned for her from the turn of the twentieth century. Rachel was small, so there was no way she could fit into my dresses or Stephanie's, or even any of Sylvia's old dresses, so I figured I might as well get her a few made for herself.

Around four o'clock that afternoon Eleanore Murdoch knocked on the back door. I answered it, wondering what had brought her to the Gaheimer House. Eleanore and I are not enemies per se, but we try to avoid each other whenever possible. She's outlandish, large, speaks in riddles half the time, and wears color-coordinated hats and socks with every outfit. Most of the time, her jewelry and her clothing have a food- or flower-related theme. Today, it was poinsettias. She had big red poinsettias appliquéd on her blouse and a black hat with a red plastic poinsettia sticking out of it. Don't get me wrong, I don't dislike her for her appearance; in fact, she can liven up any room. We just sort of clash.

"Hi, Torie," she said. "I just came by to let you know that you will be my partner for the birding Olympics. I expect my partners to be on time and quiet. Be at the park a half hour before six."

I blinked. After I'd gotten over the cruel joke of the universe that I'd be spending the next twenty-four hours with her, I said, "The Olympics do not start until six in the morning."

"Exactly why you must be there a half hour early. We must prepare and meditate."

"'Meditate'?"

"Become one with nature."

"Why?"

"It will draw the birds to us."

"Meditating will draw the birds to us?"

"Yes. They will feel our presence and will know that we mean them no harm, and they will come and be curious. And then you will write them down on our sheet. After I've identified them, of course."

"But . . ."

"No buts, Torie. We shall be the champions."

"Right," I said, with the lyrics to the Queen song running through my head. Bet Freddie Mercury never thought his song would be the anthem for a bunch of crazy birders in Missouri.

"We shall be triumphant," she said, raising her head a notch.

"Right," I said. "Wait, Eleanore, I have question. Why are we doing the Olympics in the winter? Wouldn't we see more birds in the summer?"

"Well, there is a birding Olympics in the summer, too. We've just never participated in it. This is our first year, and I am so excited!" She took a deep breath and continued. "Basically, it's just a fun way to track the migration patterns of different bird species during the winter."

"Why?"

"Because the birds that live here in the winter are different from the ones in the summer. Some are the same, obviously. But some are different. At the end of the Olympics, we turn all of our data in to the local birding chapter, which then turns the data in to whatever university was sponsoring it."

"I gotcha," I said.

"By the way, I have some photographs to give you from the horse show we had a while back. I'll bring them tomorrow." My mind was still reeling with how impressed I was with Eleanore's knowledge of birds, so I didn't really pick up what she was saying when she shook her finger at me, showing off her rambunctious red fingernail polish.

"Oh, and no bright colors. Blend."

"Blend." Did Eleanore really just tell me to blend?

"Tah tah, see you in the morning."

I shut the door and banged my head on the pane of glass. I closed up the Gaheimer House, picked up pizza from Chuck's, went home, scarfed my dinner, and went to bed. I let Rudy take care of the nighttime routine on this night, since I had to get up at like four in the morning. The next twenty-four hours were going to be the longest twenty-four hours of my life.

Three

I held an extra-big cup of hot cocoa in my left hand as my right hand scratched my tummy in the dark. I yawned as Eleanore pulled up in her big station wagon. Everybody participating in the birding Olympics was meeting at the commuter parking lot just on the edge of the south part of town. I waved, blithely thinking that she'd be happy that I was on time for this stupid meditation. I was mistaken.

"Caffeine! How do you intend to meditate if you're hopped up on caffeine?"

"Geez, Eleanore, it's not like I'm taking speed," I said defensively.

Before I could say anything more, Eleanore moved in front of the headlights on her station wagon. She was dressed entirely, from head to toe, in camouflage. Her face was painted various shades of green and tan. And somehow Eleanore had managed to find a lady's wide-brimmed hat in camouflage colors. She had a big feather of some sort sticking out of the back of it. Upon closer scrutiny, I noticed that she'd even painted her fingernails alternately with green and tan. Well, when Eleanore decided to blend, she could blend.

I, on the other hand, was wearing long underwear, a pair of jeans, Doc Martens, a Rams sweatshirt, and a big fuzzy blue hat that Rachel had knitted for me in her crafts class at school. I don't own any camouflage clothes. I don't own any khaki, unless you count my shorts, and it wasn't warm enough for those. But I thought at least the hat was the same color as the sky.

Eleanore glared at me, looking from my shoes to the floppy ball on the end of my hat. "If you ruin my chances of winning the first ever New Kassel Birding Olympics, I will hunt you down."

"Hunt me down? Eleanore, you know my address."

"I mean it, Torie. You may ruin everything, but you're not ruining this!"

"Oh yeah? Well, I was just about to say the same thing about you. So if you don't win, sweep in front of your own door!"

"But *I* am not the one—" She raised her hands and stopped mid-sentence. "We must meditate."

She spread a blanket on the gravel and sat down.

"Okeydokey," I said. I gulped as much of my hot chocolate as I could and sat down across from her.

"Ankles folded. Fingertips touching the thumb. Relax. Breathe."

"Right." I did as she instructed and wondered when in the world Eleanore had started meditating. It sure as heck had made no difference in her outward personality, so it was either something brand-new or there was no hope for Eleanore ever being anything other than Eleanore. I couldn't help but wonder if it was okay to think about Eleanore during meditation.

"Open the back of your throat," she said.

"I thought I had."

"No, no, no. You've got it all wrong."

"The back of my throat is open!" I argued.

"No it's not."

"If it wasn't open, I'd be dead, you idiot!"

"You have to sound like Darth Vader when you're breathing."

"You do? Are you sure?" I asked.

"Yes."

"All right," I said.

So we sat there facing each other, sounding like Darth Vader, although I thought we sounded like we had head colds. Even though there was a blanket beneath me, the rocks were grinding into my butt cheeks, and it was nippy outside—about forty degrees. So pretty soon my teeth were chattering and my butt was numb and Eleanore was attracting all sorts of attention with her breathing, but it wasn't from the birds.

"Imagine you have wings," she said in some far-off, dreamy voice.

I didn't want to imagine that I had wings, but I said nothing.

"Now you're soaring on the wind," she said.

"Soaring on the wind," I repeated.

"The wind ruffles your feathers. You're as light as a feather. Suddenly, you see a big juicy beetle. You swoop down—"

"Eleanore, I don't want to eat a bug."

"Oh, for heaven's sake!" she exclaimed. Then she got up and began tugging on the blanket while I was still on it. I rolled backward after I grabbed my cocoa cup, so she could get the blanket out from under me. "Let's get our numbers—they identify us to the judges—and head into the woods."

"Sure thing," I said from the ground.

Four hours later, I was yawning so loudly that I thought I would fit in more with hyenas than birds. Eleanore sat perched on a tree branch on a bluff on the side of the Mississippi River with her binoculars raised to her eyes. I was on a rock with a notebook, and I was writing down the names of the birds as she called them out to me. So far, we had seen that bird Stephanie had talked about, the Eurasian tree sparrow, a cardinal—I identified that one—a mockingbird, a starling, and about a dozen hawks. Eleanore didn't like the starling very much and made a puckered face when she reported it to me.

There was a knocking sound from somewhere in the distance. "Hey, you hear that?" Eleanore asked.

"Yes," I said.

"It's a woodpecker."

I wrote down "woodpecker," only to have her throw a stick at me. "What?" I asked.

"I don't know what *kind* of woodpecker it is yet, you moron."

"Oh," I said. I had no idea there was more than one kind of woodpecker.

A few minutes later, Eleanore said, "Oh sweet Jesus, it's a pileated."

"It's affiliated with what?" I asked.

"No, the woodpecker. It's a pileated woodpecker." She pointed across the way to a tree right on the edge of the river. I grabbed my binoculars and there was this huge prehistoric-looking bird with a bright red head banging the heck out of the tree with its bill.

"Wow," I said.

"Oh, wait until Elmer Kolbe hears about this."

I wrote down what type of woodpecker it was, wondering if I'd spelled "pileated" correctly and if it would matter in the long run. About an hour later, I pointed out another starling to Eleanore. I thought I was doing a good thing.

"That is not a starling," she said. "Really, Torie, we are doomed if you can't tell the difference between a common grackle and a starling."

I said nothing for a minute. Then I said, "So what does an uncommon grackle look like?"

Really, I'm not this stupid ordinarily. I'm much better with dead people and ancient documents.

"Just try not to speak," Eleanore said, disgusted.

"Fine, I won't speak."

Two hours later, my stomach growled so loudly that it was chasing away any birds that might have stopped by. Eleanore threw a granola bar at me from her perch. She made horrible disapproving noises as I noisily opened the wrapper, but she seemed to be all right once I started chewing. Then my cell phone rang.

"You brought a cell phone?" she asked.

"Everybody knows where I am, Eleanore, so if somebody is calling me, it's important."

"You brought a cell phone!"

Things scuttled across the forest floor and birds took flight from the trees as Eleanore screamed at me. "How could you do this! You have disturbed the sanctuary of our Olympics!"

"No, I didn't. You screaming disturbed the sanctuary."

I looked at the screen on my cell phone. I didn't recognize the number. "This is Torie," I said as I answered it.

"Mrs. O'Shea," a male voice said. "My name is Glen Morgan. I must talk to you about your grandfather's music. I've discovered something . . . amazing."

"Yes, my sister said that you'd called. I'm tied up today, but I can meet with you tomorrow."

There was a silence on the other end. "Hello? Mr. Morgan, I'm in the woods, so I'm afraid I might lose our connection."

"In the woods?"

"My town is hosting a bird Olympics."

"It is of the utmost importance that I speak to you today," he said. The only people who actually use the word "utmost" in a casual conversation are people trying to sell you something, or they're British. This guy wasn't British, but the fact that he went right by the whole birding Olympics without asking for an explanation actually had me thinking that whatever he had to say to me must be pretty important. At least important to him. "I'm not sure how much longer . . ."

"How much longer, what?" I asked.

"Do you remember a man named Scott Morgan?"

Then it hit me. Of course, I should have recognized the last name Morgan. Not that it's an uncommon name, but anytime you put the name Morgan with music in the southeast Missouri area, you come up with one family: the Morgan Family Players. During the twenties and thirties, they were famous for their music in about five states—mostly in the areas of southeast Missouri, Arkansas, Tennessee, Kentucky, and southern Illinois. They were not unlike the Carter Family, but they never established nationwide fame. Also unlike the Carter Family, the Morgans seemed to fade into anonymity once the Depression ended.

Scott Morgan was also the man primarily responsible for my grandpa being the fiddle player that he was.

"Yes, of course," I said.

"I thought you would. Scott Morgan was my grandpa. Look, I've found a tape. I really need to see you right away."

"I'm sorry, Glen, but I can't see you until tomorrow. You can speak with my sister in town. She should be at the Gaheimer House today. If you go there, she'll help you with whatever it is that you need. But I can't see you until tomorrow."

"This is very disconcerting, but I suppose if there's no way around it . . ."

"No, I'm afraid not," I said, glaring at the back of Eleanore's head.

"All right, then, I'll call you in the morning. I'll meet you in town."

"Sure," I said, and hung up the phone. "Hey, Eleanore. What do I do if I have to pee?"

She threw a roll of toilet paper down at me. "Find a bush. And put the used toilet paper in a Baggie until we get back to town. I'll not have you littering—on top of everything else that you've done today."

My, my, she could be so persnickety.

Four

Putting used toilet paper in a Baggie was a first for me, but I did as Eleanore instructed and pretty much kept as quiet as I could the rest of the day, for fear of Eleanore having a stroke in the middle of the woods.

42

By about 6:00 P.M., we had identified twenty-seven different bird species, including five different wood-peckers. Who would have thought there were so many woodpeckers in the world, let alone in Missouri? The river ran below our rocky perch, and the sun was setting behind us. Across the river in Illinois, the purple skies of dusk had already settled in, casting eerie shadows from the naked trees, and the temperature had dropped a good ten degrees. Thoughts of having to stay awake in the cold all night with Eleanore made me want to cry, but I was a big girl and told myself that I could do anything for a limited amount of time and that within twelve hours it would all be over.

"I can't imagine doing this on a day when it's really cold," I said out loud. Realizing that it was going to get down to about twenty-eight later, I shivered. Ten or fifteen years ago, it would have been down to single digits.

"Don't talk to me," she said.

"You're not still mad over that whole bluebird thing are you?" I asked.

She held her hand up in my direction. "I don't wish to hear your voice."

"Fine, fine, fine, whatever," I said.

Fifteen minutes went by. I couldn't take it. I could not take the silence any longer. I'd rather have had Eleanore running off at the mouth and saying stupid things to me than have to go on in complete silence another minute. This was unusual for me. I actually like silence. A lot of times when I'm driving in my car,

I won't turn on the radio just because I love to hear nothing for a change. As much as I love music, I will work for hours in my office with no sound whatsoever except the clacking of my keys and the white noise of the street in the distance. I think the difference there is that it's self-inflicted silence. I have control of it. It's when I want it to be quiet.

Right then, I didn't want it to be quiet, and as if God had somehow heard my prayer, the silence was broken. Not necessarily in the fashion that I would have liked, but still . . .

The gunshot that sounded in the distance nearly frightened Eleanore into jumping out of her tree. "What the . . . ?"

"Hunters?" I asked.

"Probably, but Sheriff Joachim was supposed to make sure there was no hunting activity within ten miles today."

Then another shot. Then another.

"Hey," I said to her. "Is it me, or were those shots getting closer?"

"It sounded like it to me," she agreed.

A few minutes went by and then another gunshot. This one was a lot closer than the others had been. Then another report sounded, and a bullet hit the bark of the tree that Eleanore was sitting in.

"Oh, good Lord in heaven!" she shrieked.

"Eleanore, get down out of that tree!"

"Oh, I . . ." She raised her foot to try to swing it around the tree branch that she was straddling, but

Eleanore, being the size she was, couldn't quite raise that leg up and over in a hurry. I jumped up and went over to the tree and began pulling on the leg that was closest to me.

"Ouch! Torie, stop pulling my leg!"

"Eleanore if you don't get down out of that tree now, your leg is going to be the least of your worries!"

Another bullet, but this one hit the bark right by my head.

I screamed, Eleanore cried for her mother, and then the tree branch broke. Eleanore came tumbling down out of the tree and landed on top of me.

She knocked the wind clean out of me, and for a moment I thought I was a goner. Eleanore was screaming, bullets were flying everywhere, and I couldn't breathe. It felt as though my lungs had collapsed.

Eleanore turned toward me, grabbed me by the coat, lifted me off of the ground, and banged my whole body up against the tree. "This is your doing! I know it! You ruin everything!" she screamed.

My arms were flaying all about and everything was turning sort of white around the edges. About the third time she slammed me into the tree, my breath came back to me. Big gasps of air filled my lungs and for about twenty seconds I just drank in as much sweet air as I could get.

"Eleanore, stop!" I yelled finally. "Can we run? You can beat me up later."

"I oughta—"

"Run, that's what you oughta do!"

I started running down toward the river, toward the railroad tracks, but Eleanore was not behind me. I turned and saw her messing with the tree. Somehow, her binoculars had gotten entangled in the branches, and she was determined not to leave them behind. "Eleanore!" She ignored me.

I ran back up the part of the hill I'd just descended. When I reached her, I yanked on her arm. "Let's go!"

"These binoculars cost me three hundred dollars. I am not leaving them!"

"You can get them tomorrow!" I said. A bullet whizzed by my ear. I broke out in a cold sweat. "Fine, I'm leaving you here!"

"Torie! Torie!" she exclaimed as I started running down the hill. But I couldn't leave her. As much as I should have left her, I just couldn't.

"I'll buy you a new pair!" I called up the hill.

"You promise?"

"Yes, God bless it. Now let's go!"

Finally, with the promise of new binoculars, she came bounding down the hill. We took off running through the dim light of dusk, dodging around trees, jumping over bushes, and sliding down rocks. Tree limbs smacked me in the face, and I had no idea where I was actually running to. I just knew that the river ran south and we were south of town. So all I had to do was follow the railroad tracks and the river north, and I'd end up in New Kassel within a mile or two. The thought of running a couple of miles at full speed was pretty daunting, considering I was fairly out of shape and didn't really run anywhere, ever.

Eleanore cried out from behind me. "I have to stop." She gasped for breath, half-bent over, and clutched at her chest.

"Eleanore, we have to go." I flipped open my cell phone and dialed Sheriff Mort Joachim.

She held her hand up. "Wait. I don't hear anybody anymore. Maybe they just thought I was a big old deer stuck up in the tree. Now that we're down here, they can see I'm not a deer anymore."

I listened for a second. I heard nothing but the river and Eleanore's breathing.

"God help us all, Eleanore, if we give gun permits to idiots who think a deer can climb trees."

"Whoever it was couldn't hit the broad side of a barn," she said, laughing.

This was true. As the phone kept ringing, I glanced nervously around the woods. Stopping to call him any sooner would have been stupid. I was only worried about getting away from the bullets. Now that we appeared to be safe, I felt like I could stop long enough to talk on the phone.

"It's the only reason we're still alive." She laughed harder now. I think she was hysterical.

A voice answered on the other end. "Mort," I said.

"Torie?"

"Listen, Eleanore and I are about two miles south of town on the railroad tracks. Some hunters just tried to shoot us."

"What?" he said. "That area is supposed to be cleared."

"Yes, I know. Look, it was probably just some stupid kids who are new to this whole hunting thing, but I'd feel better if you sent somebody after us."

"All right," he said.

"We'll be on the tracks."

"Okay, but if you hear any more shots, find a safe place and stay there."

"Mort, there are no safe places!"

"All right, we're on our way."

"Eleanore," I said. "We should keep moving."

"I can't run anymore," she replied, still laughing. Pretty soon, she was in full-fledged, all-out, hysterical laughter. Tears ran down her face. I thought, Gee, if we *were* the intended target of those guns, with as much noise as she's making, they'll find us for sure.

"Eleanore."

Her laughter came from the gut, and then she took a deep breath and whooped even louder with the laugh ending in a deep spasm. Finally, I just slapped her.

She stopped and stared at me. "You slapped me."

"Yes. It was a matter of survival. Can we go now?"

"You *slapped* me!"

"I'm leaving, Eleanore. We don't have to run anymore. We can walk, but I'm walking up there where there's a little more cover. I don't like being in the open like this."

"You don't think . . ." she said, rubbing her cheek where I'd smacked her.

"I don't know what to think, Eleanore, but I'm not taking any chances. Mort's on his way."

I made my way up the hill a few yards and began walking in the same northerly direction, keeping the river to my right but making sure I was under the cover of bushes and trees at least. A road ran to my left way up on top of the ridge. Sometimes the road was a quarter of a mile away from the ridge, and other times it edged right up to where the cliff dropped off. A small picnic area at a scenic overlook was just above us now, and I thought about just climbing the hill straight up, but I doubted that Eleanore would make it. Not only that, I wasn't exactly sure how steep the incline was at the top, nor was I sure how secure those rocks were. All I'd need would be to grab hold of a loose rock and go tumbling down. Besides, Mort expected us to be on the tracks. No, I'd keep following the river until it leveled out with New Kassel or Mort intercepted us, whichever came first.

Eleanore's breathing came in ragged puffs now, and so I decided to stop. She was right about one thing: Whoever it was hadn't followed us. Maybe it was a bunch of hunters who had mistaken Eleanore for a deer. Darkness was just about completely on us now, and I didn't want to surprise any more hunters. I wanted to get back to civilization as quickly as I could, but Eleanore needed to catch her breath. Not that I wouldn't benefit from resting, too. My legs burned and my heart was still thumping harder than it ever had in my whole life.

"Let's stop for a moment," I said.

She stopped and sat down on a rock. I heard something rustle in the bushes, and both of us screeched. It was a skunk. I could tell because the white stripe down its back was the only thing illuminated in the purple-gray of dusk. "Be very still," I said. All we'd need would be to scare the skunk.

About that time, I saw headlights at the top of the ridge. Somebody had just pulled into the overlook. Maybe it was the sheriff, although I would have thought he'd just head to the train depot in New Kassel and then follow the tracks to meet with us, rather than descend down a two- or three-hundred-foot cliff.

"You think they can help us?" Eleanore said.

I glanced at the skunk and back to the ridge. "It can't be more than a mile to New Kassel, and Mort's on his way," I said. "And I'm not going to scream for help with that skunk sitting right there."

Just then, we heard a crash. I glanced up at the ridge in time to see something big come flying over the edge of the cliff. It crashed on the rocks above, scaring the hell out of the skunk, which sprayed Eleanore and me with all its might. But that was the least of our worries: Whatever had just been tossed over the edge was still coming down the hill—straight at us.

"Oh crap," I said.

"Mother of God!" Eleanore cried. I pulled on her arm and she came right up off the rock. The thing was still crashing and clanking all the way down the hill, breaking tree limbs and sending rocks flying in all different directions. Finally, whatever it was hit the tree right above us and stopped.

Stinky as we were, Eleanore and I clutched each other, crying and gasping for air. Above us, precariously nestled in the tree, was a big chest or trunk of some sort. The car at the top of the ridge left. Eleanore and I looked at each other and back at the trunk.

"Torie," she said, shaking. "I think I peed my pants."

Then the lid on the trunk flew open and out popped a body, which landed at our feet. After my heart started beating again and I was finished screaming, yet again, I grabbed the flashlight that was clipped to Eleanore's belt and focused it on the body. Whoever he was, he was covered in blood.

Five

Jesus, what stinks?" Mort said as he made his way toward us.

"What's the matter, Sheriff, you never smell a skunk before?" Of course Mort had smelled a skunk before. He was a regular Daniel Boone, at one with the wild. He spent the majority of his spare time at his cabin, holed up away from the real world. Shoot, he probably ate skunk on the weekends. I suppose it was just natural to comment on the odor.

I, for one, didn't think the stench was that bad, but Deputy Miller quickly assured me that I'd just gotten used to it. Guess that was a built-in defense mechanism so that I wouldn't gag all night.

"Are you guys all right?" Mort asked, flashing his light in our faces.

"No!" Eleanore cried. "We are not all right. First, first we get shot at, then I leave behind my perfectly good three-hundred-dollar binoculars, then we run for what seems like miles and miles, then we get sprayed by a skunk, and then somebody throws a dead body over the cliff at us! *Does it sound like we're all right?*"

Mort and Deputy Miller stood very still. "What about a dead body?" Mort asked.

"Right there," I said, and guided his flashlight to the dead man at our feet. "He was in that trunk. Somebody threw it and him off the cliff. We just happened to be here when he landed."

"Oh . . . that's grand," he said. "Miller, call this in. Get the CSU and the coroner out here."

Just then, I heard footsteps crunching on the gravel and a voice in the distance. "Hey? You guys all right?"

It was Colin, my stepfather.

"What are you doing here?" I asked. "You are not sheriff anymore. How come you just show up at all the crime scenes anyway?"

"Wait," he said. "This is a crime scene? Did you guys get hurt?"

Even in the dark, I could see his concern. "No, we're fine, but he's not."

Mort shined his flashlight so that Colin could see.

"Oh, wow," he said. "And let me guess. You found the body?"

"Don't start, Colin. All right?" I said.

"She didn't find the body, Colin. It was thrown at us," Eleanore said. "You wouldn't have believed how awful it was! I swear, if I hadn't been here . . ."

"What?" I asked.

"Well, I'm not so sure you would have made it down that hill alive without me."

"Eleanore!"

"I was the driving force behind you, and you know it."

"Yeah, because you were trying to catch up with me!"

"Can somebody cover up this body?" Mort said. "Jesus, you think you two could have some respect?"

"Of course, Sheriff," Eleanore said and cast her eyes at me as though I'd started the whole thing.

"Your mother is never going to believe this," Colin said.

"Yes she will. She'll believe it because . . . well, it's me," I admitted.

"Gosh, you haven't found a body in awhile," he said. "What's it been—who was the last one, Maddie?"

"Hey, she was alive. I haven't actually found a dead one in a few years now. And you can't count the one Rachel found!"

"I'm beginning to think you have some sort of corpse-detecting software built into your brain," he said. "It allows you to zero in on dead bodies with virtually no effort."

"My mother sent you, didn't she?"

"No," he said. "Elmer and I were just north of town. We'd just seen a barn owl when I heard Deputy

Swanson's radio squawk. Mort said that you two had been shot at. So, did the guy shoot at you before he launched himself off of the cliff?"

"No, that was somebody else," I said.

"Ah," he said. "But you're fine now?"

"I'm fine."

"Well, I'm not," Eleanore said. "Torie, you're cursed."

Colin laughed and said, "I've been trying to get people to believe that for years."

"Fine, laugh all you want," I said. "But you know, there is a dead person lying here. Could we have some respect?"

"I could have sworn I just said that," Mort said. "Colin, I think maybe you should head back to whatever it was you were doing."

It was suddenly very quiet on the riverbank. Had Mort just kicked Colin off his crime scene? After a moment, Colin cleared his throat. "Oh, sure, Sheriff," he said. "Let me know if I can be of any assistance."

Colin turned to leave, and I really wanted to stick my tongue out at him, but I refrained.

"So, what did the car look like? Could you tell?" Mort asked.

"No," I said. "It was nearly dark. I just saw the head-lights and that was it."

"Well, after you clean up, I want you to come down to the station and look at some photographs of head-lights. People tend to think they're all the same, but they're not. Maybe you could at least narrow that down for us."

"Well, okay," I said. Although I doubted it seriously. I hadn't been paying that much attention to the car, and it had been pretty far away.

"So, where did the shots come from?" he asked.

"They came from the south." I pointed downriver, even though he couldn't see my hand in the blackness.

"You think you can show me where you guys were when it happened?"

"Not in the dark. If we come back tomorrow, yes."

"All right," he said. He shone his light on the dead man's face one last time. "Do you know him?"

"It's hard to tell," I said. "He's sort of bloody."

"Take a good look," he said.

I looked closer but couldn't really see any facial features. All I could see was the blood, and the cuts and the bruising. My stomach lurched and I swallowed quickly. This man had been beaten before he was sent over the cliff. All I could definitely tell was that he was older. Over sixty for sure.

"It's Clifton Weaver," Eleanore said.

"Who's that?" I asked. "Is he a local?"

"Yes," she said. "He works at a shoe store over in Wisteria. Lives in New Kassel. Has lived here for years."

"How do you know him?" Mort asked.

"He's an old college friend of Oscar."

Oscar Murdoch, Eleanore's better half, was an all-around good guy. He'd been a staple of the tourism community for as long as I could remember. He was at least ten or fifteen years older than Eleanore. Most likely in his seventies now.

"I'm sorry to hear that," Mort said.

"I haven't seen too much of him since he started dating *Rosalyn Decker*." She said the name as if it were coated in castor oil. I knew of Rosalyn Decker—and I knew her reputation as a player. Those especially not safe around Ms. Decker were widowers.

"Did he have any enemies?" Sheriff Mort asked.

"I really don't know; you'll have to ask Oscar. Now, can we please go home and change out of these god-awful clothes?"

"Of course," Mort said. "Miller, drive them home."

As soon as I had taken a shower, I put my clothes in a trash bag and headed downstairs to burn them. The phone rang, and the caller ID said it was my mother. I let it ring, because I just didn't have the energy to listen to my mother.

I love my mother. She's one of the wisest people I've ever known. Sometimes I think she's so wise because she's been wheelchair-bound since she was ten years old. She's done a lot of observing rather than partici-pating. Not that physically disabled people can't par-ticipate, because they can, but my mother has chosen to sort of sit on the sidelines. As a result, she can read people better than anybody I know.

But she is a mother first and foremost, and I didn't want to listen to her tell me how being outside at dusk during hunting season was a stupid thing, even though the Olympics had been in the papers, there were signs about it all over town, the sheriff had marked off a ten-mile radius with signs saying NO HUNTING, and all of the deputies had been posted at regular intervals just so this very thing wouldn't happen.

But it still had. And my mom was going to make me feel as though it was my fault. So, after tossing my clothes in the fire pit, I walked to the stables to be with the horses.

Rudy and I used to live in town. Our house had looked right over the Mississippi River, but now we live in this house we had built for us on several acres. We didn't go all out and have a huge house built, because our kids would be leaving home in a few years and then it would be too big. It was a two-story brick structure, and there were times I still thought it was going to be too big someday, like when Rachel went off to college, but I pushed that thought from my mind. The real charm of where we live now is the acreage and all that goes with it.

I'd taken an hour-long shower, scrubbing and rescrubbing and sudsing up until I'd run out of soap and hot water, but somehow, I noticed the faint smell of skunk still lingered in my hair as I walked through the yard and then through the gate to the field beyond.

When I reached the stable, the horses made a few noises, and Cutter sneezed. Rudy and I own three quarter horses. It had been my idea to get them, and I had not regretted the decision for a single second. Yes, they are a lot of work, and yes, we probably don't ride them nearly enough, but they have this amazing calming effect on me and the whole family, and they lend a certain ethereal quality to our property. I know that sounds strange, but it's true. When Rudy and I decided to sell our house in town and move out here, I knew there was something missing. Regardless of the beautiful vistas and the hawks and even though I still had my chickens, there was something missing. It was the river. The Mississippi had been the view out my bedroom window ever since Rudy and I had gotten married. So, when I got the horses, they sort of filled the space that Old Man River had once occupied. The horses gave me something to reflect on, like I used to with the river.

The third horse we had bought, Nessie, had a black mane and a deep brown coat. Her two front legs were white from the knees down. They were her only distinguishing marks. Nessie was the horse I could always count on to be there for me. She sensed, almost immediately, whatever my mood was.

Now was no different. She came right to me and pranced around a bit as she registered the skunk smell. Then she settled in and let me pet her. I opened the door to her stall and walked through to the outside. All of the stalls had an opening out to the field. She followed me as I strode across the dark expanse and found my favorite part of the fence to sit on. I climbed up and sat down and she nuzzled me. "You don't mind the smell, do you?"

She whinnied and stepped sideways.

"Okay, so you do mind. But at least you're willing to keep me company."

We sat there, alone like that, for at least a half hour. She ran off for a few seconds, but then she came right back. Even Cutter sauntered by briefly. Funny how I hadn't wanted to spend the night outdoors, and yet here I was under the stars, in the dark, petting Nessie.

I took in the view that moonlight had to offer and realized that there was something strange about the field.

It had one too many horses.

"What the . . ."

Just then, I saw the headlights from the van and knew that Rudy and the kids were home. I glanced back at the field and counted again. Yes, there were four horses. I was sitting there contemplating how this had happened when I heard Rudy walk up behind me.

"Hey, are you all right? Colin called me on my cell phone when we got out of the theater and said a hunter mistook Eleanore for a deer and shot at you guys."

"Yeah," I said. "I'm fine."

He grabbed me and hugged me and then said, "What is that smell?"

"It's Dial-covered skunk."

He started laughing then, and I jabbed him in the stomach.

"It's just that . . . well, I'll bet you're the only one who got sprayed by a skunk at the first ever annual New Kassel Birding Olympics," he said through laughter.

"There's no annual," I said.

"What?"

"I mean, this was it. There will be no repeat of this ridiculous event."

"Wow, Torie, usually you have a little better attitude about the things that happen to you. No matter what happens, you can usually laugh about it."

"Well, I'm not laughing this time."

"Okay," he said cautiously.

"Why do we have an extra horse?" I asked him.

"We have an extra horse?" he asked and peered into the field. The moonlight allowed him to make out the shape and movements of four horses. "I'll be damned. Was somebody pregnant?"

"No, besides, the new horse is even bigger than the ones we already had."

"Oh," he said. "I don't know. Look, why don't you come inside? Maybe Rachel told one of her friends she could board her horse here."

"All right."

We headed inside, and I played the phone messages while Rudy asked Rachel about the horse. There was a message from Glen Morgan, saying he would meet me the next day at the Kendall House. As much as I was excited about getting new info and pictures on my grandpa's music career, the thought of having to go anywhere other than to the refrigerator was pretty daunting. The next message was from my mother: "I know you're there. I know you're avoiding picking up the phone. I hope you're all right. I hope you don't have an outdoor event in the woods during deer season ever again." Then she'd hung up.

"Well, Rachel doesn't know anything about a fourth horse," Rudy said. All three kids went running past him into the night to see the horse that had magically appeared.

"So," I said. "Did Colin tell you about the body?"

"The body?" he asked, getting out the milk. Then he stopped. "Wait. There was a body?"

I filled Rudy in on all of the events of the day, not just the skunk and the hunter part.

"So, what . . . a body just came flying over the edge of the cliff?"

"And Eleanore and I happened to be there when it landed."

He leaned back and thought for a minute. Then, thinking better of it, he put the milk back and got out a beer. "Who was it?"

"Clifton Weaver? Shoe salesman over in Wisteria. Do you know him?"

Rudy shook his head. "No, never heard of him. Was he . . . shot?"

"I don't know. If he was shot, he was certainly beaten up first."

"Well, what do you think? . . . I mean, I don't understand."

"Me, neither," I said. "Somebody obviously murdered him, shoved him in a trunk, and then tried to get rid of the body."

"Which is ridiculous, because somebody would have found it eventually. People walk along the railroad tracks all the time. And it's hunting season—everybody is out."

"The only thing I can think of is that either they were

61

in a super hurry and intended to go back and move the body later or they thought it was going to go into the river."

Rudy popped the top on his beer and took a swallow. "This is terrible."

"Yeah," I said. "Do me a favor?"

"What?"

"Call my mother and tell her I'm all right."

"Why don't you call her?"

"I'm tired. I just want to go to bed."

"Sure," he said. As I headed for the stairs, he added, "What do I do about Merlin the magical horse?"

I shrugged. "Feed him. I'll have Eleanore run it in the paper."

THE NEW KASSEL GAZETTE
The News You Might Miss
by Eleanore Murdoch

Fellow New Kasselonians. I have been at my computer all night to bring you the news of the birding Olympics. Aside from the fact that my partner, Torie O'Shea, and I were shot at by targetly challenged hunters, the birding Olympics was a success. Elmer Kolbe and Mayor Colin Brooke won, with a total of thirty-three species of birds sighted, including the blue heron, which Elmer claims has existed here for the past two years but nobody else has ever seen. Now that the mayor has witnessed the existence here of the blue heron, I concede that I can no longer doubt Elmer's vision or birding skills. Second place went to Maddie Fulton and Lisa Berenger, third place to Tobias Thorley and Runa Williams.

The events committee would like me to remind everybody that we are having a *Scherenschnitte* demonstration next weekend at the visitors center. *Scherenschnitte* is the art of German paper cutting and should be a big hit with all of our tourists. In fact, the entire Wisteria German Club has signed up for the event.

Torie and Rudy O'Shea wanted me to announce the arrival of a new horse. Apparently, the Percheron just showed up in their field yesterday, and they'd like for the rightful owner to come and claim her.

Annette and Tom Lodke had their first child over the weekend, a girl!

Charity Burgermeister has handmade mittens and scarves for sale. She says she'll make you a matching hat but must have your head measurements first.

I shall go for now. Be sure to ask Sheriff Mort Joachim about the body that he told me not to give details about in the paper.

Until next time,
Eleanore

Six

"The Incredible Hulk does not have X-ray vision!" Mary screamed at the top of her lungs. My eyes had just parted to allow the morning sun to filter in when I heard this.

"But I'm pretending like he has X-ray vision!" Matthew countered.

"But that's not how it goes. Superman has X-ray vision."

"But Superman's dumb."

"Well, so are you!"

I rolled over and covered my head with my pillow and snuggled into Rudy's back. I could just lie here like this all day, right? I thought. Rubbing my feet back and forth on the supersoft sheets, I relaxed back into a semisleep state. After all, was there any reason I actually had to get out of bed?

Glen Morgan and the Kendall House. I had to open the museum. "Ugh."

"Mary! Where are my angel earrings?" Rachel screamed from down the hall.

"I don't have your stupid earrings," she said. "Why would I want those earrings. They're ugly and lame anyway!"

"Mom!" Rachel called. Her voice got louder as she bounded into my bedroom. "Mom. Tell her to give me back my earrings."

"Mary, give your sister back her earrings," I said.

"I don't have them!" Mary said, now standing in the bedroom, too.

"Mom, Mary says the Hulk can't have X-ray vision," Matthew chimed in.

"Well, he doesn't have X-ray vision, honey, but you can pretend that he has whatever you want him to have."

"See," he said and stuck his tongue out at Mary.

Mary turned and stormed out of my bedroom. "I knew you'd take their side!"

"You have to seriously do something about her, Mother!" Rachel said, her dark brown eyes furious with sisterly disgust.

"I am doing something," I said, putting my robe on and stretching.

"What?" she asked.

"I'm not killing her," I said.

Rudy rolled over, leaned as far over as he could and patted my butt, and said, "That's my girl."

"You are insufferable," Rachel said and flew out of the room. Matthew used the distraction to jump on the bed and tickle Rudy, and then the two of them descended into a massive pillow fight and tickling marathon.

After a breakfast of Raisinets and Dr Pepper, I went outside to see Merlin. Although, upon closer inspection, I could tell that Merlin was actually a girl and I'd have to come up with a new name for her. She was also a Percheron. She was head and shoulders bigger than my quarter horses, with a gray speckled coat and a happy little lilt to her gait. I thought of the people around town who owned horses, but I couldn't think of anybody who had a Percheron.

Oh well, I thought, somebody will claim her eventually.

I drove into town and made my way to the Kendall House. My newest acquisition was two stories, with white clapboard and newly painted blue trim. In the spring and summer, all sorts of blooming vines and bushes smothered the house, including some supernatural morning glories. In this part of Missouri, the old-fashioned morning glories are annuals. Meaning they don't usually make it through the winter. There are some new and improved breeds, I suppose, that would—or so I've been told. But at the far edge of the porch on the Kendall home lived some freakishly hardy old-fashioned morning glories that bloomed all morning, all day, and into the evening and came back every year, going dormant only about six weeks during the winter. As a result, the Kendall home was now on the register of haunted places, because a lot of people believed that the house was haunted by Glory Anne Kendall, thus the freakish morning glories. I personally had never seen the ghost of Glory Anne, but there were times I felt something . . . unexplainable. Someday, we'd probably discover that what was growing at the end of the porch weren't morning glories at all, but some unidentified flowering vine, and then I'm not sure if we would still be eligible to be on the register of haunted places anymore. At any rate, the place was quite gorgeous in summer and autumn.

The Kendall House was a museum. Not so much a family museum, unlike the Gaheimer House. The Gaheimer house was filled with all of Mr. Gaheimer's furniture, antiques and the likes, so that one could see how life was at the turn of twentieth century. With the exception of the World War I mural done by Glory's brother Rupert, the Kendall home was a haven for women's textiles. Not only did we have all of Glory Kendall's quilts to display but we had also acquired many other textiles from around the state, going back as far as the late 1700s—everything from quilts, chintz coverlets, rugs, and doilies to dresses, undergarments, samplers, and children's clothing.

This was my baby. Everything else I had inherited from Sylvia Pershing. In fact, most of the town still had the stamp of Sylvia and Wilma Pershing's hard work all over it, but this museum had been my brain-storm. When the house had gone on the market the previous year the owner had agreed to sell me Glory Kendall's quilts and textile-related objects. Then I bought the house. After learning the tragic story of Glory's life, I felt like I should make some sort of monument not just to her but to all women like her.

The surprising thing? It was a huge success. I had more visitors per week to the Kendall home than any other landmark in town. People began calling me up, telling me how they wanted to donate their great-grandma's things because they didn't want anything bad to happen to them, or they didn't want the family fighting over them.

There was a guest house in the back, where I kept some acquisitions in storage, and someday I planned to rotate the things I had on display. None of this would have been possible, though, without the help of Geena Campbell, a quilt historian and textile artist. I'd learned a lot from her, but without her, I wouldn't have known a two-hundred-year-old quilt from one made fifty years ago. She pulled a shift once a week at the Kendall House and said it was the highlight of her week.

At any rate, this took a lot of my time now, which is why I was hiring somebody to take over giving tours for me at the Gaheimer House. Of course, I was still head of the historical society and the only genealogist in town. Not that there was a huge rush on people needing me to trace their family trees, but I still did, on occasion, have somebody request that I find an ancestor of theirs. The sad part about genealogy as a hobby is, well, once you've sort of flushed out all of the lines on your family tree, all that's left are brick walls. Those aren't a whole lot of fun, until they come tumbling down, and then you have this whole new family to absorb. That's the point that I was at now. My family tree was pretty much traced, with the exception of those brick walls.

I opened the museum at ten o'clock, and exactly five minutes later a man walked in and rushed toward me. "Are you Torie O'Shea?" he asked.

"Yes," I said, extending my hand. "You must be Glen Morgan."

He shook my hand, glanced around the room, and said, "I must speak with you at once. Alone."

Well now, I'd been known to do some stupid things in my time, but when a perfect stranger told me that he must speak with me at once, alone, I was a bit leery. Especially when I was the only one working the museum. I'm not saying it would have stopped me from speaking with him alone—because I'd been known to do some pretty silly things—it just made me nervous.

"Well, I can't really disappear, Mr. Morgan. I'm working."

Glen Morgan was about my age, maybe even a few years younger, so late thirties or early forties. He was tall and lean, like a teenage boy. His body was sort of long in the torso and he had big hands. His face was pleasant enough, with expressive black eyes, and he had a head full of brown hair. The resemblance to his grandfather was slight, but I could find it around the chin and the curve of his mouth.

"I've made a huge discovery," he said.

"What's that?"

As he leaned in toward me, he whispered, "I don't think your family tree is what you think it is."

I laughed, until I realized he was serious. "What do you mean?" I asked, suddenly somber. Nobody, I mean nobody, tells me my family tree is incorrect.

"A few months ago, your cousin Phoebe contacted me."

"Phoebe . . . what, Uncle Ike's daughter? Why would she contact you?"

"She's been tracing the family tree," he said.

"She has? Why would she do that?" I'm not sure why the news was so upsetting to me, but it was. Maybe because Phoebe was a nutcase most of the time. She was notorious for just taking off and living in the woods in a tent for weeks on end. Then she'd reappear with some new "vision" that the spirit of the oak tree had given her. Now, I'm not knocking trees. I'm not saying that there isn't wisdom to be learned from our natural environment, because I think there is, but Phoebe was also the same cousin who'd said that Lee Harvey Oswald had impregnated her mother from prison and was really her father. So that sort of put that whole tree wisdom stuff in a bad light.

While her acid-tripping days were over, and she realized that she was the daughter of Ike Keith after all, I still couldn't understand why she'd retrace what I'd already traced. I'll be the first to admit that every family has its secrets. I'll be the first to admit that ancestors pass on their familial "knowledge" and stories to us, and I think for the most part our ancestors are telling the truth. Or, they're telling what they believe to be the truth. I also know that sometimes ancestors will do whatever they can to keep something they're ashamed of a secret, but the data on my family tree was all documented. I only used the family legends as background. The documents were what hold up all of the branches.

"Does she even own a computer?" I asked.

He looked at me weirdly and shook his head. "That's

not the point. She has information that suggests that John Robert Keith may not be the son of Nate Keith."

My head spun. Not the son of Nate Keith? I'll tell you right now that Nate Keith was a son of a bitch, but he was still responsible for me being here, and we can't pick our ancestors. Among other things, Nate Keith was vindictive and beat his wife. I'd love to not have his blood running through my veins, but I do. It's who I am, regardless of whether it makes me happy. I'd had customers come to me before, trying to manipulate data so that they could be descended from the person they thought they *ought* to be descended from. I had a friend who'd started tracing her family tree just so she could find the famous French theater actress that her mother claimed her great-grandmother had been, only to find a family tree full of Irish and Germans, no French, and definitely no famous French actress.

In my own family, I'd been told many times how my great-grandmother had died when my grandma was only four years old. But then I found her obituary and death record, which showed she'd died five years later than I'd been told she had. My grandma was actually nine when her mother died, not four. How does that happen? There are all sorts of reasons, but I had two independent records giving the exact same date, and the obituary couldn't exactly have been faked, since it was published when the event actually happened.

At any rate, I had mixed feelings about Nate Keith. I despised the man, but then, all of his ancestors that I had painstakenly researched wouldn't be my ancestors at all if he suddenly wasn't my great-grandfather. Just off the top of my head, I could think of at least two really cool families that I'd no longer be associated with, and I wouldn't be descended from the highland clan of the Keiths. This bothered me. Which was ridiculous, I knew. Because I was being just like the people I complained about. My ancestors would be who they would be, regardless. So the angst I would feel over no longer being a Keith was sort of . . . silly. But I felt it all the same. For one thing, my maiden name wouldn't even be Keith. This irritated me, to say the least, and my irritation was a bit more evident than I intended when I answered Mr. Morgan.

"Phoebe is a nutcase," I said. "What reason she'd even have to reresearch the family is beyond me."

"The music, Mrs. O'Shea. It's in the music. I'm afraid, whether you like it or not, we're cousins."

"What?"

"I'm saying that your grandpa, John Robert Keith, was actually the son of Scott Morgan."

"Based on Phoebe's discovery?" I asked, crossing my arms.

That and more. Look, I want you to listen to this CD," he said, and handed it to me.

"What is it?" I asked.

"It's a recording of the Morgan Family Players," he said. "Never-released recordings. Your grandpa is the main fiddle player on at least four songs."

"How do you know?"

"Just listen, you'll know. There's more where this came from. After you've listened to it, please call me. I'll meet you," he said.

"Mr. Morgan . . ."

"Call me Glen."

"Glen, I'll be honest. If it came from Phoebe, I'm skeptical. I love her, but she's not always all there. She once said that a rosebush told her to bet four thousand dollars on a horse named Gidget. She lost the money."

He waved his hands in protest. "I know," he said. "I can barely have a normal conversation with her, but her research deserves some closer scrutiny. I'm aware of your credentials. My mother told me if there was anybody in the Keith family to go to with this, it was you. I'm trusting you that you'll give this an unbiased, clinical study. I've got Phoebe's research at home. After you hear the CD, we'll talk more."

I blinked at him. "All right, Glen," I said with a big sigh. "I'll listen to it."

He exited the museum quickly, and I glanced down at the CD he'd given me. He knew exactly what buttons to push. I itched to hear this CD so badly that it actually felt heavy in my hands.

Seven

Stephanie sat in the chair across from my desk with her chin resting in her hand. I put the CD in the player and waited for music. Nothing happened. I checked the cord and made sure it was plugged in. Still nothing. Then I banged on it. Finally, it spurted and kicked in and music began to play.

"Is that him? Is that our grandpa?" I felt sorry for Stephanie. She was the product of an affair that my father had had, and he hadn't known she'd existed until she was grown. As a result, Stephanie had missed out on weekends in the country at Grandma and Grandpa's house. She had missed out on all the crazy sleepovers and strawberry-picking frenzies that all of us cousins had engaged in on a regular basis, as well as running through the orchard at night catching fire-flies, nearly drowning in the pond, chasing the dogs down the road, pulling ticks off of the back of your legs at the same time you nursed the stings inflicted by nettles. But most of all, she had missed out on the music—the endless jam sessions of all of our uncles and our dad in Grandma's living room or, in the summer, out in the front yard. The question of whether or not Grandpa was actually going to treat us with playing a song on his fiddle would hang in the air. Then inevitably, at some point, he'd pick up his instrument and scratch out a few old dance tunes.

Stephanie had missed all of that, through no fault of her own. It was at times like this that I could have kicked my father a good one for the careless way he'd sauntered through life. But, at the same time, if it had been any other way, I wouldn't have had one of my newest dear friends sitting across from me. I was beginning to believe that there was no healthy place for regret.

I listened to the music carefully. It was definitely in the style of my grandpa, but I'd really only heard him as an old man. Sometime during the fifties, my father had taped my grandpa, but even then, he'd hardly been young. Besides, it wasn't as if I was a musicologist. A fiddle is a fiddle, right? Probably the only time I could pick out a specific musician was because I could recognize certain guitar styles. My father and his brother had a definite style all their own that I could pick out in a crowd. I'd listened to my father play every single day growing up. It would be hard not to be able to pinpoint him, but—the fiddle? My ear just wasn't that well trained.

"I'm not sure," I said. There were no liner notes that came with the homemade CD that Glen had given me, so I wasn't even sure what I was listening to. The first song ended and then I heard a voice come on.

"Hey, Johnny, how many babies you got now?" I had no idea whose voice it was, but the man spoke in that clipped and fast way that people did during the Depression.

"Next month's gonna be my third," he said. "I wrote this next song for Jed."

Jed would have been my grandpa's eldest son. He couldn't have been more than a few years old if the third baby was on its way. "That was Grandpa," I said.

"Which one?" she asked.

"The second voice," I said. We both strained to listen to the next song, even though the volume was up plenty. It was as if we were listening for what we couldn't hear, whatever was supposed to be between the lines.

The song was a comical tune about a boy who liked to fish all day. "Why, little Jed even slept with the fishes," the lyrics went. Then the chorus to the song: "Fishes, fishes, little fishes, Momma likes to beat him with the dishes. Take your time, sleep all day, those fishes aren't goin' anywhere anyway." Then there was the fiddle solo. It was a typical jaunty dance tune written during that era. Goofy lyrics were often applied to happy music, anything to make the American people smile, even if just for an evening. Quite often, there was some hefty satire going on, too, and there was no shortage of morbid songs, either. But the happy songs were what people latched onto, especially in the Midwest.

But this song . . . there was something about this song.

"I don't understand," Stephanie said. "What are we listening for?"

"I'm not sure," I said. "But . . . there's something . . ."

"What?"

"I've heard it before," I said.

"Well, wouldn't that be the case? You said Grandpa played all the time."

"Yeah, but that's not where I've heard it."

I went to my computer and Googled the lyrics to the song. A couple of Web sites popped up. Imagine my surprise when right there on the computer screen was the song "Jed's Fishin' Days," written and copyrighted by none other than Scott Morgan. That was where I'd heard it before. It was a Morgan Family Players song.

"What?" Stephanie asked.

"This says the song was written by Scott Morgan, but Grandpa just said there on the recording that he wrote the song for his son Jed."

"What's the copyright date?"

"Well, that doesn't necessarily mean anything," I said. "These old songs—what I call Americana music—some of them are old English ballads or Scottish highland music. They came to this country with the immigrants, who then sang them and changed them, until they evolved into what groups like the Carter Family recorded. Some of these songs are hundreds of years older than their copyright date. So you can't really go by that. Not always. Scott Morgan would have put whatever date he recorded the song as his copyright date, even though it could have been in his repertoire for years. Obviously, the date on this is six years after Grandpa would have written it. My point being, if anybody would have said anything to Scott Morgan about the authenticity of this song, he could easily have said, 'I wrote that song years ago.' Unless Grandpa or somebody took him to court, nobody would be the wiser."

"So . . . this isn't bluegrass, right?" she asked.

"No, bluegrass came later, but bluegrass is descended from this music. You wouldn't have bluegrass without it. It's very difficult to explain the subtle differences in some of this old music, especially when each is so dependent on the other for its existence, if you know what I mean."

"No, I don't," she said, smiling.

"Well, it's like bluegrass borrowed the old highland music from Scotland and England, but then added the African influence of the banjo . . . but then it also has a very American country feel to it. Like the style of picking the banjo. The clawhammer style, that's fairly unique to bluegrass. After the musicians had spent years living in the mountains of Kentucky, Virginia, and the like, those songs from the old country had become distinctly Americanized. It's very complicated but also very organic. At any rate, the stuff that our Grandpa played wasn't bluegrass. He did play it eventually, when it became popular, but not this, not his early stuff."

She shook her head. "How do you know all of this?"

I smiled. "Several reasons. One, our dad's a musician, and I was just interested. When I was growing up, I discovered Dad's recordings of Grandpa. Grandpa could play a breakdown better than anybody I've ever heard. When I started hosting the music festivals here in New Kassel, I began reading up on it more."

"Wow, I had no idea," she said. "So, where did Grandpa learn to play?"

"Well." I sighed. "I was always told that his father, Nate, played but that Grandpa and his sister both learned to play from their neighbors who lived down by the creek bed. The Morgan family."

"Who were they, exactly?"

"Well, they were a fairly famous musical family. At least in this area," I said. "They had recording deals and everything. There was even a petition going around to change the name of Progress, Missouri, to Morganville back in the thirties, but it didn't pass."

Her eyes grew large. "And you're telling me that Grandpa learned to play from them?"

"Well, according to this recording, it seems as though he actually wrote some of their material, too." I typed in the name of another song that was now playing on the CD, a sadder song about the ghost of girl who lived in the meadow and wore daisies in her hair. That song, too, was credited to Scott Morgan. By the time the CD was over, an hour had passed, and in some form or another, my grandpa had claimed to have written at least nine songs that I had Googled and found Scott Morgan taking credit for. "But nobody ever knew."

"Is that what Glen Morgan wanted to tell you?" she asked.

"No, actually," I said. I glanced at the clock. "We need to reopen the museum."

She walked with me as I went to the front door and flipped the sign to OPEN. I turned to her then. "He claims that our grandpa was actually the son of his grandpa—Scott Morgan."

"What?" she asked. Her gaze searched my face, trying to read my feelings about the whole mess. "Is that possible?"

I shrugged. "Well, sure, Stephanie. Anything like that can happen. I mean, you're a good example."

Something flickered in her eyes, and immediately I knew I'd said the wrong thing.

"I didn't mean it like that."

She turned away and headed back to the office.

"Steph," I called out after her. "Stephanie."

When I caught up with her, I grabbed her arm and swung her around in one motion. She wasn't crying, but the look of hurt was heavy in her eyes. "You know I love you," I said. "You know our whole family accepts you. I didn't mean any disrespect by what I said. You know my mouth just opens and out fly ridiculous, often thoughtless things. I just meant that of course these things can happen. That's all I meant. Please don't be offended."

I often felt like I walked on eggshells around Stephanie. Not because she was supersensitive or melodramatic, or prone to tantrums, but because it had taken me thirty-something years to be given the gift of my one and only sister and I was afraid that at any moment she'd realize what a screwed-up family we were and leave. I mean, it wasn't as if she *had* to associate with us.

"It's just that . . ." she began.

"What?" I asked.

"I don't know, maybe I expect too much."

"What? Stephanie, you can't expect too much from me. There's nothing I wouldn't give you. You know that," I said.

"I know," she said. "It's not you. It's everybody else, like that Glen Morgan guy. I am John Robert's grand-daughter, too, but he wouldn't speak to me at all about any of this. He had to speak with you."

"Steph, that's just because of what I do. I've got a reputation as being the family historian, that's all."

She shrugged, not entirely convinced. "I . . . I just wish I could go back in time and spend one day at their house."

"Whose?"

"Grandma and Grandpa's. Just one day."

I grabbed her hand and squeezed it. "I wish you could have been there, too. But look, you can help me with this. Maybe this—whatever this mystery is we've stumbled upon—maybe you can help me with it. Then you'll have contributed to the family his-tory."

"Yeah, I guess," she said. "You must think I'm silly."

"Not at all," I said. And I meant it. I would have felt the same way, probably worse, had I been in her shoes. "All right, I've got to talk to Glen Morgan."

"Off and running," she said, laughing.

"That's me."

"You still smell like skunk, by the way," she said.

"Great. Glen must have thought I was some sort of freak."

We were laughing as I turned to pick up the phone, but before I had the chance, Sheriff Mort knocked on the door frame. "Hey, are you busy?"

"No, come on in."

"I need you to come down and look at headlights. Remember?"

"Right, sorry."

"It's all right," he said. "Look, I just wanted to let you know that the body was positively identified by Rosalyn Decker as that of Clifton Weaver."

"Is she a suspect?" I asked.

"Everybody's a suspect until I say different."

"What was the cause of death?"

"Believe it or not, a gunshot wound to the stomach."

I could feel my brow creasing. "I don't . . ."

"You want to know what I think?" he asked.

For the record, I like Sheriff Mort Joachim. He's young, spiffy, and always immaculate, even if he does spend the majority of his time in the woods. But I like him because he doesn't view me as a threat of any kind. He sees me as a resource. He doesn't know this town like I do. And he knows it. So it doesn't hurt his ego in the least to come to me for help. I like it when a man has a reason to have a huge ego but doesn't have one. It's a good thing when people are more concerned about the world around them than what that world thinks of them. It's also not as easy to manage as one would think. We're all guilty of worrying about what everybody else thinks of us. And if your mouth and your brain don't always have the greatest connection, like mine, then you've got reason to worry. Because, like me, you're probably always offending somebody.

"What do you think?" I asked him.

"This man was beaten terribly. I think he was beaten,

then shot, then shoved in a box and dumped over the edge of the cliff. And I think whoever shot him was shooting at you and Eleanore, too."

"How do you know?"

"It makes sense to me that when they saw you and Eleanore, they assumed you both had witnessed something."

I sat down then, feeling for the chair behind me. Stephanie disappeared into the kitchen and came back with a can of Dr Pepper. "Here, drink," she said.

I took a big gulp. "So, they were actually trying to kill us. Not just—they weren't just hunters who got lost."

"I won't know for sure until you take me out there and show me where you guys were when the shots were fired. I need to analyze the crime scene and collect evidence. But I think it's a good assumption. In fact, those first few shots you heard may have even been the shots that killed Clifton Weaver."

"But . . ." My blood ran cold and I found it difficult to form words.

"Put your head between your knees," Stephanie said.

I did as she instructed.

"But what?" the sheriff asked.

I raised my head and the room spun. "But damn, that's awfully brutal, don't you think? That means Clifton Weaver probably knew he was going to die."

"Yup."

"But why beat him up first?"

"Information."

"Huh?"

"What kind of information?" Stephanie asked.

"There are only two reasons to beat somebody up first when you're going to kill him anyway. One, you're just a sadistic bastard who wants to inflict pain, or you think your victim knows something that you can learn by beating it out of him."

My mind reeled, and the Dr Pepper wasn't strong enough.

"Like I said, that's just my theory for right now. I need you to come out soon and show me where you were when the shots started."

"Right," I said and swallowed.

"For now, I'm running down everything I can on this Weaver guy."

"What do we know about him?" I asked.

"What, you don't know him?"

"I don't know everybody in the town, regardless of what you may think. This is one guy I don't know."

"We know . . . nothing much. He was born south of here—in Progress."

"Progress?"

"Why?" Mort asked.

"Nothing, that's just where our dad was born. His whole family is from Progress," I said.

"Huh," he said, tapping his chin and mentally filing that for future reference. "At any rate, he was born down there, his parents moved up here when he was about seventeen, he graduated from New Kassel High School, went to a community college with Oscar Murdoch for two years, joined the army for several years, maybe even did a tour in Korea—I'm still checking on that—lived in Wisteria for a while, then moved back here. In general, there's not much to report. He's been a shoe salesman almost his entire life."

"I don't get it. What does a shoe salesman know that would get him killed?"

"I don't know," the sheriff said. "Is there any way you can get away?"

I glanced at Stephanie.

"Of course," she said. "I'll hold down the fort."

I grabbed my jacket. Just as we were about to head out the door, Mort glanced around and said, "You did a great job with this place."

"Thanks."

"I like your office at the other house better, though," he said. "I like all those things you have hanging on the walls."

"Oh," I said. "Well, I haven't decorated this one yet."

Who would have thought that the new sheriff paid attention to interior design?

Eight

Seeing our bird-watching place by daylight made no impression on me one way or the other. I stood next to Sheriff Mort on the side of the hill, overlooking the river, where Eleanore and I had been the night before when somebody had, apparently, tried to kill us.

The wind was a little brisk, whistling through the bare branches of the trees. "This is the tree Eleanore was sitting in," I said.

If I had realized that the tree was a redbud, I might have suggested to Eleanore to sit in a more secure one. The redbud wasn't very big or very old, and Eleanore had put her butt square on one of the smaller branches. I hadn't really been paying attention to the tree. There was no reason for me to have paid attention to it. I had been counting down the hours until the whole event would be over and I could go home. However, I suppose it was a good thing that Eleanore had chosen that tree, because if it had been a sturdier one, the branch wouldn't have given way and she might have been shot.

I must have been under a lot of stress, because at any other point in my life, getting rid of Eleanore once and for all would have sounded like a good thing. No, honestly, I'm not a murderer, I just wish sometimes that I could magically make her disappear. It had worked with the old mayor. Of course, a lot of people got hurt in the process of getting our old mayor out of town. So I figure maybe I should just grin and bear Eleanore's existence.

Sheriff Mort examined the marks in the tree left by the gunshots. He clicked on his walkie-talkie. "Send Darla down from CSU." Then he smiled at me. "I want to check ballistics on these bullets and see if they match the one found in Weaver's body."

"You found a bullet?"

"Weaver was shot twice; one of the bullets lodged in

a bone. We got lucky. If it matches the bullet right here in this tree," he said, pointing to a hole in the bark, "then I'd say my theory is correct."

He glanced up to the ridge above and then looked south. "If these bullets are from the same gun, and you said they came from a southerly direction," he said, "then I think we'll find evidence of Weaver's murder and beating somewhere down that way."

"Evidence?" I asked.

"Blood from his gunshot wounds. He was most likely shot outside. No point in getting the inside of your car dirty if you don't have to. So he had to have dripped blood somewhere," he said. "And we might get lucky and even find the first bullet that went through him. And maybe his tooth."

"His tooth?"

"During the beating, they knocked a tooth out. It wasn't on his clothes or in the chest they shoved him in, so I'm laying bets it's still at the crime scene."

"Oh," I said and swallowed. My gag reflex gave a nice little jerk. "God, that's just gross."

"That's why I try not to eat before going to work."

"You don't eat all day?" I asked.

"If I've got a crime scene to investigate, I don't eat until I go home. It was especially true when I worked in New Orleans."

"You used to work in New Orleans? I didn't know that."

"Five years," he said. "Worked two years in Billings."

"Montana?"

"Yeah. Did you know the population of the whole state of Montana is less than St. Louis? Well, if you count St. Louis County, as well."

"Not much crime up there?"

"Billings is a good-size town. It has its share."

"You surprise me."

"Because you didn't know these things?"

I shrugged. "I guess."

"People talk every day. They have no idea what little snippets of personal information they give away. It's just a matter of if you're paying attention."

"Right."

"What?" he asked.

"What, what?"

"You got that faraway look in your eyes."

"Oh, it's nothing."

"Nothing is never 'nothing' with you. That much, I learned within the first week I knew you."

"It's just what you said can be applied to other things, not just criminals and investigations. I'm wondering if I need to listen to a certain CD again."

"New music?" he asked.

"New old music. A recording of my grandpa that somebody gave me. I need to really listen to it to get the 'snippets' of personal information that you were just talking about."

"Glad I could be of help," he said and glanced up at a hawk flying overhead. "You can go now. But I want you to go straight to Wisteria and have Fletcher show you the headlight book."

"All right," I said. "I will."

A few minutes later, I was walking through town and noticed that the holiday decorations were coming along quite nicely. White string lights were wound around the lampposts and looped along the chain that kept tourists from sliding down a large hill to the river. Garlands were strewn around every shop doorway, and single battery-operated candles were placed in the windows. Some shop owners had taken it upon themselves to add further to the decorations, like putting that fake snow in the windows and signs that boasted of holiday cheer.

Large groups of people milled about everywhere and it seemed to me that the town was bulging at the seams with people. Then I realized they were there for the choir festival. I'd completely forgotten.

My cell phone rang. "Hello?"

It was Mary. "Mom, Alexa wants to know if I can come over and help her paint her room?"

"Have you returned your sister's earrings?"

"I don't have her stupid earrings. Mom, seriously. Have you seen those earrings? They are butt-ugly. I wouldn't be caught dead wearing them."

"That doesn't mean you didn't take them."

"Why would I take them if they're too ugly to wear?"

"To make your sister crazy."

Silence. I'd either hit the nail on the head or she was having trouble believing that her mother could think this deviously. Honestly, I'd had much more devious thoughts in my life, so this shouldn't have surprised her.

"Whatever," she said finally.

"No, listen," I said. "I know you think you're really proving something to your sister, but you're actually proving a lot more to your father and me."

"Oh, like either one of you cares."

"We do care."

"No you don't. All you care about is your perfect little angel, Rachel."

"That is not true!"

"Fine, whatever, can I go over to Alexa's or not?"

"Not until those earrings are returned."

"But I don't have them! Ugh, never mind. Just, just don't talk to me."

With that, she hung up. I noticed then that there were people staring at me. The reason would be because I was standing in the middle of the street holding up traffic with one finger in my ear and speaking quite loudly. I moved over to the side of the road and stopped in at the Gaheimer House.

Helen Wickland was there, giving tours and showing Rachel the ropes. Helen waved, dressed in her blue-and-white-striped Civil War-era dress. I motioned for Rachel, and she came quietly, trying not to disturb the tourists. "Hi, Mom!" she said. "This is so awesome. I am learning so much!"

"Great," I said.

"When do I get neat costumes to wear?"

"They're being made as we speak," I said.

90

She couldn't help herself. She squealed—and all the tourists turned to look in our direction. I just smiled.

"I cannot wait to see them! What time era did you pick for me? What color are they? Oh, what kinds of patterns? You know, I really like those dresses that are like tight around the waist but then it looks like somebody stuck a bucket under the dress, right in the back, where your butt is. Oh, and all that lace, and oh, my gosh. Although, Helen's dress is really neat as well. I'm hoping mine is purple. Or blue."

"Rachel, shut up."

"Oh," she said. "Sorry, I'm just so excited. And the great part is, I get paid for this! I mean, it's the bomb. How did you ever luck out on such a great gig?"

"Rachel, shut up."

"Oh, yeah."

I had to speak quickly because I could tell she was going to burst if I took too long to get out what I had to say. I could almost see her skull popping as I opened my mouth. "Are you sure Mary took your earrings?" I asked.

"What? Why?"

"Just because. I want to know, is there any other way those earrings could have gone missing?"

"You mean other than her sneaking into my room while I was at school and putting her grimy little hands all over my dresser and then *stealing* them? No."

I rubbed my eyes. I have done many things in my life. I have hosted music festivals with twenty bands and hundreds of patrons. I've moved thousands of jars of strawberry jam from one house to another without breaking or losing any. I've solved hundred-year-old crimes and faced dangerous criminals, thinking I was about to take my last breath. I've traced family trees that people thought were untraceable. For years I kept the town of New Kassel from eating Sylvia alive. I've nursed my husband's tummy after every pie-eating contest he's ever been in, and believe me, he's been in every single one. *But I can't get my children to live peacefully!* What is wrong with me?

I was a complete failure.

"Mom?" Rachel said. "Are you all right?"

"Why?"

"You look like your head is about to burst."

Funny, I'd just been thinking the same thing about her. "Look, I'm going to Wisteria to identify head-lights."

"Huh?"

"Don't worry about it. I'll be home later. Tell your dad not to cook. We're going to Chuck's for pizza."

"Cool. Can Riley come along?"

Riley, her boyfriend. He'd proven himself worthy, so I had no complaints.

"Uh . . . sure," I said.

She kissed me on the cheek and I left for Wisteria, wondering if I'd accomplished anything at all with that conversation. By the time I'd reached the sheriff's department, I had pretty much concluded that no, I hadn't achieved anything at all this morning, except to correctly identify a tree for Sheriff Mort.

Nine

I'd arrived home before Rudy, which wasn't unusual. Riley was standing at the corral, looking at the newly discovered horse, and he waved to me as I pulled in the driveway. Matthew ran up to me, full of verve, with his arms waving about wildly. "Mom, that horse is *big*!"

"Yes, he is."

"I think the Incredible Hulk could ride him!"

I laughed. "Probably."

"So, nobody's claimed him yet?" Riley asked.

"Nope," I said.

Riley was an all-around good kid, I have to admit. He had dreamy blue eyes and dark hair, and he was completely infatuated with my daughter though not in a serial-killer-stalker type of way. For now, it was cute and sweet. I just hoped that it wouldn't become suffocating and controlling later. And I have to admit that I was a bit concerned about how he was going to take Rachel going off to college. As if he'd read my mind, he said, "Has Rachel made up her mind about which college she's going to attend?"

"She hasn't told you?"

"No."

"I think she'd tell you before she told me," I said. I understood where he was coming from, though. He was worried that she was going to go far away to another state and that she'd either forget about him or just plain old never move back home. I worried about the same thing. It was selfish, and neither of us was going to say a word to her about it, but we felt it all the same. It was natural.

"This is the weirdest thing," he said and glanced back out at the Percheron.

"Yup," I said, because there was nothing else I could say. I headed into the house and Matthew followed me, talking the whole way about some creature he'd drawn that had a wingspan the size of the Empire State Building. He'd never actually seen the Empire State Building. He'd just seen King Kong. Either way, the Empire State Building had become his new measurement of exactly what big was.

"I'm going upstairs to listen to music," I said to him. "You want to come with me?"

"Yeah," he said. He trotted up behind me and sat himself on the floor with an action figure that had been secured in the back pocket of his jeans. I put the CD that Morgan had given me into the CD player and pushed the play button. I glanced over at Matthew and saw that his head was keeping time with the music.

"You like this?" I asked.

"Yeah," he said. "It's fun-sounding."

"It's my grandpa and your great-grandpa," I said.

"Great-grandpa?" he asked. "He must be *old*. Like old, old. Was he after the dinosaurs?"

It was really difficult to explain history to a person who could only remember three or four years of his own life, max. We'd had this history discussion before.

For Matthew, there was before dinosaurs, after dinosaurs, and then the knights with their swords. Then he went straight to the here and now.

"After the dinosaurs," I said. "And after the knights."

"Still," he said, his eyes huge. "If he's *your* grandpa, he must be, like, really old."

"Actually, he's dead."

"See, told you he's old."

"Right," I said. I went back to listening to the music. The whole CD had played and I still hadn't found anything that stood out, aside from my earlier discovery. I played it again while Matthew bounced his action figure off of every bookcase in the room. Every now and then, he'd stop to dance a little jig when my grandpa would play a particularly fast breakdown on the fiddle. I can't explain the feeling that overcame me. My grandpa had been dead for years. And here was the next generation of our family enjoying his music. It was a connection linking the generations, separated by decades, yet . . . the connection had been made. John Robert's music was really his legacy, even if he'd never been famous or made a million dollars, and he deserved the credit.

"Hey, who's playing the hillbilly music?" Rudy asked, coming into the office.

"Hi," I said. "This is my grandpa playing."

"Really? That's neat. Where'd you get it?"

"Some guy . . ."

" 'Some guy'? Please. Give me more credit than that."

I laughed. "Glen Morgan, who is the grandson of Scott Morgan."

"Oh, yeah," he said. "I've heard of Scott Morgan. How'd this Glen get recordings of your grandpa?"

"Well, you knew the Morgans were neighbors, right? Family legend says that my grandpa *almost* married one of Scott's daughters," I said. "Which, if what Glen has to say is correct, would have been a nightmare."

"Why?" Rudy asked.

"Because according to Glen, my grandpa's father wasn't Nate Keith. It was Scott Morgan," I said. "Of course, I don't really believe that."

"Why not?"

"Because he seems to have gotten his info from Phoebe."

"Your cousin?"

I nodded.

"The same Phoebe who claimed she had an affair with Scotty from the *Enterprise*?"

"Not just Scotty from the *Enterprise*, but while she was *on* the *Enterprise* somewhere in the Alpha Quadrant."

Rudy laughed, but then his laughter faded as quickly as it had come. "Then why do you look so worried?"

I explained to him about the music on the CD being Morgan Family Players songs and how my grandpa had actually written them. "My guess is the original recordings of this were never supposed to be found. They stole those songs from my grandpa. Which lends credence to the other family legend that I've heard."

"What's that?"

"That sometime they had a falling-out and my grandpa had forbidden any of his children to even speak to that family," I said. "My dad used to say that even if they headed up the creek bed in the direction of their home and it got back to my grandpa, they all got the spankin' of their lives."

"Okay . . . so how does this correlate to your family tree being wrong?" he asked.

I shrugged.

"You're thinking if you didn't know this stuff, what else didn't you know?"

I nodded.

"Well, why don't you call Phoebe and see what information she's got?"

"I don't want Phoebe to know I know about any of this," I said.

"Why not?"

"It's better not to involve Phoebe," I said.

"So, what then? Are you going to ignore this information?"

"No," I said. "I'm going to try to meet with Glen later. After dinner tonight."

"Oooh, what's for dinner?" he asked. "You gonna make those chicken and dumplings again?"

"No," I said. "We're going to Chuck's for pizza."

"Oh," he said. "That's just as good."

Glen Morgan had agreed to meet with me. He lived in a suburb of St. Louis, and so I drove up there after dinner. It was dark by the time I reached his house in Kirkwood. It was December, after all, and the days were almost as short as they would get before they would grow longer again. The air was nippy and brisk, and everywhere I looked, houses were decorated with their holiday regalia.

Kirkwood is a great little community, located just west of St. Louis, with wonderful two- and three-story homes with big wraparound porches. Entire blocks were like that, with trees taller than the three-story houses. I passed the train station and then watched for the street that I wanted, turned and followed it down several blocks until I came to the address that Glen Morgan had given me over the phone.

The steps on his front porch creaked as I walked up them and rang the doorbell. I couldn't tell exactly in the dark, but I thought his house was painted a pale yellow with white trim. He answered and ushered me in. The inside of his house was a veritable shrine to his grandfather's music. Everywhere I looked were framed album covers, framed sheet music, instruments, old photographs, and magazine covers.

"Wow," I said.

"Yeah," he said, running his hand through his hair. "It's an obsession."

"I don't know what to say," I said. "I'm fairly obsessed, too, when I get on something. But I think you take the cake."

He laughed. He seemed more relaxed than the other times I'd spoken with him.

"Do you play?" I asked.

"Actually, I'm in a band."

"What instrument?"

"Uh . . . gee, I play piano and banjo and harmonica, but with the band, I play the guitar. We played in New Kassel once at one of your musical festivals."

"Really?" I asked.

"Yeah, I had no idea who you were, though. Or I would have introduced myself. Of course, back then I didn't fully understand the connection we have," he said.

"Yeah, about that . . ."

"Wait," he said. He handed me a manila envelope. "These are for you."

I searched his face for some sort of clue as to what I'd find in the envelope, but I couldn't decipher what lay in his eyes. I opened the envelope and inside were photographs of my grandpa, dozens of them. Mostly, they were of him onstage at hoedowns or box socials with the Morgans. I knew this because I recognized Scott Morgan in the photographs. I also knew from family legends that my grandpa had played on occasion with the Morgan Family Players.

There were a few candid shots in the bunch, one of which was of Grandpa sitting at a picnic table with his fiddle at his chin and a giant watermelon sitting in front him. The smile on his face was one of pure joy. I wondered what was happening at the moment that photograph was taken. Was it a church picnic, or just some local gathering where his mother had hauled out the watermelon and a pie or two and everybody just jammed? That's how it always happened when I was a kid.

"I don't know what to say," I said. "Thank you."

"You're welcome," he said. "Have a seat."

I sat down, and he offered me a glass of iced tea. "I have to tell you, Mrs. O'Shea, I've discovered the most amazing things."

"Yeah, about those things, Glen. What proof does Phoebe have about the parentage of our grandfather?"

He smiled but hesitated to speak. "I know this is hard for you. Your reputation precedes you."

I smiled, because honestly, I'd heard that before. And let me tell you that my "reputation" isn't always good. Not that it's necessarily bad, just that, well, I can be difficult. Rudy assures me that I'm worth it, but still. Glen had either heard from Phoebe or from somebody else in the family that I'm a bit particular when it comes to other people writing the family history. I've already done it, darn it. I'll admit I'm a bit vain about this, but I suppose it's more than that. I'm the one who worked my fanny off to trace the family tree—a total labor of love—when nobody else even cared. So to have somebody come along and suddenly care seemed both exciting and unfair. Don't get me wrong. I'm not one to hoard my research or my discoveries. I'll share anything I have with anybody who's interested. I believe that genealogy and one's family history should be shared. If people were interested now, that was great. It was fantastic. I just didn't want anyone to come along and tell me that I didn't know what I was talking about after I'd spent twenty-something years of going it on my own.

"Right now, I'm in a very precarious situation," Glen said.

"Why?"

"There are people who don't want this news to come out," he said. "By now, I'm sure you've realized that your grandpa wrote a great number of the Morgan Family Players songs."

"At least nine, judging by the CD you gave me."

"My family recorded hundreds of songs. Of those hundreds, your grandpa wrote twenty-seven of them, that I know of, and never got credit for any of them. Nor did he get paid for them. And during the Depression, that money could have come in handy, I'm sure. As you can imagine, if word of this got out, Scott Morgan's reputation would be stained and your family would have legal rights to royalties on the Morgan family's music."

"Right," I said. When he spoke of my family having rights to the Morgan family's music royalties, I'm fairly certain he meant my father and his siblings. In Jed's case, maybe his children would benefit from this, since Uncle Jed was dead now. But in my case, it would go to my father. If all of this were true, I'd be much more interested in my grandfather getting the credit he deserved than in the money. "So why are you telling me this?"

"Because it's not right, for one thing," he said. "For

the other, if John Robert was Scott's son, then the sin is doubly worse. Scott Morgan cheated his own son out of money and fame."

"So, all this is out of a chivalrous notion?" I asked. I knew there were people who did the right thing, but when it came to money, more often than not, they didn't.

"If all of this is true, and I believe it is, then John Robert is as much a part of the Morgan Family Players legacy as my father. I want the history of my family right. And adding John Robert to the roster is right, so to speak."

"What's her proof?" I asked again.

"Letters from your great-grandma to Scott Morgan. They come right out and say that he is the father. I believe, and I quote, they say, 'The boy looks more like you than any of your own sons. He is yours. How can you be so cruel?' End quote."

"What's she referring to? So cruel about what?" I asked.

Glen shrugged. "I'm not sure. But those letters were written when John Robert was young. The letters give no indication that she was thinking about leaving Nate Keith."

"Nor would she," I said. "It would have been suicide to even think it."

"I've heard of Nate Keith's . . . wrath."

"Nate Keith gave no indication ever that John Robert wasn't his son. In fact, he left him the home place in his will," I said.

Glen made the palms-up gesture. "I don't know how to explain it; I just know what the letters say."

I stood then to look at the items hanging on the walls. "May I take a closer look?"

"By all means."

As I walked to the wall, I got a glimpse of his hallway and a room that I could just see the corner of. It looked like an office. There was a computer, and it was surrounded with books of some sort, sheet music pinned to the wall, and recording equipment. He was in the middle of a big project. I knew, because my desk and office looked like that when I was in the midst of something huge. He followed me to the wall and pointed to the people in the photographs as he told me who everybody was. "That's my dad, Roscoe. This is his sister Miriam, and that back there is their cousin Toot."

"Toot?"

"Yeah, his real name was Charlie, but they called him Toot. This is my dad's brother Eddie, and, of course, that's Grandpa Scott. Scott had two other sons and another daughter, but they were never in the band."

"Why not?"

"Uncle George was tone-deaf and just never took to any instruments, Uncle Cletis didn't care about music, and Aunt Em was . . . touched."

" 'Touched'?"

"Yeah, not all there."

"Oh," I said. I understood a thing or two about

touched relatives. "Who's the other woman? Playing the guitar."

"That's Belle. She was married to Uncle Eddie. She disappeared one night."

" 'Disappeared'?" I asked.

"She and Eddie had a big fight; she said she was leaving, and she did. Never came back. None of us ever heard from her again," he said.

"So, I have to ask, where did Phoebe find these letters?"

"She told me her dad had them. When her dad retired last year, they downsized and were going through stuff and found them," he said.

"If they were letters that our great-grandma had sent to Scott Morgan, how did they come back to be in our family's possession?" I asked.

"I'm not sure." He shrugged. "Who knows what went on in the decades before we were born?"

"Why did Phoebe contact you?" I asked.

"I suppose she recognized the name of Scott Morgan."

"And the music? That you just recently discovered?"

"You sound as though you're skeptical."

"Of course I'm skeptical," I said. "I've spent my whole life doing this sort of thing, and then out of the blue, my nutty cousin manages to find letters indicating the pedigree of our grandfather is all wrong and you find long-lost recordings that indicate he wrote much of the music for the same family that Phoebe is suddenly laying claim to. Sounds like a scam to me."

"Scam?" he asked, glancing about nervously.

"Like maybe you're wanting to conjure up some cheap publicity for the Morgan family. What, have you got a book in the works? Are you writing a book on the family and this is your way of getting publicity for it? Introduce some equally talented fiddle player who just never got a break and make him the illegitimate son of your subject, who just happened to write some of the music? It would cause quite a stir," I said.

He swallowed. "As a matter of fact, I am writing a book on the family."

"Yes, as I thought. Thank you very much, Mr. Morgan. It's been nice meeting you. I'll treasure these photographs," I said and headed for the door.

"But there's more," he said.

"More what?"

"More music where that came from. I've got more recordings of your grandpa."

"Great, that's wonderful." I didn't care. I was not going to be a part of this.

"I am writing a book, Mrs. O'Shea, but that's the only part you've got right. Sure, the publicity will be great for it, but I didn't *plan* it. I just got lucky."

I stood at the door, knowing that if I stayed and listened to anything else that he had to say, it could change the way I thought of everything. If I walked out right then, I could keep my heritage intact. What had I just been thinking about? Those people who tried to manipulate the family tree to be what they wanted? Was that what I was doing? Staring real evidence in the face and refusing to believe it because I didn't want to give up the pedigree I'd come to love? "Where did you get the music?"

"Toot's wife. She's so old now. When she found out I was working on this book, she gave me all of the old recordings that she had. Boxes of them. I haven't even made it through all of them yet. As I come to them, I put them on CD. When Phoebe came to me with the letters, I didn't believe her at first. Then the more I listened to the recordings, and I started finding these songs by your grandpa, the more I started to believe her."

"So what do you want from me? Obviously, you're not just giving me all of this information for the heck of it."

"Well, you're the family historian. You should be the one to have the new information to hand down to the next generations. Aside from that, I want you to do a quote for the book. Not only are you descended from the subject in question but you're a leading authority."

I thought about it a moment. I knew he was playing to my ego, that elusive little thing that doesn't really exist, when you think about it. It's more like personality or opinion. It wasn't something I could actually take out and club to death with a hammer but the tug of it was so real. I found myself saying, "Okay, here's what I want. I want those original recordings analyzed by a technician—one that I choose. If he says they're authentic and they've not been doctored, fine. But if he's not thoroughly convinced of their authenticity, then when your exposé comes out, I'll deny everything."

"Fair enough."

"And the letters from Phoebe, I want those, too. And I'll have them analyzed."

"I only have copies, Phoebe has the originals."

My eyes rolled in the back of my head. "Oh great," I muttered. That meant I'd have to go visit Phoebe. And not only would I have to visit her; I'd have to convince her to give me the original copies of the letters long enough to have them tested. A task that seemed overwhelmingly daunting, considering Phoebe's disposition.

"I'll call you to bring me the tapes and I'll take them to the person I want to analyze them," I said.

"This is great," he said. He shoved his hands in his pockets and rocked forward on the balls of his feet. "This is why I wanted you involved. I knew you'd help. I knew you wouldn't just blow me off or accept it at face value. This is what I was hoping for."

"Mr. Morgan, are you sure this is what you want to do? I doubt your family will like the offspring of John Robert laying claim to your kingdom."

"Oh, I know," he said. "They'll be furious, I'm sure. But I can't help it. It's the right thing to do. And . . . well, some of them have already gotten a whiff of what I'm doing. And they aren't happy. That's why time is of the essence. I've got to prove or disprove this before the whole family is in an uproar."

"And it will sell more books, I'm sure."

"That doesn't hurt," he said and smiled.

At least he was honest.

Ten

On Thursday, everybody overslept. I have no idea why, but every now and then the little motor that keeps the family functioning just burps or runs out of gas or something and the whole damn house falls apart. We oversleep, or forget lunches, or miss the bus, or, like this Thursday, all three. Why have one screwup for the day when you get three for the price of one?

"How do all of the alarms in the house stop working on the same day?" Rudy asked as he jumped out of bed.

"Well, it all starts with you. Your alarm goes off, which wakes me up, and then I get Matthew up. Rachel, on the other hand, has her own alarm, but if she doesn't hear you and me get up, she's convinced that her alarm is broken or set wrong and waits for us to wake her up. Mary? Well . . . Mary doesn't get up until somebody goes in her room and screams at the top of their lungs, so we can't exactly count on her as backup."

Rudy stared at me with that frightened look he gets every now and then when he realizes that he's living with the most unusual family in the world. He says nothing, though, because he knows if he does, I'll remind him that they sprang from his loins.

As Rudy was pulling on his pants, I said, "Oh, by the way. I think we should let Mary be Santa Lucia this year." In Scandinavian countries, Santa Lucia Day is celebrated by having a young teenage girl dress in white and wear a wreath of candles on her head while offering sweet rolls to her guests. Every year, we have a parade on or around Santa Lucia Day, and we have a young girl from town lead the procession as Santa Lucia. I thought it would help Mary feel like a part of what I did in our town. Maybe all that was wrong with Mary was just jealousy about Rachel getting to work with me. It was one more thing that I was proud of Rachel for. So why not give a chance to Mary?

Rudy got two legs in one hole of his pants and flopped on the bed. "Wait, you're suggesting we let our darling, though clumsy, daughter put candles on her head?" he asked. He yanked the pants off, and they were inside out. He took the time to turn them right side out and then very carefully put a leg in each hole. "Her head will go up in flames, and you know it."

"That's not necessarily true," I said. I went to our bedroom door and yelled down the hall, "Girls, get out of bed. You're oversleeping!"

Rudy pulled his socks on, then his T-shirt, then his button-down shirt. He was getting that middle-aged paunch, not a lot, just enough to separate him from the boys. Which was fine by me. I like my men with meat on their bones. "You're crazy," he said. "She doesn't know if she's coming or going half the time, Torie."

"Well, we have to start somewhere. We have to let her think we have confidence in her."

"Okay, but do we have to start with fire?"

"Rudy . . ."

109

"What?" he said. "We're talking about fire!"

"Your socks are mismatched and your T-shirt is on inside out."

He glanced down at his feet, one sporting a black sock to match his pants and the other one a tan sock that didn't match anything. "I hate it when I oversleep."

"I know," I said. "I'm letting her be Santa Lucia."

"What, I get no say-so?" he said.

As I walked out of the room, I heard him say, "Fine, I'll call and take out extra insurance coverage on her today!"

When we were all finally ready to leave, Mary stood by the corral, looking at the horses, while I shoved Matthew in the car. "Hey, Mary, let's go!"

She offered her hand up to Cutter, and he nuzzled it. Then she turned toward the car. "I still can't believe nobody's come for the other horse," she said.

"I know."

"If nobody comes, can we keep her?"

"I don't know the first thing about Percherons," I said.

"Well, you didn't know anything about quarter horses, either, until you bought them."

"This is true, but I don't know. I just hate to say the horse is ours and then a year from now some family comes to our door and says she's theirs, you know?"

She shrugged.

"We'll see. Let me talk to your dad about it."

Mary got into the front seat. She rode shotgun

110

because she quite often got sick in the backseat. Rachel used to claim that Mary was just faking it to get to sit up front, until Mary threw up a few times; then Rachel conceded. I suppose a vomit-free ride was worth giving up the front seat for.

"I wanted to ask you if you'd be Santa Lucia this year?" I said.

"Who do you want for Santa Lucia?" Rachel asked from the backseat.

"Mary."

"What about me? I never got to be Santa Lucia!" Rachel said.

"Not everything's about you!" Mary shouted back.

"Whoa, wait, this is not intended to be a fight. I just want to know if you'll do it."

Mary shrugged.

"Well, I need to know, because otherwise I'm going to ask Charity's niece."

"Wendy?" she said, incredulous. "She doesn't need a bigger head than she's already got. I'll do it."

"Great," I said. "It's Saturday during the procession."

"Okay," she said.

I dropped all of them off at school, and for the first time in a while I felt as though I'd accomplished something, even if they were over an hour late. Since Geena Campbell was covering the Kendall House and my sister was covering the Gaheimer House, I decided to go to Fräulein Krista's Speishaus for breakfast. It's my favorite place to eat in New Kassel. I even have my own booth. Of course, I've never had to remove anybody from my booth; it just always seems to be empty when I go there. Thursday morning was no different.

I was about to tear into my waffle and hash browns, when Sheriff Mort and Colin stepped inside. It wasn't unusual for them to be seen together. They were friends, after all. Colin was the one who'd endorsed Mort for sheriff, but when they turned and walked toward me, an uneasy feeling settled in my stomach. The sheriff and mayor appeared to have business on their minds.

"Hey, Torie," Colin said. "Can we sit down?"

"Depends," I said. "What's up?"

"Your mom said you've discovered some old recordings of your grandpa's?" Colin said.

"Well, I didn't discover them. In fact, I've got a friend in Wisteria who's supposed to be listening to them today to authenticate them for me. It's going to take him awhile, I'm sure."

"Who is it?" Colin asked.

"Leo King," I said. "His band, the Granite County Fire Pickers, always plays at our music festivals. He told me if I ever needed anything to give him a call. So I did. Why?"

Colin shrugged. "Just curious. Just makin' conversation."

"Why are you two really here?" I asked. I took a bite of hash browns and swallowed.

"We found blood and a bullet where I thought we'd find them," Mort said. "Up on the ridge, but farther south. The bullet matches the one that came out of the tree Eleanore was sitting in."

"And the blood?"

"We're still waiting on that. Ballistics happened to be free and clear when I sent off the bullets, so they got it done quickly. DNA lab is a bit more backed up. I should find out tomorrow or Saturday. But I'll bet next month's salary it's a match to our victim."

I sighed heavily. "So most likely it wasn't hunters who shot at us."

Mort shook his head in the negative. "Though it seems like you've gotten over being shot at fairly quickly," he said.

"She's been shot at before," Colin chimed in.

"It's not like I can identify the shooters," I said. "They have to know that."

"*They* are cold-blooded killers. They don't have to know anything," Mort said.

A chill danced down my spine. "Well, it was so far away. There's no way they identified us, but I have a feeling this isn't all you wanted to tell me."

Both of them shifted in their seats and finally Colin spoke. "Well, I thought it would be a good idea if Mort brought you in on this one, officially."

"Officially" meant that Mort would consult me. I was a special consultant to the sheriff's office now. Mort had arranged that, not Colin. What I didn't understand was why Colin had to be the one to make this call.

"What's going on?" I asked, and shoved my perfectly

good waffle to the side. It would get soggy now, so I figured I might as well just accept the fact that breakfast was ruined and that I'd just have to come back for lunch.

"Nothing," Colin said. "Other than Clifton Weaver is from Progress, and you've got connections down there. So Mort would like you to go down to Progress and poke around."

I looked at Mort. "Why didn't you just ask me? Why bring him into it?"

"Because I want to send Colin with you," Mort said.

"What do you mean?"

"I mean this was a very brutal attack and murder on a Granite County resident, and as far as I can tell, there was no reason for it. So far, everybody I've interviewed had no reason to hurt Weaver, no beef with him . . . and all have alibis. I would just feel better if you had somebody with you when you go poking your nose around in Progress."

"Then why don't you go with me? Or send one of the deputies?"

"I've got one deputy out on sick leave and another on vacation, and there's just too much for me to do here. I can't leave," Mort said.

"So, you came with Colin to smooth things over, thinking I would just agree to whatever you said."

They exchanged nervous glances and then gave me sheepish grins. "Well, yeah," Mort said. "But, Torie, I'm gonna say this in front of Colin. You call the shots. He's just there as muscle."

"Wait. Don't you have some sort of mayoral duties to do or something?" I asked Colin.

"Golf game at noon and a small business matter at four that I can postpone until tomorrow."

"Is he going to carry a gun?" I asked. "Brawn doesn't get you everywhere, you know."

"Yes," Colin said. "I have a permit. I'll bring it as backup only. I'll leave it in the car."

Mort said nothing, just glanced at me to see if this would pass my approval.

"Because I've had to rescue him a few times even when he *was* armed," I said.

"So I've heard," Mort said.

"All right," I said. "Let's do it today, while I've got coverage on both museums."

Mort gave me notes on his investigation, including the names and addresses of Clifton Weaver's living relatives in Progress, Missouri. I paid for my breakfast and then Colin and I headed out of town.

Progress is one of those towns that—excuse me for saying so— progress has sort of passed by. It is about an hour due south of New Kassel. My dad grew up in the country surrounding Progress, but when he would talk of "going to town," Progress was the town he was speaking of. It has a population of about twenty thousand now, but when my dad was a kid, it was probably about eight thousand. It boasts several fast-food restaurants, a school, a teeny tiny library, and—what else?—a Wal-Mart.

Several of my aunts and uncles still lived down

there, including Uncle Ike and his daughter Phoebe.

Colin was unusually quiet as he sat next to me in the front seat. About ten minutes from Progress, he finally began to speak. "Do you ever look back and wonder what you should have done differently in your life?"

"Please tell me you're not divorcing my mother," I said.

"God no. Jalena is the greatest thing that ever happened to me. The only good thing that ever happened to me," he said.

"You know, good things don't just happen to people, Colin. You have to help them along sometimes. Which you did. If I remember correctly, you pursued my mother."

"True," he said.

"So what gives?" I asked, but I already had a pretty good idea what he was going to say.

"It's this blasted job," he said. "I hate it."

"I know that. Everybody knows that. So when your term is up, do something else."

I glanced over and saw him look off at the rolling countryside and farmland. "It's not that simple," he said. "The job I really want is taken."

"Sheriff."

"Yeah, and Mort's good at what he does," he said. "I don't want to horn in on that."

"Well, not to burst your bubble, but the townspeople like Mort, too. I'm not saying they didn't like you as sheriff, because they did, but Mort has endeared himself to us."

"I know that," he said. "So, even if I ran for the job, you're saying I might not win?"

"That's exactly what I'm saying."

He pinched the bridge of his nose and sighed.

"Why did you do it? Why did you run for mayor if you loved your job as sheriff?"

"I don't know," he said. "That's what I've been trying to figure out. I think part of it was that Bill was such a lousy mayor for such a long time that I wanted to make a difference. Part of it was, maybe I just wanted to try something new. And maybe I was getting a little bored."

"Bored?" I asked. I put on my blinker and got in the turn lane as my exit came up.

"Not bored as in there was nothing to do, just bored with it being the same old stuff to do," he said.

"Well, you've made your bed now."

"I know. I know. That's why I was asking the question about looking back on your life and doing things differently. Do you think this is normal? Do people second-guess their decisions all the time?"

"I think people second-guess their decisions some of the time. I think the people who second-guess themselves the most are either paranoid—"

"I'm not what you call paranoid," he interjected.

I held my finger up. "Or they're the ones who know they either compromised what they believe in or made a decision based on the path of least resistance. You know why?"

"Why?"

"Because those rarely ever work out."

"You think that's what I did?" he asked.

"No," I said. "In your case, I think you took a chance and it turned out poorly. So here's the real question. What do you do about it now?"

"Yeah," he said, watching the cows in the fields go by.

Our first stop was the high school. It was a newer building sitting in a big meadow just on the outskirts of town. Their school colors were red and blue, which were represented in the banners hanging on all the light poles in the parking lot. "What are we doing here?" Colin asked.

"Yearbooks."

He gave me a questioning glance.

"I just want to see who his classmates were. You know, sometimes those relationships last a lifetime. In a small town like theirs and ours, it's almost a given. I've spoken to a lot of people who haven't talked to their former classmates in years. But in smaller towns, it's more likely they will stay in touch and it's more likely they'll marry somebody from their school."

"I didn't."

"I know that. And I didn't, either. But unless somebody moves away and stays away from their small-town roots, the chances are more likely that they will keep their old acquaintances," I said.

"You really do think of everything as one big genealogical chart, don't you?" he said.

"Yup," I replied.

As soon as we entered the school, I was overwhelmed with that school smell. It was a completely unique and completely indescribable smell. I think that's because it was a combination of many things. "The thing with Clifton is that he didn't graduate from Progress High. According to Mort, his parents moved to New Kassel when Mort was about seventeen. So what is that, his junior year? I just want to check out who was in his class before he moved."

The school secretary gave us guest passes and sent us on our way to the library. The only problem was, I couldn't remember what year Clifton Weaver was born. "Call Mort and ask him what year Clifton graduated from high school," I said to Colin.

"My, aren't we bossy."

I glanced through some of the yearbooks and found photographs of my dad and Aunt Sissy before Colin finally told me what year we were looking for. "Class of '52." He hung up the phone and frowned. "Will they have the yearbooks back that far?"

"They should. The historical society has the yearbooks for all of the one-room schoolhouses, one of which my dad attended until eighth grade, and some of the smaller schools on the outskirts of the county. Around 1949, all the smaller schools within a twenty-mile radius consolidated into this one big school."

"How do you know this stuff? I swear, you're just like this walking encyclopedia of completely useless information," Colin said.

"My dad's family have lived in and around Progress for at least a hundred and fifty years. You get to know these things. Besides, I wouldn't exactly say it's useless information."

I pulled out the yearbook for 1951, when Clifton would have been a junior. I made a photocopy of all the pages of Clifton's fellow classmates, then made copies of all the freshmen, sophomores, and seniors, too. In 1951, that totaled fifteen pages. "If it comes in handy, it's not useless knowledge."

"Show-off," he said.

Colin and I spent most of the remaining day in Progress, tracing down people who had died, moved, or were not at home. We got lucky on the second-to-last name on the list that Sheriff Mort had given us. A woman named Etta Chapin lived in a small white house, which I would almost have bet was built by the original owners, not by a construction company. It just had that handmade look to it—the same look that my grandparents' house had. The largest mimosa tree I'd ever seen grew right next to the house. I could just imagine how pretty it must be in June or July, when it bloomed. Right now, it was bare, save for the small seed pods that the wind hadn't jarred loose yet.

We knocked on the door and a woman around sixty years old answered. "Hi," I said. "You don't know me, but I'm an acquaintance of your . . ." I looked at the paper. "Cousin. Clifton Weaver."

"Yes?" she said.

"Are you Etta Chapin?"

She glanced at Colin nervously and then back at me. "Why?" Which meant yes.

"Have you been contacted about his death?"

The expression on her face changed, softened, and then morphed into curiosity. "Yes, another cousin of ours just called to tell me yesterday."

"Well, I live in the same town as he did," I said. "And I've been asked by the sheriff 's department to ask his family some questions." I reached in my purse and got out the formal letter from Mort saying that I was a consultant to his office.

"Questions about what?" she asked.

It was cold on her front porch. I stamped my feet together and said, "May we come in?"

"All right," she said, although her eyes said no. "Can I get you something?"

"No, thank you, ma'am," Colin said. "This will just take a few minutes of your time."

"When was the last time you heard from Clifton?" I asked. Once we were standing inside, Colin flipped open a notebook and wrote down Etta's answers.

"Oh, Uncle George's funeral. Two years ago. That man lived to be ninety-seven. Oldest man in our family, Uncle George was," she said.

"Two years ago," I said, deflated. Chances were that anything Clifton had been involved in to get him killed had come about more recently. She most likely couldn't help us.

"How exactly are you related?" I asked.

"His mother and my father were brother and sister," she said.

I asked a few more questions and really felt like I was wasting this lady's time, so I asked my last question. "Can you think of any reason why anybody would want to hurt Clifton?"

"No," she said. "I was just tellin' that to my husband last night. How I couldn't understand how this could happen to Clif, of all people."

"All right," I said. "We won't bother you anymore." But just as I turned to leave, I saw one of those embroidered samplers hanging on her wall—the type that give the names of both the husband and wife and the date they were married, and which are usually surrounded by lots of flowers and a set of wedding bells. The sampler read MARTIN CHAPIN AND ETTA MORGAN, 25 JANUARY 1963.

Etta *Morgan*? "Mrs. Chapin," I said, "your maiden name was Morgan?"

"Yes," she replied.

"Are you by chance related to Scott Morgan?"

Colin gave me a quizzical look, but I ignored him.

"Why, yes," she said and smiled. Clearly, she was proud of her connection. "He was my grandpa."

"So . . . Clifton Weaver was the grandson of Scott Morgan, as well?"

"Yes, he was Miriam's son. Miriam married Clifton Adam Weaver."

"Let me get this straight," I said, a feeling of dread spreading throughout my chest. "Clifton Weaver was the son of Miriam Morgan, one of the fiddle players for the Morgan Family Players. Is that correct?"

She nodded her head. "Why, is there something wrong?"

"And which one was your father?"

"Cletis," she said. "He never got into music much."

"Ma'am, do you know a man named Glen Morgan?"

"Well, of course, he's Uncle Roscoe's son. Roscoe was on the young end. I think he was second to the youngest. At any rate, little Glen was born just a few years after I got married. Even though we're first cousins, we're a generation apart."

The room spun. This had to mean something. This couldn't just be a coincidence.

"He's a talented one. Inherited all of our grandpa's musical ability. I hear he's writing a book on the family," she said.

"Mrs. Chapin, do you know the name John Robert Keith?" I asked.

She glanced from me to Colin and back to me. She fiddled with her necklace and said, "Yes."

"How do you know him?" I asked.

"Well, he was a neighbor to my grandparents. What has this got to do with poor Clifton?"

"I'm not sure," I said. "What do you remember about John Robert?"

"I remember my dad telling me that Johnny Keith was the best fiddle player west of the Mississippi. That's what. I've heard Johnny Keith play. I was just a kid. He was playing at the church for some dance

123

fund-raiser. I just remember my dad leaning over and saying that he was the premier fiddle player of the valley, not Scott Morgan. He was adamant about that."

I'm not sure why I reacted to this news the way I did, but tears rose to my eyes. I swallowed and fought them back. This all had to mean something. This could not be a coincidence, I thought again.

"Ma'am?" she said. "Are you all right?"

"John Robert Keith—Johnny Keith—was my grandpa," I said.

Her hand covered her mouth, and after a long moment of watching me for some reaction or some hint of an unnamed emotion, she said, "You're that historian who lives up in New Kassel."

"Yes," I said and glanced at Colin. "This is—it's a small world."

"It sure is," she replied, but that was all she said. She crossed her arms in front of her chest. I couldn't help but feel that she was either hiding something or was keeping something to herself.

"Well, we won't bother you anymore," I said. With that, Colin and I walked out to the car, just as a cold gust of wind stirred up the leaves in her front yard and flung them all about.

Once in the car, I sat there, numb.

"You want to explain to me what just happened?" Colin said.

I filled him in on what I could. Glen Morgan coming to me with the recording—which Colin already knew about—and my cousin Phoebe's discovery. And how

124

I'd just met with Glen Morgan a few days ago and he never once mentioned that a cousin of his had just been brutally murdered. Why wouldn't he have at least mentioned it to me? Is that why he'd been acting so nervous when I first met him?

"What does it mean?" he asked.

"Maybe nothing," I said. "But it certainly makes me question Glen's motives."

"Why?"

"Well, isn't it strange that the very day he contacts me with this earthshaking discovery, his first cousin is horribly beaten and shot to death? I mean, so far as coincidences go, this has to be astronomical. Do the math. What are the odds? Like a bazillion to one."

"Nothing is ever easy with you," he said.

My mouth dropped open. "I didn't *do* anything!"

"Let's get back to New Kassel and discuss this with Mort," he said.

"Right." I just sat there looking at the small white cottage in front of us.

"What's wrong?"

"I don't think I can drive," I said. "I'm pretty wigged."

"Okay, I'll drive." When Colin got where I'd been sitting, he got wedged between the steering wheel and the seat. "God, I hate midgets," he said, reaching beneath his leg to release the seat and readjust it.

"No, you don't. My mother's shorter than I am," I said.

"Okay, she's the only exception."

THE NEW KASSEL GAZETTE
The News You Might Miss
by Eleanore Murdoch

Have no fear, fellow New Kasselonians, our brave and wonderful new sheriff is hard at work, trying to discover who shot at me last weekend! I'm doing fine and have gotten over the shock of the traumatic events. Although somebody still owes me a new pair of binoculars.

That surge of electricity last Tuesday when the lights dimmed all over town was just Elmer Kolbe getting electrocuted when he was putting up the Christmas lights on the river overlook. Other than some singed hair and an insatiable thirst, he says he's doing fine.

This year, the cookie bake-off will be headed by Charity Burgermeister. We are looking for at least five-hundred dozen cookies to be donated to the Give a Kid a Cookie Foundation. Father Bingham and the nuns will distribute them to children in the foster homes and hospitals throughout three counties for the holidays. Please have your cookies to Charity by next Sunday.

May everybody have a fun holiday procession this weekend and may those cash registers sing!

Until next time,
Eleanore

Eleven

It was Saturday, just before sunset, and Mary was about to become New Kassel's forty-seventh Santa Lucia. I have to admit that I was a bit nervous, and Rudy had brought the fire extinguisher along with us. I made him keep it in the van, though.

The drum and fife corps sounded first, coming from the direction of Ye Olde Train Depot at one end of town. Slowly, they marched down River Pointe Road. Behind them, the children's choir of the Catholic church began to sing, "Come they told him, pa rum pum pum pum."

Following closely behind was Patty Greene, riding on my neighbor's mule. She carried her newborn daughter, wrapped up in a blanket, who was supposed to be baby Jesus. Joseph, played by her husband, walked alongside. There were no electric lights involved in the procession, only candles or propane lights. After they passed by, my daughter Mary came along, dressed in her long white robe, with a plate of sweet cakes in her hand, the wreath of candles atop her head.

"Oh my God," Rudy said. "You didn't tell me she'd have to balance a tray at the same time she'd be walking."

"Just shut up, Rudy. You're ruining the moment."

She walked with her head held high, her face illuminated by the candles and the flashes of cameras.

Speaking of which, I stepped out from the crowd and snapped three photographs of her. She smiled and kept walking. After Santa Lucia came a long line of people dressed as Father Christmas, Saint Nicholas, and Santa Claus. Then Elmer Kolbe carried a huge lighted menorah. Eleanore followed with a cage full of doves and let them loose. The birds took off quickly and disappeared into the sky. Children wearing wooden shoes from Holland clopped down the cobblestone street, and the only family of African-Americans in New Kassel, dressed in brilliant African robes to represent Kwanza, threw candy out at the onlookers. The procession ended with four archangels, their wings flapping behind them in rhythm to their steps. The archangel Gabriel was played by Chuck Velasco, and I want to state for the record not only that angels should not wear construction boots but that Chuck is about the furthest thing from an angel that you'll find in New Kassel. But that's okay; he took the part seriously, boots and all. After the parade, the New Kassel sixth-grade choir stopped at every intersection and sang "Joy to the World."

The whole event took about twenty or thirty minutes, but people drove from miles around to see it.

"I don't believe it," Rudy said. "She didn't burst into flames."

"What?" Matthew said. "I want to see her burst into flames! Who's going to burst into flames?"

"Nobody," I told him.

Rachel was with Riley somewhere in the crowd. All the tourists who had gathered now went about shopping. The only time our gift shops stayed open past five o'clock on a Saturday was during the holidays. There were big sales and nearly every shop was offering baked goods and refreshments. "I think we should celebrate," Rudy said. "Our insurance rates won't go up."

I jabbed him in the ribs. "You're terrible."

"You know as well as I that it could have gone either way."

I smiled, but the smile faded when I saw Sheriff Mort headed toward me through the crowd. "What's up?" I asked.

"The blood matched our victim. He was definitely killed south of here in that little roadside rest area."

"Could they really get a clear view of Eleanore and me from there? It was nearly dark."

"My bet is somebody had binoculars and was watching out for witnesses. When they saw you guys, they couldn't take any chances," he said.

"That's silly. There's no reason Eleanore and I would have thought they were anything other than hunters."

"I know," he said. "But there you have it. Murderers are quite often just as stupid as they are paranoid."

I shook my head.

"Is there a reason we have to talk about blood and bullets after a holiday procession?" Rudy asked.

"Sorry," Mort and I said in unison.

"So, how's it going with the music?" Mort asked.

"What do you mean?"

"You're having it analyzed," he said.

"I'm going to e-mail Leo tonight when I get home. Haven't heard anything so far," I said.

"Oh, okay," he said.

Just then, Mary came running up to me, her wreath in her hand and the white gown already gone. "How'd I do?" she asked, eyes sparkling.

"You were wonderful!" I said and hugged her.

"Thanks."

"Your head get hot?" Mort asked her.

"Actually, yeah, it did."

These kind of days are wonderful and exhausting all at the same time. I'd been gone all day at the museums, then I'd attended the holiday procession. I wouldn't have traded one moment of the day, since I'd been completely in my element and had a great time, but as we pulled into the driveway, I could feel my muscles sort of tighten up and scream.

Mary instantly headed to the corral before the car engine was even off. Anytime Mary went to the corral, the horses came to the edge to greet her. I'm not sure what magical power she's got, or maybe they just like the way she smells, but they will follow her wherever she goes. "She's still here!" she called out.

The mystery horse was, indeed, still in the corral. "All right," I said to Rudy. "We need to get the vet out here next week and take a look at this new horse."

"Are we keeping her?" Rudy asked.

"I don't know. Somebody had to put her in the corral. Last I knew, draft horses couldn't exactly jump a five-foot-tall fence. She's got shoes, so you know she belongs to somebody. I don't get it," I said.

He shrugged. "Why us?"

"Don't ask that question. Bad things happen when you ask that question."

I grabbed the mail out of the mailbox and headed inside. "Matthew, you need a shower before you get on your jammies!"

Matthew made some disgruntled noise. I'm fairly certain he was worried that the grime was the only thing keeping the skin on his bones and that by taking a bath he was endangering his life, but so be it. As I walked in the house, Matthew was already stripping his clothes off—not happily, I might add—to get his shower over with. Before he ran to the bathroom, he stopped and said, "Mom, what are we going to do about that guy in the woods?"

A large envelope that was nestled among the bills, advertisements, and newspaper got my attention. It was addressed to me. The return address was none other than that of Clifton Weaver, so I was a bit distracted. "What, honey?"

"There's a guy living in the woods," he said. "Should I keep feeding him, or what?"

I thought about this a minute. "No, don't feed him anymore. Talk to your father about it."

He ran off to the bathroom and I stood there staring at the envelope in my hand. How could it possibly take a week to deliver a package to me, when Clifton Weaver and I lived in the same small town? It had to have taken a week, because he'd been dead that long at least. Obviously, he couldn't have mailed it to me after he was dead.

I opened the envelope, hands trembling the whole time. What could Clifton Weaver have sent me? I wondered. I didn't even know him. I didn't think I'd ever met him. A lot of people in town knew who I was because my job was a high-profile one for a small town and my name was in the New Kassel paper once a week over something. But I didn't always know everybody, and I hadn't known this man.

I dumped the contents of the envelope on the kitchen counter. Inside was a CD and a letter. The letter read:

Dear Mrs. O'Shea,
I am not certain that you know who I am, but I have been a resident of New Kassel for a very long time. My grandfather was Scott Morgan. I believe your grandfather knew him. I am aware of your special skills at solving old crimes. When you listen to this CD, I believe you will understand why I have chosen you to give this to. Once you've listened to it, call me at the number below. I'm not sure what to make of this recording. It does not sound like a hoax to me. The original is in a very safe place. My only regret in sending you this is that I'm not certain if there is any danger involved.

I feel as though I am being watched. But maybe that's just the old military man in me. Please listen to this carefully.
Yours respectfully,
Clifton A. Weaver

Gooseflesh tickled my arms, and the hair rose on the back of my neck. A letter from a dead man. God, I hated those. I didn't even notice that Rudy had walked in the house until he asked, "Where are you going?"

"Up to my office," I said. I never even glanced his way. I took the letter, envelope, and CD upstairs and put the CD in the player. Then I sat down and listened. At first, it sounded like a recording done in somebody's house, the living room probably, which wasn't unusual. Back then, that was quite often the makeshift studio. The music was the same type I'd been listening to for the past week. I didn't recognize my grandpa's voice anywhere, but he could have been playing the fiddle. I heard some names thrown around—Scott and Toot. So it was definitely the Morgan Family Players. Scott called the session quits. "We'll go back at it tomorra," he said. I heard the recorder click off.

I sat in the dark for a second, wondering if this was some sort of joke. Then the recorder came back on and there was a tapping sound on the microphone. Then I heard a woman's voice say, "I'm going to sing you a murder."

A guitar kicked in, wonderful harmonies in the chords, and then the mystery woman began to sing.

133

It was a bright and shining autumn morning,
When I found her with my only love.
I thought my eyes they were deceiving,
Until I heard the voice from high above.
The voice said, "You must go and show her
That she cannot take him away . . .
He was meant for your heart only
Regardless of what she'll try and say. . . .

Then the chorus kicked in.

The beautiful Belle, well, she's going straight to hell,
For doin' to me what she did that day.
And let it be said, that the face of the dead,
They don't e-ver truly go away.
Now I waited softly in the barn loft
For her to return and speak her lies.
But she could not know that I'd seen her
And she should prepare for her good-byes.
The ax it was sharpened and so pretty
It gleamed just right in the light.
She couldn't see this coming, could she?
I pulled it back and swung with all my might.
The beautiful Belle, well, she's going straight to hell,
For doin' to me what she did that day.
And let it be said, that the face of the dead,
They don't e-ver truly go away.
Now Belle was so beautiful, I have stated,
And all the people there they did weep.
But it was she who I most deeply hated

For takin' the love that I did need.
So now she's a rotting under the bridge of stone
Nobody will ever know her lips.
Her body is cold, and Eddie, he moans.
I don't regret a one of those licks.
The beautiful Belle, well, she's going straight to hell
For doin' to me what she did that day.
And let it be said, that the face of the dead,
They don't e-ver truly go away. . .
No, they never truly go away. . .

When she was finished singing, the sound of her breathing into the microphone was all that could be heard. Then a muffled sound, like she'd set the guitar down. Then one last haunting sentence before she turned off the recorder: "I wrote that one myself."

"Oh crap," I said. I grabbed the envelope and examined it. The return address may have been for Clifton Weaver in New Kassel, but the postmark was another story. The package had been mailed from Wyoming. So Clifton had either been in Wyoming on the day he was killed and he'd posted the letter before flying home to meet his demise or he'd mailed this to somebody in Wyoming and requested that they mail it to me on a certain day. Or in the event of his death. Or had it been sent by somebody in Wyoming who was pretending to be Clifton Weaver?

I didn't think it really mattered. What mattered was

that Clifton Weaver had thought to send me this . . . this . . . blood ballad.

I picked up the phone and dialed the sheriff. "Mort, we have a huge problem."

Twelve

I opened the door and let Mort in at almost midnight. I handed him the envelope by the very edge. "As soon as I realized what it was, I stopped handling it. I know you're going to find the postman's prints on it, but maybe, just maybe, you'll find a print from the person who sent it to me."

"Hang on. Slow down," he said.

"I also touched the CD and the letter inside, so I suppose you'll check those for prints, as well. Here's a transcript of the lyrics to the song," I said.

Mort read the lyrics. In the amount of time it had taken him to drive out to our house, I had played the CD several more times and had written down the simple yet perplexing words.

He glanced up at me with a sharp expression. "You think this is for real? It could just be the lyrics to a dumb old song," he said. "Those mountain people are always singing about dying and lost love and dying . . . dying, mostly."

"Well, this wasn't written by mountain people; this was written right down here in southeast Missouri," I said.

"You know what I mean," he countered.

"The voice says, 'I'm going to sing you a murder.' Then after the song is over, she takes credit for writing it. The names in the song, Eddie and Belle . . ."

"What about them?" he asked. He removed his hat and scratched his head.

"Eddie Morgan is one of the members of the Morgan Family Players, and his wife, Belle, played the guitar for the band as well. Now, I've been told that Belle Morgan just up and disappeared one night," I said. "What if she never disappeared at all? What if she was murdered?"

"Like the song says," he stated.

"Exactly. I mean, it says right in there that whoever the narrator is takes an ax to Belle, and then Eddie 'moans,' which you could take to mean he's grieving."

"Oh boy." He glanced around the room.

"What?"

"Well, what has this got to do with Clifton Weaver? I don't have the manpower to investigate a cold case when I've got Clifton Weaver in my morgue," he said. "It's not even my jurisdiction!"

"I'll investigate the cold case," I said. "That's what I do best. Besides, Clifton Weaver either sent this to me because he was worried about what he'd discovered or somebody else sent it to me to let me know what Clifton Weaver had discovered. Either way, Sheriff, I think this song is the reason Clifton Weaver was murdered."

"I'll see what I can do," he said. "In the meantime, what are *you* going to do?"

"Libraries are closed tomorrow, so there's not a whole lot to be done right now. But I think I'm going to go talk to a few of the family members and see what they have to say about Belle Morgan's disappearance."

He nodded. "All right, let me know if you need anything."

"I will."

The next morning, I called my dad and met him at Denny's in Arnold for breakfast. Denny's is usually packed because Arnold doesn't really boast many other breakfast-type restaurants. It's situated right off of Highway 55. I found my father in what used to be the smoking section. Arnold passed a no-smoking law in restaurants a while back. My father's been planning on setting the city hall on fire in retaliation but hasn't gotten around to it.

"Hey!" I said.

"Hey, kiddo," he said. Dad was getting old. It was starting to worry me. I mean, we're all getting old, but dad seemed to be noticeably aging. Of course, I didn't see him on a daily or even weekly basis like I did my mother or grandma. Sometimes a whole month went by before I'd see him. Still, I was fairly certain that people weren't supposed to age noticeably in a month. He seemed thinner, grayer.

"You feeling okay, Dad?" I asked.

"I'm fine," he said and fiddled with the cigarette pack on the table next to him. "Actually, no, I feel like hell. This is against my civil rights. No smoking in a public place! What the hell kind of crap is that? I'm telling you, there's some snooty hausfrau in city hall, what do you want to bet?"

"Calm down, Dad." I decided not to tell him that New Kassel was about to pass the same law. No use in him having a stroke at breakfast. "It was voted on."

"Well, the majority of this city is stupid, then. So what's up?"

"Well, how much do you remember about Scott Morgan and his family?" I asked.

The waitress came, and I ordered a Belgian waffle, hash browns, and orange juice. Maybe I'd finally get to have the breakfast that was interrupted at Fräulein Krista's. He ordered the Grand Slam, eggs over easy, extra coffee, extra black.

"What you really want to know is what I remember about my family and the Morgan family, isn't it?" he asked.

"Has Mom talked to you?"

He smiled. "No," he said. "But usually if you've got a question like this for me, it's family-related."

"Oh," I said. "Well, sorry I'm so transparent."

He waved a hand at me. "If it's the worst thing you do . . ." he said. "Well, my dad learned to play the fiddle from Scott Morgan. Him and Roscoe Morgan were good friends. Dad told me he almost married Miriam Morgan. Said her fiddle playing turned him on."

"Dad," I said.

"What?"

"I really don't want to hear about my grandpa being turned on."

"Well, it's the truth," he said. "Told me nothing was hotter than Miriam with a fiddle in her hands, and if she hadn't been so darned sexy, Dad told me, he woulda never been the fiddle player that he became. Because he spent an extraordinary amount of time down at Scott's place, learning the fiddle, when he was really just wanting to be with Miriam."

"Oh, brother," I said and rested my chin in my hand.

"I think he also wanted to impress her. So he'd just practice the hell out of that fiddle," he said, laughing. Then he looked me straight in the eye and said, "What is it you really want to know?"

I didn't tell him about Glen Morgan or Phoebe's theory that my grandpa was actually the son of Scott and not Nate Keith. Instead, I told him everything else. "Glen is convinced that Scott stole some songs from my grandpa—your dad," I said. "I've heard the recordings."

He perked up then, and his eyes got a sparkle. "You've got new recordings of Dad?" he asked.

"Yeah," I said. "From the early days. Dad, they're really neat."

"Well," he said with a sigh. "I've often thought something like that happened. Because Dad told us we were forbidden to even talk to the Morgans. Kind of hard when they went to the same little church in the valley. But that's all right. Us Keiths, we'd sit on one side of the church, and the Morgans, they'd sit on the other."

"You think that was it? The music?"

He nodded. "Absolutely. Imagine barely being able to feed your family, and then the man you helped write songs for went on to be fairly rich with your music!"

"Why didn't Grandpa take him to court?" I asked.

Dad shrugged. "Who knows? Dad was just a country boy. Probably didn't even know that option was open to him. All he wanted to do was plow corn and play the fiddle. Drink a little whiskey once in a while."

And walk his property. Grandpa would get up every morning and "walk the place," as he'd tell my grandma. He'd start on one end, walk down through the orchard, down the gully by the sinkhole, back up the other side, then down past the pond and back home. Then he'd walk every garden and check the plants, the soil, the rocks, you name it. He had an almost supernatural connection to his land.

"So, you believe Glen Morgan, then?" I asked.

"Why not?"

"Have you ever met him?"

"Once," he said.

"Your impression of him?"

"Hell of a banjo player."

Musicians often judge a person's character first by how good a musician that person is. Then afterward they consider things like personality, behavior, and intelligence.

"Poor George, now, he was tone-deaf," Dad said.

"George Morgan?"

"Yeah, I think he was the oldest brother. His wife, Ava, she was my mom's cousin."

"Okay, Dad, I have to ask you: What do you know of Belle Morgan?"

"Eddie's first wife?"

"Yeah," I said.

He shrugged. "Don't know. She took off and left Eddie and both those boys before I was even born. Eddie remarried and had three more kids, I think. Why?"

"What do you mean, 'she took off'?"

"She told Eddie she was going to the mill one afternoon, and she never came back. But Eddie said she'd packed her things. Eddie thought she'd been having an affair and she wanted out. Scott was all torn up over this because Belle did a lot of the singing. He didn't understand how she could just leave them. But she did. And it ruined the band."

I said nothing. I glanced out the window and was happy when the waitress brought us our food. My stomach rumbled. I hadn't realized how hungry I was.

"Why?" he said. "What's going on?"

"There's just been some new evidence come to light that, well, maybe she had help disappearing," I said.

"What do you mean?" he asked as he cut his eggs up and peppered them generously.

"So you've never heard any stories that would lead you to think that anything else happened to her other than she just ran off with a lover?"

"That's not what I asked," he said.

142

I smiled. "I know."

"What do you know that you're not telling me?" he said.

"Nothing for sure—yet. Hey, listen, I'm meeting with Leo King later. He's analyzing some old reel-to-reel recordings that belong to Glen. He's going to put them on CD for me. Do you want to tag along? I'm telling you, Dad, you've got to hear these recordings. They are so awesome."

"Sure, what time?"

"Later today, around four."

"I'll be there," he said. "Oh, by the way. Can Matthew have a snake?"

"What?" I nearly shrieked.

"Well, a friend of mine needs to get rid of his snake, and I think it'd be perfect for Matthew. He'd love it." He swallowed his food and glanced up at me. Then he added, "Or not."

Thirteen

All the way back to New Kassel, I debated the pros and cons of Matthew having a snake. In the con column were things like "slithery," "have to feed it mice," and "gets loose and gives me a heart attack." The pro column had yet to have an entry.

I went to the Gaheimer House and worked the afternoon shift in my reproduction green velvet dress with chenille ball trim, an outfit that reminded me of a pair of curtains. Since Sylvia was gone, I could splurge on getting myself a few new dresses and retiring the decade-old ones. Just as I was about to close up the museum and go back and change, there was a knock on the back door. *Irritation* is a mild word for what I felt, because, well, as much as I love my new dresses, you just can't go to the bathroom in them, and I was looking forward to getting this thing off. Now it would have to wait.

I answered the door and my breath caught in my throat. A lot of things could be said about my cousin Phoebe Keith. One of them was that she was by far the prettiest grandkid in the family. She had emerald green eyes, dark auburn hair that fell to her hips, a cute little squared-off chin, and dimples. She was also impulsive. Phoebe was standing in front of me, wearing pink cotton capris, sandals, and a flannel pajama top with sleeping bears all over it. The mercury said it was about thirty-six degrees outside. She either had nerve damage in her toes and didn't realize they were frozen or she was superhuman. She would claim to be superhuman. Phoebe was about thirty-seven, the baby of Uncle Ike's family. Uncle Ike had always been fairly normal. In fact, of my father's siblings, I'd say he was the most normal of them. Uncle Jed, on the other hand, had never really been "all there," but I used to explain it away as alcohol overload. Taking in Phoebe on the back porch of the house made me wonder if alcohol was really to blame or if weirdness was something that just ran in my family.

Well, at least I'd escaped it.

I know what you're thinking.

"Torie," Phoebe said with a smirk. "I've come to settle this once and for all."

Oh boy.

"What's that?" I asked.

"Why are you dressed like such a freak?" she asked, glancing down at my dress. "You look like you're wearing a curtain."

Then she just whisked by me, into the kitchen of the Gaheimer House.

"I went by your house, but somebody else is living there now," she said.

"Yes, we moved out to the country."

She glanced around the room and smiled. "I always liked your house. Why'd you move?"

"Oh, you know, the country air," I said. "How's everybody?"

"Good," she said. "But you know why I'm really here."

"Why's that?" I asked. "You want something to drink?"

"I've discovered a flaw in your *history*," she said. She spoke the word as if it were a joke. "And here are the letters to prove it."

She handed me the letters from our great-grandmother like they were yesterday's grocery list. I cringed at the thought of the eighty-year-old letters being tossed about in her bag and folded and refolded time and again. I took the yellowed letters gingerly from her and instantly began reading them.

"I'm gonna look around while you take all that in," she said.

"Okay," I replied, barely looking up in her direction. The letter paper had been folded so many times that the words were more faded at the creases. I read through the letters, then read through them again. I all but ran to my office and turned on the copier. While I waited for it to warm up, I read through them again.

. . . I cannot believe you refuse to acknowledge what you have done. Peggy is out of her mind with what to do. She has no income. You must give her some money. You have plenty. There is no reason for this. I know that you're away in Arkansas, but you must send her something. God will judge you, Scott William Morgan. What you have done to all of us is a crime. Johnny will someday see this for himself.

How can you deny the boy? He looks more like you than any of your own.

The next letter was similar, my great-grandma more insistent.

I will ruin you, and yours, Scott Morgan. Unless you do right by this boy, I will ruin you. How many more like him are there, scattered about while your wife sits at home, believing you love her? The boy is starving. Feed him, for God's sake. For I cannot keep doing it . . .

Then a third letter, written a few years later.

Why Johnny has anything to do with you, I'll never know. I told him to watch his back, as you'd be sticking a knife in it first chance you get. He'll learn. He'll learn the hard way. As you've never done right by anybody in your life.

Nowhere did she say he was John Robert's father.

I quickly made photocopies before Phoebe came back and changed her mind about sharing this with me.

As childish as it was, I smiled with relief. Everything would stay the way it was. My genealogy was intact.

Phoebe came sauntering back into my office and leaned up against the door frame. "So, what do you think? It really rocks the socks right off of your world, doesn't it?"

"It's very interesting, Phoebe. It's an amazing discovery," I said. "But it doesn't mean that Scott Morgan is our grandpa's father."

"But it says so right there," she said.

"No, what the first letter says is that there is a boy who Scott Morgan needs to take care of, but she never says it's her own John Robert. In fact, she alludes to the boy's mother being named Peggy."

"But right there it says Johnny."

"She says that Johnny will learn someday what Scott is, but she never says Scott's his father. I think it's pretty clear that it's a boy by a woman named Peggy."

"I knew you'd be too dense to understand," she said and snatched the original letters from me.

"Phoebe," I said. "This is an amazing thing you've come across. Who is Peggy? Who is the boy? And what does she mean when she talks about God judging Scott for what he's done to the boy? I mean, honestly, Phoebe, this is really amazing."

She laughed at me then. "You always were the slowest one in the family," she said. Then she glanced down at my dress again. "And the worst dresser. But we love you anyway, Torie. Don't think that we don't."

I blinked at her. "Well, that's great, Phoebe. I love you, too."

"How's your mom?" she asked.

"She's doing good," I said.

"I have told her many times that if she would just project herself as walking, she could get out of that wheelchair and walk."

My mother had polio at ten and could not walk at all. After decades of sitting in a wheelchair, she no longer had the muscle mass and her bones were entirely too brittle for her even to attempt to stand. Everybody knew that. Still Phoebe insisted on my mother "projecting" herself. On the one hand, it was annoying, but on the other hand, I had to give Phoebe credit for being so blasted optimistic all the time.

"So, what made you come by and share this with me?" I asked.

"Glen said you were ready to be shown the truth, finally," she said. "Boy, was he wrong."

"I'm sorry to disappoint you, Phoebe, but in my line of work, I need something a little more concrete than disjointed fragments of sentences to prove or disprove a pedigree. She must state 'John Robert is your son' for me to believe it."

"You don't know the first thing about faith, do you?" she asked.

"What do you mean?"

"Faith. You know. F-a-i-t-h."

"I know what faith is, but what do you mean?"

She moved closer to me then, a wisp of her auburn hair falling just over her left eye. "I feel it in my bones that our grandpa is the son of Scott Morgan. Just listen to him play."

My eyes narrowed on her. "What do you mean?"

"It's like listening to Scott play."

"Scott was Grandpa's teacher. The student always retains some of the teacher's style and discipline."

She smiled and made a dismissive noise. "Whatever you say. I'll see you around, Torie."

Phoebe was a kook. I knew she was a kook. So why did I worry about what she'd just said the whole time I tried to worm my way out of my dress?

Fourteen

Leo King's studio was located in the upstairs loft of his apartment in Wisteria. Wisteria is located just west of New Kassel and is the largest city in Granite County. That's not saying a whole lot, but the jail, sheriff's office, and community college are all within Wisteria's city limits. It's also a fast-food haven, home to the county library, and boasts a movie theater, the only movie theater in the whole county. You must understand that Granite County is mostly made up of farms and little bitty towns.

Since my dad didn't know exactly where Leo's studio was, he rode along with me. We arrived about 7:30. I still hadn't shaken the uneasy feeling Phoebe's visit had given me. The fact that she had just showed up with those letters unnerved me. There was something not quite right about it. I figured she would have fought me tooth and nail even to look at the letters. Instead, she'd just sauntered in and handed them to me. Of course, she'd snatched them away from me so quickly that I knew I'd never get a chance to have them looked at by a professional, but I was about as close to a professional as you could get in this area, and they looked authentic to me. The paper had been soft and yellowed, small, and lined with a faint blue. The handwritten ink had faded to sepia, but what really did it for me was the handwriting. A person might be able to fake old paper and old ink, or even find old paper and old ink to use in a new letter, but people wrote in a distinctive way back then. The cursive style was a little more formal in those days than it was now, a little blockier. In the letters Phoebe had shown me, it was definitely old cursive. So unless she'd hunted up a hundred-year-old person to write the letters for her, or gone to a lot of time, trouble, and expense to hire a professional forger, I'd say they were authentic.

But I couldn't help it. The whole thing felt odd to me.

Leo King was an old musician. Meaning he was from that school of honky-tonk from the fifties and sixties that had brought us the likes of Patsy Cline and Hank Williams. Even though nowadays he chose to play a more mountain style of country picking, rather than the slower crying-in-your-beer music. That didn't take away the fact that he'd been one of the great crying-in-your-beer music musicians. So had my dad. So they hit it off quite well. In fact, I just stood back for a good ten minutes while they discussed music. Finally, Leo remembered why I was there.

He was in his seventies, with a huge belly and hairy ears. Don't let that fool you. When he picked up a guitar, the man was magic. "Torie, I've got to say that these are some awesome recordings. Absolutely awesome."

"Yes, but have they been doctored?"

"Not at all." He handed me a stack of CDs. "I've put them on these CDs for you, and whenever they identified a song on the recording, I wrote it down on the liner notes. Quite a few of the songs, I just knew and recognized on my own. This is the Morgan Family Players, isn't it?"

"Most of it. With the help of my grandpa," I said.

"I knew it," he said, and rubbed his hands together. Then he turned to my father. "Hey, Dwight, you want me to burn you some copies?"

"I'd love it," my dad said.

"Actually, if you could burn another set for my sister, I'd be totally indebted," I added.

"Sure thing," he said. "It's not often I get to work with original recordings of such a noted and talented family. So, what's your connection?"

"Apparently, my grandpa—his dad—" I said, pointing to my father—"wrote quite a few of their songs and jammed with them. Scott taught my grandpa to play the fiddle."

"Wow. It's amazing to have that rich a musical history," Leo said. "Wish I had that in my family. I'd be so proud."

"Well, it seems we haven't had a chance to really be all that proud, since we just discovered it. Scott wasn't on the up-and-up, and my grandpa didn't get credit or money for any of the songs he contributed."

"Oh, wow. *Yee-haw*," he said. "Sounds like you're getting ready for a court battle."

"No, not really," I said. I glanced over at my father, who didn't seem to dismiss it so quickly. "Well, at least my generation isn't. His might."

"Well, if you need an expert witness," Leo said to my father. "I'd be happy to go to bat for you guys, saying these are authentic tapes."

"I appreciate that," Dad said.

"I'll give these copies to Torie," Leo told him. "When I get them done. Will that be all right?"

"Sure," Dad said.

"So, do you have any more?" Leo inquired.

"Any more what?" I asked.

"Recordings. I'd be happy to put whatever you've got on CD for you."

I thought about the CD of "The Blood Ballad," my name for the recording of the confession of Belle's murder. I couldn't help but wonder who had the original tape. And I wondered if I'd get back the one I'd given the police as evidence. Not that it mattered, since I'd made a dub onto tape before I'd handed the CD over to the sheriff. Still, the CD that I'd received would be better quality than the tape I'd made from it.

"Not right now, but I'll let you know if I do," I said.

"Well, I hate to cut this short, but I've got a date with the libraries tomorrow, so I need to get home."

"Libraries?" Leo asked. "What for?"

"I've got to find out everything I can about the Morgan family."

"And when she says 'everything,' " my father added, "she means everything."

It was true, so I just laughed along with them.

The next day, Mary's picture as Santa Lucia was on the cover of *The New Kassel Gazette*. I bought ten copies and set them aside to distribute to all of her grandparents and to put in her scrapbook. She seemed pleased about the whole situation, and I thought her stint as Santa Lucia even garnered her some attention from that boy Tony, whom she was always mooning over.

As I dropped the kids off at school, Rachel couldn't

possibly let the morning go down as one of the most pleasant ones in the history of our family. As she got out of the van, she turned to Mary and said, "I guess because you got your picture in the paper, you think you can keep my earrings. But you can't!"

Oh, for the love of God.

"Mom, tell her I want my earrings back," Rachel said.

"Rachel, I've told her."

"Then do something. Chain her to a wall and torture her until she confesses or returns my earrings!"

"Get out of my car," I said and rubbed my now-throbbing head.

Mary grabbed her book bag, slammed the car door, and yelled at her sister across the parking lot. "Loser!"

I drove the quarter of a mile until I came to the elementary school building. "Your turn, big guy," I said to Matthew.

He rolled his eyes. "I can't wait until all of this is over."

"What's over? Rachel and her earrings?" Because I had news for him: Rachel was as stubborn as a rock, and she would not let this whole earring thing rest until Mary either returned the earrings or Rachel got to draw blood. I'd been through this before. Last time, it had been Rachel's bath sponge. It went missing and then turned up in the garbage disposal three days later.

"No, I mean school. When do I not have to go anymore?" he asked.

I hated to tell him that he had at least a decade to go. "A long time, buddy."

He grabbed his Yu-Gi-Oh book bag and his Darth

Vader lunch box—he believes in having broad inter-ests—and climbed out of the van. "So there's no way at all I can hurry this up?"

"Afraid not, honey," I said.

Then he turned, very dejected, and walked into his building as the bell rang. Poor kid. I hated school, too, when I was younger. Well, I loved to *learn* and I still love to, but that's not the same thing as liking school. Matthew was just like me. I probably would have liked school much better if I could have taken all the other children out of it—too many judging eyes for my unconventional self—and I suspected that was Matthew's issue, too.

When we lived in town, the kids used to walk to school unless the weather was bad. Now that we were out in the country, several miles from town and the school, they either rode the bus or I'd drop them off on my way to do something. Just as I was doing now.

I drove over to Wisteria and stopped by my mother and Colin's for breakfast as I waited for the library to open. It was a spur-of-the-moment thing, because that's the way I always was. My best friend, Collette, says I'm too tame and not spontaneous enough, but I think I do all right.

Colin was at the office, but my mother was waiting with a butterscotch/brown sugar breakfast roll type of thing, as if she knew I would be coming. I kept thinking that this built-in sense of knowing when people were about to arrive at my house would kick in any day, since my mother seemed to have had it her whole life, but so far, no luck. People showed up at my door and they got a bowl of cereal or Fritos, depending on the time of day that they arrived.

My mom, for the record, is very pretty. Not in that "Oh, gee, I hate you" sort of way, but in that "Wow, I'm enthralled" way. She really does have that effect on people. Which can be a bit annoying when you're standing next to her, looking like your father. That's okay, because one thing I can say about my mom is that she's not arrogant about it in the least. She's always very humble and very polite when people gush about her beautiful doe eyes and her creamy skin. It never goes to her head, and most of the time, she actually still blushes. Part of her allure is the way she holds herself. She comes across as somebody who's gone to finishing school, when in actuality she never graduated from high school—due to an unfortunate encounter with polio—and grew up barefoot and wild as a polecat in the hills of West Virginia. I'm not sure where the magical metamorphosis occurred, but it did. I'm still waiting for my metamorphosis.

"How are the girls?" Mom asked.

"Fighting."

"Typical," she said.

"How would you know? They're always well behaved around you."

She sighed and said, "Colin hates his job."

"I know."

"Is there anything to be done about it?" she asked.

"I talked with him a little bit about it the other day."

"You did?" she asked, surprise tugging at the corners of her eyes.

"Yeah."

"Like, a real conversation? No snide remarks?"

"Yeah, like a real conversation."

"Wow," she said.

We were both quiet a moment, and then I added, "I don't know if there's anything to be done about it or not. I guess it's really up to him."

"I guess so," she said. "He's driving me crazy."

"I know."

"And *you*," she said. "I can't believe you were outside at dusk during hunting season!"

"It doesn't matter, Mom. Turns out it wasn't hunters after all," I said.

A grave expression crossed her face, as if she were still somehow right, but I just let it go.

After breakfast, I headed to the library. The Wisteria library was much closer to me than the St. Louis library, and I didn't think I'd need the St. Louis library, for this research anyway. Most of the information I was in search of had to do with Progress, and, believe it or not, the Wisteria library boasted more records on Progress than the library in Progress. That might be because when I inherited all of the money from Sylvia, I donated a good chunk of money to the Wisteria library specifically for the genealogy department. Now there was a whole wall of books and records with a plaque that read: MADE POSSIBLE BY SYLVIA AND WILMA PERSHING, NEW KASSEL, MO.

First, I checked for the census records. I knew I could find most census records on-line at most of the major genealogy dot-coms, but aside from the fact that I was a dinosaur and preferred the library, I didn't always trust the information on the Web sites. Call me paranoid—many already have—but I wanted to look at the original microfilm, handle it myself, and see it with my own eyes. Completely ridiculous, I know. Besides, it's always much more interesting to go to the library than just to sit at home on the computer all day. Since there were other records to look for, why not just do it all at one place?

I found Scott Morgan and his wife, Louise, living four households away from my great-grandpa, Nate Keith, and his family. The children were listed: Cletis, Eddie, George, Miriam, Emma, and Roscoe. What I really needed was the name of the woman my great-grandmother had referred to in her letter as Peggy. Peggy was not an uncommon name, although it wasn't as common as Doris, Louise, or Sarah in the first half of the twentieth century. It became much more popular in the fifties. Prior to 1900, Peggy was actually short for Margaret, and every now and then, I'd still find it used like that these days. Patsy was the nickname for Martha, back in the day. I'd never been able to figure how either one of those nicknames derived from the actual name. But if you know all of that when you start tracing your family tree, you're less likely to spend months looking for two daughters, Patsy and Martha, when the names belong to one and the same person.

I had no idea where to begin. My cell phone buzzed, and I answered it with a whisper. "Hello."

"I think we should challenge the results of the birding Olympics," Eleanore stated.

I glanced at the clock on the wall; it was just past 9:00 A.M. Had Eleanore gotten up and decided she needed to start trouble? "Eleanore," I began.

"No, I'm serious," she said. "Getting shot at should mean something."

"It did mean something, Eleanore. We got shot at."

"But . . . Elmer gets all the glory. We got shot at!"

"Well, we got to live! You should be happy about that," I said, trying to keep my voice down.

"But it's not fair. We would have seen more birds than he did if we hadn't been interrupted by flying bullets."

"How do you know we would have? What's your guarantee that we would have seen more birds?" I asked.

It suddenly occurred to me that my side of the conversation would sound very strange to people passing by.

"Because I'm a better birder than Elmer, that's why." The venom in her voice was almost palpable. Damn, when she got ticked, she got *ticked*.

"How can you be so sure? I mean, isn't it just luck? A bird happens to land in the tree, you spot it, and then you write it down. It all depends on where that bird decided to land at that moment. How does that make you better at it?"

"Because it's all about the essence you emit and what you bring to it. The birds can sense that, you know?"

"What, have you read *Zen Birding* or something?"

"Oh, is that a book?" she asked. I could hear paper rustling. She was writing it down.

"Eleanore! I'm not contesting anything," I said.

"It's not fair," she persisted.

"Okay, and neither is training your whole life for the real Olympics, flying thousands of miles away from your country, only to pull a hamstring or fall in the first ten feet of the race. It totally stinks, but there's nothing you can do about it! We got shot at. Simple as that!" I screamed.

The librarians didn't bother to stare at me. They understood that, well, I could be a difficult patron sometimes. But the other librarygoers *were* staring. One woman grabbed her little blond-headed toddler and slinked behind a Dr. Seuss display.

"Oh, I forgot to give you those pictures from the horse show," she said. "When can I bring them by?"

"Eleanore, how did you get my cell phone number?" I asked suddenly, ignoring her question. "Never mind. Don't answer. I'm hanging up now."

"Fine, but you owe me new binoculars!" she screamed into the phone.

I hung up, and instead of leaving the phone on vibrate, I turned it off completely.

I went through the census, scouring the statistics for each family within the township that Scott Morgan had lived in. It would most likely be a futile effort, I knew. The Peggy I was looking for could have been from anywhere in the county, but I got the feeling from my great-grandmother's letters that she was a woman who'd lived close by. Somebody in the valley, maybe, or somebody at their church. Back then, people didn't go to the end of the county to socialize. My grandpa would travel several counties to perform, but when it came to socializing, most people did it in their own backyard, so to speak. If I was going to find this Peggy, it would be within a five-mile radius.

After four hours, my head throbbed and my eyes felt stuck in one position, but the census records gave me a total of two Margarets and three Peggys. One was seventy years old at the time, so I figured she was out, and another was about ten years old. That left me with one Margaret Brown, a Peggy McKee, and a Peggy Kiefer. My great-grandmother had indicated that the Peggy in question was unmarried, because the boy was starving, and she had nobody to help her feed him.

If she were an unwed mother, it was possible that she'd lived with her parents for a while after the baby was born. So I followed the Margaret and Peggys in question to the census for 1930. One Peggy and the Margaret had disappeared, meaning they'd probably gotten married and were living under their married names with their husbands, but one Peggy remained: Peggy Kiefer. Peggy Kiefer lived with her parents, Al and Joanne, one sister, and a little boy named Rufus. Rufus was listed as the grandson of Al, the head of the household.

Rufus was listed as Rufus Kiefer. So he was either Al's grandson by a son who'd died before 1930 or he was a grandson by one of Al's two unwed daughters. I will say that it's not unusual to find grandchildren in a census who bear the name of the head of household. I'd seen where this happened numerous times in my own family. It happened sometimes because the census taker just put down the last name of the head of household and assumed everybody else had the same last name. There was any number of reasons why this might happen, but the point is, it usually didn't happen.

I went back and checked the 1920 census, and Al and Joanne Kiefer had two boys to go with their two girls. I jotted down their names and then went forward to 1930. Both were alive and well, married and living with their own families.

So little Rufus Kiefer had to be the son of either Peggy or her sister, Ann. Or it might have been an error on the part of a sexist census taker. Since Ann would have been about thirteen when Rufus was born, and my great-grandma's letter mentioned Peggy specifically, I was going to go with Peggy.

Grabbing my notebook, I went outside and made a phone call to the library in Progress. One thing they had there that I couldn't look at in Wisteria was the baptismal records of the churches. Based on the township that they were living in, I deduced which churches would have been closest. It helps when you've studied a county your whole life. The fact that

I knew all of the churches in that township was actually pretty scary. I could also name all the creeks and rivers in that township. When the librarian answered, I told her what I was looking for and for which churches, and an approximate year. She said she'd call me back in half an hour.

I went back inside and checked the marriage records for all of Scott Morgan's kids. Cletis married Rosa Cook, Roscoe married Hattie Jones, Miriam married Clifton Adam Weaver, George married Ava Moony—who was indeed my grandmother's first cousin— and Eddie married Belle Mercer. I then checked for cousin Toot, Charlie Morgan; he'd married Nancy Yates. There was no marriage record for Emma. I remembered what Glen Morgan had said about his Aunt Em being "touched." I supposed if that were true, she most likely wouldn't have married. Depending on how "touched" she was.

So, enough of all of this. I went to the biography section and pulled out a book on the Morgan family, written by somebody outside the family nearly thirty years ago, and a book called *Olde Tyme Music of the Mississippi*. I found a few CDs of the Morgan Family Players and photocopied the liner notes. I took all of my notes and the photocopies, checked the two books out of the library, and went to lunch.

Snuggled in a corner at a local buffet, I began to read while munching on a salad with a scrumptious buttermilk dressing. The first book on the music of the Mississippi literally covered everything from Missouri, southern Illinois, Arkansas, and western Tennessee to Louisiana and Mississippi. So there were a great many types of music represented. I flipped to the index to find the pages that mentioned the Morgan Family Players. I turned to the first of these pages and began to read.

The Morgan Family Players, made up of Papa Scott Morgan, his daughter Miriam, his sons Roscoe and Eddie, his daughter-in-law Belle, and cousin Toot, were one of the most influential music families of the twenties and thirties. Their music has been covered by some of the most famous country musicians in the world, and nobody could mistake the unique vocal qualities of Belle, Miriam, and Scott in the harmonies they created. Their songs usually had a lead fiddle and harmony fiddle, much like a lead guitar and a rhythm guitar in today's rock bands. In later years, Scott Morgan was quoted as saying, "No man was prouder of his daughter than I was of Miriam. She played that fiddle better than I could. She took what I taught her and ran with it."

The Morgan Family Players burst onto the scene about the same time as the Carter Family, pre-ceding them by a few years and representing the midwestern "everyman" influence, as opposed to the Appalachian influence of the Carters. The first hit for the Morgans was "Daughter, Don't You Cry," and they followed it up with "Crawdad Dance" and "Appaloosa Love Triangle." The sense of humor in their lyrics was always evident, and their influence on fiddle playing in the boot-heel region of Missouri was unmistakable.

In 1936, at the height of their popularity, the group was plagued with controversy. Scott Morgan's daughter-in-law Belle left with a lover and was never seen or heard from again. Besides breaking Eddie's heart, she left behind two children, Dora Kaye and Johnny. The Morgan Family Players were never able to rebound from this loss, and the band dispersed. Most musicologists agree that if the band had stayed together, they would have gone on to be the most famous musical family of the early twentieth century.

I went to the buffet table, loaded up on some *mostaccioli* and garlic bread, and returned to my seat. I read the liner notes next. Most of them gave only who wrote the songs and who was playing what instruments on what song. On the three liner notes that I had copied, there were at least five songs that were listed as "traditional," meaning that the origins were unknown and the song was as old as dirt. At least three were songs I now realized had actually been written by my grandpa.

I was learning a lot, but I felt like I was getting nowhere.

I finished off lunch with a slice of carrot cake and then went back to the library. This time, I went straight to the source to read about Belle's disappearance: the newspapers. I thought it possible that a story like hers, the disappearance of a celebrated musician, would make even the St. Louis papers, but I started with the papers in Progress.

"It was a bright and shining autumn morning . . ." The lyrics of "The Blood Ballad" came back to me.

In a paper from October 1936, I found what I was looking for.

FAMOUS SINGER ABSCONDS WITH LOVER

Belle Morgan of the famous Morgan Family Players, sources say, has run off with her lover, abandoning her children, her husband, Eddie, and the band. It was the morning of the twelfth when Eddie Morgan says his wife, Belle, went to the mill and never returned. Authorities are convinced that there was no foul play. Eddie stated that his wife was scheduled to take a leave of absence to "clear her head," but he didn't think she was leaving for another two weeks. Sources close to the family, however, think that Belle's lover convinced her to leave early. It is thought that they have gone west, where they can blend in and live in anonymity for the rest of their lives. Inquiries as to who Belle Morgan's lover is have gone unanswered. Some people around town speculate that Eddie Morgan was unaware of her lover's identity. When Eddie Morgan was asked about his wife's infidelity, he had no comment.

The article then went on to name all of the accomplishments of the band and those of Belle Morgan in particular. The newspaper had three photographs next to the article. One was of Belle, looking beautiful and demure in her flowered dress and coiffed hair, the second showed her onstage with Eddie, and the third was of her packed suitcases sitting on the living room floor.

I printed out the article and had Sheriff Mort's phone number dialed before I made it to my car.

"Joachim," he said.

"Mort, it's Torie."

"Yeah?"

"You're going to have to pull some strings for me."

"What strings?"

"I want the original case file for Belle Morgan's disappearance. I'm particularly interested in what was packed in her suitcases," I said.

"What?"

"Oh, sorry, you have no idea what I'm talking about. Just get me the file if you can. I'll call you from my office. I have something else I need you to do."

"What's that?" he asked.

I threw my briefcase on the seat next to me and started the car. "Exhume a body."

"Oh, is that all?"

"Let me get to my office with my maps. I'll call you back."

Fifteen

All the way back to New Kassel, I felt as though there was something I was missing, a tree that I couldn't see for the forest in the way. I put in a CD that Leo had burned for me and listened. The harmony created by the trio of Scott, Miriam, and Belle was magical. It was as if their voices had been made to blend together. Then I listened closely when Miriam would take a solo part. Soon I was convinced that whoever it was singing "The Blood Ballad" on the recording that Clifton Weaver had sent me, it was not Miriam Morgan. Leo King would probably be able to tell me better, so I called him and asked if he would analyze another recording as soon as I got it back from Mort.

When I arrived at my office at the Gaheimer House, Mary was waiting for me. "What are you doing here?" I asked.

She shrugged.

"You want something to drink?"

"Yeah," she said. I gave her some quarters, and she went to the soda machine that Sylvia had installed over ten years ago. She came back with a Dr Pepper because she is my daughter.

"Wait, if you're here, who's at home with Matthew?"

"Rachel took the bus home with him. I walked here from school."

"Oh," I said. "You bored?"

She nodded.

From my briefcase, I pulled out the stack of research I'd done at the library and spread it out on the table. I also had a copy of the lyrics from "The Blood Ballad."

"What's up?" she asked, and took a drink of her soda.

"Well, I've got a song that's a confession to a murder," I said.

"You're so weird," she said. "Couldn't you just get a job at a bank or something?"

I smiled at her. "Now, hear me out. I've got this song, in which a woman confesses to hacking up a woman named Belle. And Eddie, the Eddie in the song, is in mourning."

"Okay," she said.

"This song is on a tape with other Morgan Family Players songs. Two of the members of the band were named Eddie and Belle, and they were married."

"So, then, the song is about them," Mary said. "Why is this so difficult?"

"Because according to the newspapers, her husband, and the police, she ran off with a lover," I said.

"Then she ran off with a lover. Why do you have to blow everything out of proportion?" she said, waving her arms around. " 'Ooh, Rudy, our next-door neighbor is a Mafia leader.' 'Ooh, Rudy, those dead people aren't really dead at all.' 'Ooh, Rudy, if I try hard enough, I can find an unsolved mystery in the elementary school cafeteria!' "

I just stared at her, openmouthed. "Wow, Mary. You got some issues there you want to talk about?"

"*I* don't have issues. *You* have issues. You're psycho."

I crossed my arms. "Are the kids at school making fun of you because of me?"

"No, they make fun of you. They leave me out of it," she said.

"Well, I'm no stranger to kids at school making fun of me," I said. "And they're all losers, as you so eloquently like to say."

"Normal moms don't do this kind of stuff," she stated.

"Who says I want to be normal?"

"Well, maybe *we*," she said, indicating herself, "would like to be normal."

"So you do have issues."

"Only because of you," she countered.

"Look, I don't have time for this. I've got to—"

"Discover Atlantis?" she asked.

My temper flared—finally. "Now just a minute!" I said. "I've never even searched for Atlantis. *That* would be my cousin Phoebe. What is wrong with you, Mary? I mean, what is *really* wrong with you? Are you beaten? Are you starved? Do you live in a shack with no toys, no computer, no TV? I mean, are you mistreated in any way? Because if you're not, then shut the heck up. You can be perfect when you're the mom. All right? Until then, please, for the love of God, give me a break and realize that I love you."

She blinked then.

"That's right, Mary. I love you. I know you think I don't. I know you think I only love your perfect sister—

who isn't perfect, by the way—and I know that Matthew gets a lot of one-on-one time because he's still really young. But you . . . you are the sparkle in our family," I said, making wiggly motions with my fingers.

"What? Maybe I don't want to be a sparkle," she said, shaking her head back and forth.

"Oh, I know, I understand. You with your black-hole, life-sucking attitude. You try very hard not to sparkle. But guess what? Like it or not, you are the shining spark to our family, the person who sets us apart from everybody else. Because when you shine, girl, the whole town can feel it. You keep our family out of the dark. Now, maybe none of that matters to you, and that's fine, but regardless of what you say, you are a part of us and we love having you.

Now, try all you want to push us away and make us miserable," I said, walking right up to within inches of her. "But I'm going to love my little spark anyway."

She gulped down her Dr Pepper and looked away.

Since she wasn't going to respond to anything I had just said, I took out my maps of Progress and the surrounding areas and began to study them.

"What are you looking for?" she asked.

"A stone bridge on the way to a mill."

"Why?" she asked.

"Because that's where they're going to find Belle's body."

She began flipping through the photocopies and the notes I'd taken, while I studied the maps. I pulled a reference book on old mills from the shelf. It gave me

171

information, like when the mill was built, what sort of mill it was, who built it, and what became of it. My cell phone rang then. It was the woman from the library in Progress.

"I found your baptismal record for Rufus Albert Kiefer. There is no father listed. Mother is one Peggy Kiefer. Godparents are Ann Kiefer and Louis Kiefer."

This Ann was most likely Peggy's younger sister, and Louis could have been an uncle or a cousin or any one of a number of other relatives. No father was listed. The boy was definitely Peggy's illegitimate child, and he even had his grandpa's middle name. Albert, or Al for short. "Thank you so much," I said. Before I hung up, she added something.

"I know Rufus Kiefer," she said.

"What do you mean, you know him?"

"He's the accountant at our church. I didn't put it together when you called," she said. "Until I saw his middle name. He has this very distinct way of signing his name with this big A in the middle. It's bigger than any other letter in his name. Then it hit me who you were inquiring about."

Only in a small town. All that I'd accomplished in my life would never have happened if I'd lived in a big city. The librarian gave me the name of the church that she attended, and then I apologized. It had never occurred to me that Rufus could still be living. I don't know why. He'd be in his late seventies, I figured. I wrote down the name of the church and made a mental note to go and see Mr. Rufus A. Kiefer.

After I hung up with her, I studied the book on mills and found only two that were even still working during the time period that I needed. The Babcock mill had been partially turned into a little trading store. So Belle could have been going there for any number of reasons. There was only one stone bridge the song could be referring to—Hahn's Bridge.

"I've got it."

I dialed Sheriff Mort, who answered on the second ring.

"Hahn's Bridge. I think if you check under there somewhere, you're going to find the body of Belle Mercer Morgan. It's totally off the beaten path, not on a major road. But it is in the vicinity of the Babcock mill. Whoever killed Belle could have waited until dark to actually dig the grave. It could have been a day or two before anybody even crossed the bridge."

"Wait, wait. Torie, you're going too fast."

"The Hahn stone bridge was on private property. Unless Godfrey Hahn decided to go to town or to the mill or what have you, he'd have had no need even to cross the bridge. People back then, they didn't go to town every day. Sometimes days would go by and they wouldn't leave their property. During the Depression, they couldn't afford the gas to go anywhere, and everybody had to do chores, so that they had food and clothes. I mean, going to town was a once-a-week event. Her killer could have had a window of a day or two, even."

"All right, all right," he said.

"I remember my grandma telling me once how they had to wait for the chickens to lay a full dozen eggs one Tuesday, so they could sell them to get the gas money to take my uncle to the doctor. One of the chickens got stubborn and took four hours to lay that last egg. So it's not like people just traveled to town on a whim."

"Okay," he said. "I understand."

"Mom," Mary said.

"Hahn's stone bridge. Is it still standing?" he asked.

"Yes, it is. It gets more traffic today, since Godfrey Hahn's very large plot of land has since been divided and sold to several families. So there're more people in and out of there, not to mention a school bus every day."

"Mom," Mary said.

"All right, I'll send somebody out."

"Mom," Mary said for the third time.

"What?" I asked.

"This woman . . . Belle Morgan. Isn't that Isabelle Mercer?"

"Who?" I asked.

"What, who, what?" Mort asked on the line.

"Rachel did all of that research to impress you. When she was auditioning for the job. Isabelle Mercer, who disappeared one night. It looks like it could be her. And the name is similar."

I blinked and then blinked again. "How would you know what she looked like?"

"Because I helped Rachel with the research."

"You did?"

"Yes."

"Of course, you did. . . . But why?"

"She needed it done fast. So I took notes while she made that ridiculous costume out of the shower curtain. Then she typed all of the notes into the presentation that she gave."

"Mort, I'll call you back. Send a team to the bridge anyway."

I hung up the phone. "What was your original source?" I asked her.

She walked over to the bookcase in my office, ran her fingers along the spines of the books, and then stopped and pulled one out. "*Unsolved Mysteries of Granite County*, written by Sylvia Pershing. 1962."

I gave her a big wet kiss on the forehead. Like it or not, she was definitely my daughter.

Sixteen

I wasn't sure what surprised me more, the fact that Mary had actually helped Rachel with her research—and then later pretended to be bored with the presentation—or the fact that Mary had actually remembered any of it. She could be pretty flighty at times, and unless there was a "hot guy" involved, she didn't remember a whole lot. She rarely remembered to do her homework, and if she did, she never remembered to turn it in. She couldn't remember which of her clothes were clean or dirty, so I ended up washing clean clothes more often than not, while she wore dirty ones over and over.

So the fact that she remembered the whole Isabelle Mercer story made me think that maybe, just maybe, there was a part of her that cared if her sister did well or not. She just didn't want to *appear* as though she cared.

Sometimes, teenagers are just twisted.

I sat in my office at home, reading the book about unsolved mysteries that Sylvia had written in 1962, while Rudy cooked dinner. The more I flipped through this book, the more I learned about Sylvia. Or, well, I should say, the more layers of Sylvia that peeled away.

I couldn't remember a time when Sylvia hadn't been the queen of New Kassel. And she'd ruled it with an iron fist. I was thinking Queen Elizabeth I had nothing on Sylvia Pershing. Sylvia's sister had been just the opposite. Where Sylvia had been lean and hard, Wilma had been round and soft. Sylvia expected the best out of everybody, and Wilma had just expected love and kindness. But the two took care of each other, neither had ever married, and they complemented each other.

At some point, Sylvia had had an affair with the owner of the Gaheimer House, and he'd left her everything. She'd begun building on that, buying houses and buildings in the business district, until she'd accrued half the town. She took great pride in her accomplishments, but none of it had she done for herself. It was done for the sake of Mr. Gaheimer and the town of New Kassel. And, dare I say, for future generations. She could have a soft spot once in a while; you just had to blast through rubble to find it.

I'd loved Sylvia as if she were my own flesh and blood. She was my mentor. When she died, she left me everything she'd accumulated. Not only was that a huge responsibility but also a very humbling experience. I owed most of everything I was to her.

That's why, when I found new things out about her, long after she'd died, it drove me crazy. Just as I thought, Okay, *that* was the real Sylvia, I'd find something new that shattered that image and I'd have to start all over again. I knew Sylvia had written a lot of books on local history and had compiled many genealogical publications, like cemetery records of the county, and so on, but I hadn't read all of them.

This book on unsolved mysteries made me wonder if Sylvia had been more like me than I had suspected. Because in describing many of these cases in this book, she'd relied on her own expertise, or her knowledge of the families involved. She never really came out and said what she thought the answer to the riddle was, but she always put in her two cents' worth all the same. Made me think she would have been a great sleuth.

According to Sylvia, Isabelle Mercer was a very beautiful young woman who was born to a second-generation New Kasselonian. Her father, Huxley Mercer, was the mayor of New Kassel for three terms. Her mother was descended from one of the original ten German families that founded the town. Isabelle would have been a contemporary of Sylvia's, and so I trusted most of the observations that Sylvia made. In fact, one of the photographs in the chapter devoted to Isabelle's disappearance showed a group of people on a Sunday outing. After church, they'd all gone to the river overlook for a picnic. To the left of Isabelle Mercer was none other than Sylvia Pershing, flanked on the other side by her sister, Wilma Pershing. Also in the photograph was a woman named Verna Wilson, who, according to Rachel's earlier research, had been Isabelle's best friend.

Sylvia went on to say that Isabelle was not happy or satisfied with life in New Kassel and longed for the glitzy life of society up in St. Louis. Isabelle began dating a man who was the son of one of St. Louis's wealthiest families. They were to be married, and Isabelle spent less and less time in New Kassel. Then one day, the fiancé called it off. She was distraught for weeks, and contemplated suicide, according to Sylvia, who found Isabelle standing on the edge of a cliff overlooking the river. Weeks went by, and everybody thought she was getting better. Then Isabelle announced to her maid that she was headed to her friend Verna's house. She walked out the door and was never seen by her parents or the townsfolk again. Authorities said she either ran away or jumped into the river.

Sylvia went on to state that a few people had noticed Belle Morgan's uncanny resemblance to Isabelle Mercer, when Belle happened along a few years later.

Back then, there was no MTV or VH1 to bombard people with a musician's image, and based on the research I'd just done, there were only a handful of motion picture clips of the Morgan Family Players. In their publicity photos, Belle was either slightly turned or looking down or away. I supposed that it wouldn't have been impossible for Belle to be successful with the Morgan Family Players for several years before somebody finally noticed who she was.

Sylvia said that she'd called the authorities over this, and when they went to interview Belle Morgan, Belle claimed that her birth date, parents, and birthplace were completely different from Isabelle Mercer's. Thus, Belle said, the resemblance was just a coincidence— they were not the same person.

But what about her husband, Eddie? Surely, Eddie knew the truth, because their marriage record clearly stated her maiden name was Mercer. Had Eddie helped Belle hide her past from the investigators when they showed up? It wasn't as if she was a minor or a murderess. If she didn't want anybody to know her past, that was certainly no crime. I checked the dates. Sylvia said she'd contacted the authorities about Isabelle Mercer, which was just a few months before Belle disappeared . . . the *second* time.

Sylvia concluded the chapter on Isabelle Mercer by saying, "Although the authorities believe that there is no connection to Belle Morgan, one must question their enthusiasm and results. After all, Isabelle Mercer looks very much like Belle Morgan, and on the day I went to visit Belle and Eddie Morgan, she refused to see me. Has the mystery of Isabelle Mercer been solved at last? Well, if Belle Morgan really was Isabelle Mercer, she was only found for a short time before disappearing into the mists once again."

Could "The Blood Ballad" really just be a song? If Belle Morgan had a history of disappearing when things got too rough, she could have just done it again. She might have figured she'd walked away from everything once, so what was one more time? Or had she met with a more nefarious fate? Was "The Blood Ballad" really a confession?

Just then, the smoke alarm went off in the kitchen. I ran downstairs, to find smoke rolling out of the oven and nobody in the house. I pulled open the oven door and yanked out the roast that Rudy had been trying to cook. It was, well, *roasted*. The timer on the microwave was beeping. Who knew how long this roast had been cooking? Where the heck was everybody?

I peeked out the kitchen window and saw Rudy down by the corral. I went outside, and as he saw me walking across the yard, he said, "I think I figured out who the horse belongs to."

"Who?"

"The homeless guy in the woods," he said.

"What? What homeless guy in the woods?" And then I remembered that Matthew had mentioned some man living behind our property. Why hadn't I thought of that? Why hadn't I remembered that?

"When Matthew asked me if he should keep feeding the man in the woods, I decided to check it out. Right back there"—he pointed—"with a perfect view of the corral and your office, is evidence of a campsite. There were wrappers from those hand-warmer things and traces of food."

"Are you serious?" I asked, feeling the blood drain to my toes.

"Completely," he said. "So, this guy shows up in our woods right about the time the mystery horse shows up in our corral."

"You think they're connected."

"Yes," he said. "I've got Mort coming out here right now."

"So what does Matthew say?" I asked. Matthew was off in the yard, chasing a butterfly with a stick. "Did he actually talk to the man?"

Rudy shook his head. "No. He says he saw the man out there once and decided to take him some food. He just left the food at the campsite. The next time he went back, the food was gone, so Matthew thought he was supposed to keep feeding him."

"Oh, Jesus," I said.

"Yeah," Rudy agreed. "I've already talked to Matthew and told him that he can play in the yard, the stables, and the corral but that he can't go into the woods without a grown-up."

"I didn't even know he was going into the woods. I mean, most of the time when I check on him, he's playing on his swing or the trampoline, or he's with the horses. I've never seen him go anywhere near the woods."

"Maybe this was a first. Maybe he saw the guy and just followed him, not really realizing where he was going."

"Oh, my gosh," I said.

"Yeah, pretty creepy."

"So, you really think the horse belongs to the squatter?"

"It's the most logical explanation," Rudy said.

"Okay, I've got two questions."

"What?" he asked.

"One, how does a guy living in the woods afford a well-taken-care-of and well-fed Percheron?"

Rudy shrugged, as if to say that was a good question.

"And two, what are we having for dinner? Because you burned the roast."

Seventeen

The next day, I made myself a permanent fixture in Pierre's Bakery. I was not leaving until I'd tried every one of his new line of muffins. So far, my favorite was cranberry/orange. I know it's probably not the healthiest thing in the world to eat just muffins for breakfast, but nothing else appealed to me at the moment. Besides, the reason I'd decided to take up residence at Pierre's was because my hideout at Fräulein Krista's had become entirely too well known.

It wasn't as if I was just sitting there doing nothing besides stuffing my face. No, I was reading. Often when I got stuck on some sort of research, I would head to the cellar of the Gaheimer House. The reason? Sylvia's old files. In the dungeon-like basement of that ancient building, Sylvia had kept filing cabinets by the dozens. They contained newspaper clippings, genealogical charts (which I'd since put on the computer—I'm not entirely prehistoric), and other things she'd found of interest. Once, I found file folders full of original German recipes for wonderful old food dishes: some sort of potato pancake; *Schweinebraten*, which is roast pork and sauerkraut; and hasenpfeffer, a recipe for rabbit with spaetzel and cabbage. Okay, none of that sounded too good to me, except maybe the sauerkraut, but Krista nearly snatched those recipes from my hand, and now those dishes often appeared on her menu at the Speishaus.

The moral of the story is, sometimes there are good things to be found in dark, damp, icky places. So before I went to the bakery, I'd spent a few minutes going through Sylvia's files. I knew Sylvia's system. Basically, she'd filed everything under the first letter of the first word of whatever it was she had information on.

It didn't take me long to find the file she'd amassed on the Morgan Family Players. I think it's safe to say that Sylvia had been convinced that Belle Morgan was indeed Isabelle Mercer. She couldn't have proved it without speaking to Belle, which had never happened, and since Belle had committed no crime, I think Sylvia must have felt guilty pursuing it much further. The only reason I can think of that Sylvia would have pursued it in the least was because she probably knew the family in New Kassel that Belle had left behind. I'm assuming that family missed her and wanted her back. Again, it is only my assumption; I have no proof. But I think when Sylvia went to visit Belle Morgan and Belle wouldn't see her, that was as good as an affirmation for Sylvia. Maybe she then realized that Belle didn't want to be found, and so Sylvia had let it rest, although not before she'd done a ton of research on the family.

In typical Sylvia Pershing fashion, she'd done a chart of the Morgan family tree. She'd traced their lineage back to Ireland, not that any of it was relevant to what I was doing. It had been more like a compulsion for Sylvia. What was of interest to me were Belle's children. Dora Kaye and Johnny Morgan had been born in 1928 and 1931, respectively. At the time Sylvia did the research, they were just little tykes. But at some point, Sylvia had gone back and made notes all over her original research, including a note that read: "New Kassel resident Torie O'Shea's grandfather was a neighbor of Scott Morgan." It gave me goose bumps to see my name written in Sylvia's hand. Which I'd seen before, of course, but I hadn't been expecting it this time, so it took me by surprise. My eyes teared up and I took another bite of my chocolate-chip muffin as I sat in the bakery.

Also in 1987, Sylvia had scribbled, "Dora Kaye Morgan married Tiberius O'Roarke, lives in

Columbia, Illinois. Johnny Morgan, alive, in Imperial, Missouri." She'd listed their addresses and dated the note so that she would remember when it was made. She'd also tacked on a sticky note that gave the names of Dora's and Johnny's children. Dora had two daughters. At the time of the note, one daughter lived in Philadelphia, the other in San Antonio, Texas. Johnny had four children; two were in Arizona, and two were here in Missouri. A daughter lived in Independence, and a son lived in Festus.

I wrote all of this down and decided to take a drive to see if Johnny Morgan was still living in his home in Imperial. It was a purely selfish reason. I wanted to see if Johnny could tell me anything about his mother's life between being Isabelle and becoming Belle. I couldn't help but wonder if he even knew his mother had been born in New Kassel.

Before I had the chance to go anywhere, Helen came into the bakery. "Helen!" I called out.

She spun around and held a finger up to indicate to Pierre that she'd be right back. "Whatcha doing?" she asked.

"Research, what else?" I replied.

"Well, sometimes you're sticking your nose where it doesn't belong," she said.

"Even so, that would technically be called research," I said, smiling.

"Are we still on for Christmas shopping?" she asked.

"Sure thing," I said. Just then, Colin came into the bakery, glanced around, and saw me sitting in the corner.

"I'll talk to you later," she said.

"All right."

"Hey," Colin said. He exchanged pleasantries with Helen and then smiled at me. "Thought I'd find you here."

"Why?" I asked.

"Why, what?"

"Why would you find me here? I'm always at Fräulein Krista's."

"Right, but everybody I asked said they'd seen you here."

"Oh," I said. Mental note: Must find new *new* hideout. "Okay, what's up?"

"Just wondering if you've heard from Mort?"

"Well, he was over last night," I said. "Why?"

Colin pulled out the chair across from me and straddled it like a horse. "Why was he at your house last night? Something wrong?"

"We got a squatter in the woods," I said. "And we think he left us his horse."

"Oh, the Percheron?" he asked.

"Yeah, that horse just showed up in our corral. Somebody had to have let him in. So now Rudy and Mort both seem to think that the guy in the woods couldn't afford to feed and care for the horse anymore and decided we take good care of our horses, so he left it with us."

"If he's homeless, why didn't he just sell it? He could have gotten lots of money for that horse. She's beautiful," he said.

186

"When did you see her?"

"I was looking for you today. I drove out, but nobody was home."

"Oh," I said. "Well, yeah, that's my thought. Why not sell the horse?"

"Maybe he's thinking his luck will change and he can get the horse back later. Like slip in and take her back, the same way he dropped her off. But for right now, he can't afford to feed her."

I blinked at him. "That makes sense and all, but what if *we* decide to sell her? Then what's he going to do? I mean, hasn't he thought of that?"

"He's desperate. Probably not thinking straight," Colin said. He reached over and took an errant chocolate chip off of my plate and plopped it in his mouth. "Did Mort say if he thought the guy was still out there in the woods?"

I shrugged, because neither Mort nor I could really answer that question. "Why have you been looking for me?"

"They found a body."

"What do you mean? Where?" I asked, the hair standing up on my neck.

"At the bridge. That stone bridge—"

"Hahn's Bridge!" I exclaimed. I stood up so fast, my head spun. "Are you serious?"

Colin glanced around the room. "Hey, calm down."

"No way. Are you serious? They found a body. A *human* body?"

"Yes, they found human remains. . . ."

187

I grabbed the files and my coat and all but ran out of the door of Pierre's, with Colin close on my heels. "Where are you going?" he asked. It irritated me just a little that all he needed to do was walk briskly, when I was actually running. It stinks being short.

"I'm going down to the bridge!"

"Wait," he said. "If it's a crime scene . . ."

"Look, Colin. They've found her! This woman's been missing since 1936, and now they've found her. I was right."

"Torie . . ."

I stopped at my car and threw my things in the seat. Then I smacked the top of my car and repeated, "I was right."

"I'm going with you," he said.

"Please, you'll just be in the way."

"Oh, I will forgive you for saying that," he said.

"Good, forgive me and get out of the way."

"Torie," he said. "*Please* take me with you."

I stopped then and studied his face. He was begging me to take him. I was a special consultant on this case. Invited by the sheriff. I was the one who had given the sheriff the location of Hahn's Bridge. He would let me onto the scene of the crime. Colin, well, Colin was just a little old mayor of a small town that had nothing to do with Hahn's Bridge or Progress, Missouri. He could go only if I took him along. I think it was the first time in my entire life that I'd actually, really, totally, felt sorry for Colin. Okay, well maybe that time in Minnesota. But I'd seen Colin poisoned and shot in the leg, and I remembered thinking both times that I'd wished I'd done it.

What? It's not like he died either time.

But right then, Colin standing there begging me to take him to a crime scene . . . I was overcome with pity. It must have temporarily made me insane, because I heard myself saying, "Okay, but don't tell Mom."

I was chomping at the bit the entire ride down to Progress. We got off the exit and took one of the back roads past an old feed and seed store. We traveled another eight miles out into the country. Eventually, the sprawl of subdivisions that used to be farmland gave way to actual farmland. We'd pass by an occasional house with a cluster of outbuildings, and I'd think to myself how scary it was to see civilization encroaching on the American farm. If we weren't careful, another twenty years and the "family farm" would be a thing of the past.

Blacktop turned into gravel road, and a few miles later, I pulled up at the old Hahn stone bridge. The CSU was present, along with the Progress police and sheriff, and a few Granite County squad cars. Honest to God, I had no idea why I'd actually come down to the bridge. It wasn't as if I could do anything. But I wanted to be there when they brought her out of the ground.

I found Mort amid the crowd of people and the ever-increasing cold fog that had seemed to settle in the valley as Colin and I arrived. The dark, heavy clouds overhead made it feel as though evening were just around the corner, when, in fact, it was still hours away. "Hey," I called out to Mort.

"Torie," he said. He glanced at Colin and nodded his head.

"I, uh, brought Colin with me. For security reasons."

Mort just raised his eyebrows and flipped open his notepad. "Well, I think you may have done it, Torie. It's a human skeleton, small; they think it's a female. Clothes have all rotted, but she's wearing some jewelry that looks old. So they're thinking whoever she is, she's been there a while."

"Are they gonna—"

"They'll do carbon testing to determine exactly how long she's been there, and I'm going to request one of those fancy facial-reconstruction things." He glanced over his shoulder and gestured to another sheriff. The man was about fifty and had a head full of white hair and belly the size of a watermelon. "But it's really his call. This is his county, not mine."

"Well, does he seem game or not?" I asked.

Mort cleared his throat. "Well, when I told him that I suspected the skeleton was the body of Belle Morgan, he sure as hell perked up. So I think he'll spend the money for it."

"If not, I will."

"What?" Mort said.

"Well, I mean, I guess. How much does it cost? Tell him I'll split it with his department," I said. Seriously,

I had money just sitting there doing nothing, thanks to Sylvia. The least I could do was find out if this was truly Belle Morgan.

"All right, I'll tell him."

"You know what this means, don't you? If this turns out to be Belle?"

"What?"

"It means the song that was sent to me by Clifton Weaver really is a confession of murder. I mean, it goes from being just a song about a murder to a confession of Belle's murder. Or it was written by somebody who witnessed her murder and wrote it down as a confession. One of the two."

"Which makes Clifton Weaver's murder take on a different slant, as well."

"I think whoever killed Clifton Weaver was looking for 'The Blood Ballad.' That's what got him killed. I know it."

"But why?" Mort asked. "So it's a song. Big deal."

"Well, it would be the song of the century. It would solve the country music industry's greatest mystery."

"True," he said and scratched his head with his pencil. "Or maybe it points the finger at a loved one and whoever killed Clifton Weaver doesn't want his loved one revealed as a murderer."

"That could be, too."

I glanced over at Colin, who was standing away from the CSU at a respectful distance, but wanted to jump right in. I could tell by his body language. At one point, he knelt down to watch as they started lifting bones from the unmarked grave. He was waiting to see what was lying beneath the remains. Classic Sheriff Brooke. I'd seen him do that a few times.

A hush crept over the scene as they lifted the first bone. I shook my head, still amazed after all these years that people could do really horrible things to one another. I blew warm air into my hands, as they were beginning to go numb. Then I turned to Sheriff Mort. "Look, my daughter pointed out a resemblance between Belle Morgan and a girl named Isabelle Mercer, who disappeared from New Kassel a few years before Belle showed up in Progress, married Eddie Morgan, and began singing with the family."

"Your daughter?"

"Mary."

"What, are you *breeding* historical sleuths? How did Mary just happen to see the resemblance?"

I explained how she'd been doing research to help Rachel. I shrugged. "Sorry, I don't do it intentionally. I guess from living with me, they just look at things differently and have access to things that other teenagers don't."

"So, you think she's right?"

"I'd almost bet on it. Sylvia thought so, too. She wrote a big long chapter about Isabelle Mercer in a book she wrote on unsolved mysteries. She went to call on Belle Morgan, who refused to see her."

"You think that's proof of guilt?" he asked.

"I think it means Belle had something to hide."

"Or maybe she just didn't want to talk to some

crazed fan? You know, if she really wasn't Isabelle Mercer, that's how Belle Morgan could have taken Sylvia's visit," he said.

He had a point, and I admitted it to him. "Still, the photographs are uncanny. I really wish I could get my hands on some of Eddie Morgan's personal family photographs to compare to the ones of Isabelle Mercer."

"Well, becoming a famous musician would be a really stupid thing to do if you wanted to disappear," Mort said.

"That's just it, Mort. I'm not sure she was trying to disappear. I think she just wanted out of her life. She wanted away from New Kassel. I don't think she especially cared if she was found. But then, when Sylvia showed up . . . I dunno, maybe she didn't want to have to answer to those she'd left behind after all."

"Well, we can speculate all we want, but first we need to find out if these remains are hers or not," he said.

"They're hers," I told him.

"Hey!" Colin called out. "There's something under the hipbone!"

Mort and I ran over and stood as close as we could get. Someone from the CSU called out, "This is a crime scene, not a circus!"

"Right," Colin said and shoved his hands in his pockets. He was on the other side of the unmarked grave from us. He raised his hands in a motion that implied he was striking something with a hammer. Then he mouthed to us "murder weapon."

The white-haired sheriff of Progress came over to us then and held out some jewelry in a transparent evidence bag. "Look familiar?"

Like I was supposed to know what Belle Morgan's jewelry looked like, but I took the bag and examined it closely anyway. The first piece looked like a wedding ring. It was most likely white gold, since it wasn't yellow gold, and silver was not normally a choice for a wedding ring—and besides, silver would have tarnished. This ring, other than being covered in dirt, wasn't tarnished. It had four diamonds, about the size of a quarter karat each, lined up in a perfect row. "This should be easily identifiable by family photographs or even by her children, if they're still alive."

"I thought her kids were young when Belle disappeared," Mort said.

"True," I said. "Well, maybe there's a photograph of her we could find that shows her wedding ring."

Mort jotted it down in his notebook. Then he pointed at another ring with his pencil. This one was also white gold and had what looked like two small rubies and three diamonds all in a cluster. "Those real diamonds, you think?"

I shrugged. "Possibly."

"You think even a successful music family would have bought diamond rings during the Depression?"

"I honestly don't know. It looks older than that, though. Like from the early twenties."

"I'll take your word for it," he said. "Ask Colin; he owns an antique store."

"Oh, right," he said. Mort held up the evidence bag and pointed at it. Colin nodded and walked around the hole made by the CSU, careful to make a wide path around the crime-scene tape. There were no prints or fibers that he could disturb, not after this many years, but old habits die hard. "How old would you say this ring is?"

Colin took the bag and looked at it. "Um, I'd say early twenties."

Mort made another note in his notebook.

"Can we get pictures of the jewelry?" I asked.

Mort nodded. "I'll ask. Sheriff Marceau is probably going to want to ask you a bunch of questions. Since you led him to a dead body."

"Of course," I said. I had sort of forgotten about that. Colin reached in his pocket and pulled out a pair of reading glasses. I assumed he was blushing considerably because he was embarrassed. I'd certainly never seen him wear them before. Then he held the jewelry bag closer. He rubbed the bag, as if that would make whatever he was looking at clearer.

"What is it, Colin?" I asked.

"This necklace . . . look here," he said.

I leaned over and looked. The dainty chain was silver, or possibly white gold, and there was a locket hanging from it. There was no fancy inscribed initial on it, but, rather, a delicate filigree design.

"What's inside?" I asked.

"I don't know," he said. "Right now, I'm more interested in this."

"What?"

Colin flipped the locket over to look at the back. Down at the very bottom was a tradesman's mark, the mark of the jeweler who had made the piece. "Cunningham Brothers."

"Famous jeweler?" I asked.

He snorted a laugh and then looked at me over the edge of his new glasses. "Only in Wisteria."

"What?" I asked, confused.

"There are no jewelers in New Kassel. In fact, the only jeweler in Granite County, then or now, is Cunningham Brothers."

"Are you telling me this necklace was made by a jeweler in Wisteria?"

"Yes," he said. "I'd say anywhere from 1910 to 1925. I'll know for sure when I go home and check my book."

"I don't believe it," I said.

"So we know our dead body here bought at least one piece of jewelry five miles from New Kassel," Mort said.

"Right," I agreed.

"Our first connection to Isabelle Mercer?" Mort said.

"Possibly," I replied.

One of the crime-scene investigators then bagged and tagged an ax that was found with the body.

"Oh my God, it's the murder weapon."

Sheriff Marceau was kind enough to bring it over for us to inspect. I flipped the ax over inside the bag and my blood ran cold. The air around me seemed to drop twenty degrees. I sucked my breath in hard.

"What is it?" Mort asked.

There, inscribed on the blade of the ax, were the initials J.R.K. John Robert Keith. "I think this was my grandfather's ax."

Sheriff Marceau clicked his teeth and said, "We need to be having our talk now, Mrs. O'Shea."

Eighteen

Snow had begun to fall on the crime scene by the time Colin and I left. Sheriff Marceau didn't really have anything earth-shattering to ask me. Just the usual questions somebody would ask a person who'd led them to a dead body. I stared at the bridge as the heavy wet snow began to accumulate on the edges of it. How many snows had those remains witnessed, how many scorching days? How many times had people passed right over her, none the wiser that she lay below?

It made me want to cry.

"So," Colin said as we got in the car. "What have we got here, exactly?"

"Providing the body is Isabelle Mercer's?" I put the car in drive.

"Yeah," he said, and rolled his eyes. "I think it's a pretty good bet."

"What we have is a woman who disappeared from New Kassel, only to show up sometime after that in Progress. She married Eddie Morgan and joined the family band, which really came into its own about two or three years after that. Then one day, she packed her bags, but she left without them and was never seen again. Her husband said he thought she left to be with her lover. She turns up seventy-something years later, buried under a bridge."

"And how did you know she was there?"

"I received a letter and a recording of a song. I call it 'The Blood Ballad.' In the song, a woman confesses to murdering Belle because Belle was having an affair with this woman's husband or lover. 'The beautiful Belle, well, she's going straight to hell for doin' to me what she did that day. . . .' "

Colin made some disgruntled noise and crossed his arms. "Are you okay to drive in this mess?"

"I've driven in snow before."

"Yes, but maybe not quite so distractedly," he said.

"I'm fine."

"Okay," he said and held up his hands in surrender. "So, who did the recording come from?"

"It came from a dead man. Clifton Weaver. Who just happened to be the nephew of Eddie Morgan, Belle's husband."

"So, Clifton came upon this recording and, like you, thought it solved the long-lost mystery of what happened to his aunt Belle."

I nodded. "I'm hungry."

"Me, too," he said. Like I thought he would argue. One thing is for certain, Colin has a healthy appetite. "But right after he gets the recording to you, he ends up dead."

"Right."

"So somebody else knew about the recording. And they either didn't like what it implied or . . . what?"

"Or he or she wanted to be the one to unveil it to the world."

"Right, they wanted credit for it. They wanted to blow the lid off of the mysterious disappearance of Belle Morgan. Who would want that?"

"Right now, the only person I can think of would be Glen Morgan."

"Maybe we should go see him," Colin said.

I glanced over at him. He thought he'd slipped that "we" in there much more casually than he actually had. I smiled. "No, I'm going to see Johnny Morgan."

"Who is that?"

"Belle's son. He lives in Imperial."

"He's still alive?"

I shrugged. "He'd be about seventy-five. It's a chance I'm willing to take. His address is right there on that sticky note. If he doesn't live there anymore, all it will have cost me is a trip in the snow."

Colin and I got off of Highway 55 at the Imperial exit and made a left back across the highway. Imperial is just south of Arnold, which is just south of St. Louis County. It's one of those places that has really built up in recent years, but when I was a kid, it was just a main street with a few houses and businesses scattered along it. It butted up to Barnhart. Both were home to some pretty rolling hills and brand-new subdivisions.

Johnny Morgan did not live in one of the new subdivisions. Instead, he lived in an older ranch-style home, sitting on a slight hill. Behind the house were lots of empty trellises, which would have been covered with flowers were it not for the fact that it was December.

"So, you got your Christmas shopping done?" Colin asked.

I rolled my eyes. "No. I've got two Bionicles for Matthew and a padlock for Rachel."

"Padlock?"

"Something to keep Mary out of her room. Believe me, she'll be thrilled with it. Otherwise, I've gotten nothing done. What's on your list?" I asked.

"What I want for Christmas, nobody can buy," he said.

Melancholy is not a word I would usually associate with Colin, but he did seem to be a bit more . . . introspective than usual. He really was very unhappy as mayor. "Well, I've got ideas for everybody else," I said as I pulled into Johnny Morgan's driveway. "Just haven't been able to go out and actually get any of it. My sister's, I'm going to have to make."

He chuckled. "What?"

"You? Make something?"

"Hey, you know, I'm not as useless as you think," I said. "I can make stuff."

"Like what?"

"Well, like, *things*," I said. I turned off the car. "Let me do the talking."

"Right," he said. We got out of the car and I took a

deep breath, drinking in the smell of snow. I really wished I could bottle that smell to save for hot humid days. Looking out at the big flakes falling lazily on the house and trees in front of me, a hot humid day was a faded memory. If I hadn't known better, I'd have sworn those days would never come again. But they would.

I knocked on the door, and an elderly woman answered. "Hello, I hate to bother you," I said. "My name is Torie O'Shea, and I'm a historian. I live just down in New Kassel. I was wondering if I could speak with Johnny Morgan."

She gave me a quizzical look. "Why?"

I gave a heavy sigh and glanced at Colin. "I'd like to ask him some questions about his mother."

"He doesn't really remember her," the woman said.

She'd started to shut the door, but I thought to play my only trick that might actually get me in the door. I had a feeling that Johnny Morgan had been named after my grandfather, John Robert Keith. Quickly, I said, "I'm the granddaughter of Johnny Keith."

Then I heard a voice from somewhere in the house say, "Let her in."

The old woman fixed a serious stare on me. "He's not well. Do not upset him."

"I'll try not to," I said. "This is Colin Brooke. He's the former sheriff of Granite County and now he's the mayor of New Kassel."

"How do you do," Colin said, and nodded his head at her. At one time, he would have tipped his sheriff's hat, and unless I was imagining things, it seemed as though he almost reached up to tip it now. Colin was giving me room to lead without any fuss, though. Guess he was just happy to ride along.

Johnny Morgan, I must admit, looked a lot like his grandfather Scott Morgan and held himself with a certain authority. He might not have been well, but you wouldn't have known it by looking at him. His shoulders were wide and straight, no humps anywhere, and he didn't shuffle when he walked. He was tan and blue-eyed, and he looked as if he'd just come in off the golf course.

As we entered his living room, Johnny Morgan gave a winning smile and gestured toward his wife. "You have to excuse my wife," he said as she walked into the other room to leave us alone. "She's a bit protective. What can I do for you? You're Johnny Keith's granddaughter?"

"Yes," I said. "I am so sorry, but there doesn't appear to be any easy way to tell you this. Your cousin Clifton Weaver sent me a recording just before he died."

Johnny was stoic, never moved. I saw no emotion, no indication of any hidden thoughts or feelings. It was as if he'd just braced himself for whatever it was I was about to tell him. "I'm so very sorry to tell you this, but it appears that the recording contains a woman singing a song that seems to be a confession to your mother's murder. I am sorry, Mr. Morgan. At any rate, I turned the recording over to the authorities, and with the clues in the song, we were able to conclude that someone had been buried under Hahn's Bridge."

"And?" he said, his hands in his pockets.

"We're not sure on identification as of yet. But there was a body of what appeared to be an adult female. I suppose there is a chance that it's not her, but I'm fairly certain it is. Please accept my condolences."

He sat down then and stared for the longest moment at some invisible object on his coffee table. "What is it you want?"

"Well, sir, here's the tricky part. It does appear that your mother, Belle Morgan, was the same woman as Isabelle Mercer, who used to live in New Kassel. She disappeared from New Kassel shortly before Belle Morgan appeared in Progress. Buried with the body we found a piece of jewelry that was made by a Granite County jeweler, to further connect the two women. I suppose my question to you, sir, is this. Did your father ever talk about your mother's past? Where she came from? And, of course, do you have any idea who may have wanted to harm your mother?"

"Why are you interested?"

"Well, I got interested at first because your cousin Glen had come to me with proof that some of the Morgan family songs were actually written by my grandpa. And he also had this preposterous notion that my grandpa was the illegitimate son of Scott Morgan. That's how I got involved. I suppose I'm wanting to know if my grandpa has any connection to any of this, and I'd like to solve the mystery of what happened to New Kassel resident Isabelle Mercer."

"Sit down," he said. "I got a story for you. You may not want to hear it."

I sat down on a fluffy beige couch and wondered if I should just cut and run right then.

"My grandpa was what you guys today would call 'a player,'" he said. "I know of at least three illegitimate children he had."

"Rufus Kiefer?" I asked.

"You know your stuff," he said and nodded at me. "Rufus was my half-uncle as sure as the sun comes up tomorrow."

Colin was, of course, lost, and gave me a questioning look.

"Your great-grandma did have an affair with my grandpa. No proof to it, other than talk amongst the family. And my grandfather's own admissions."

My mouth went dry, and I blinked. He had to be mistaken.

"Nobody blamed her. Nate Keith was a son of a bitch and nobody within a hundred miles would have blamed your great-grandma for finding comfort with another man. My grandma knew about it. Knew about all the affairs. She just kept quiet. However, your grandpa is not Scott Morgan's son. It was your grandpa's sister, Rena, who was Scott Morgan's offspring. She's long dead now. Her people may not want to know this, since there's no real proof other than what we all just knew."

Colin reached over and patted my knee. "You all right?"

The tears were spilling over my lower lids. My whole world spun. My heritage was still the same, but if this story was true, how could any of us ever really know if our ancestors were who the documents said they were? The foundation that I'd stood on for twenty years just cracked wide open. Not to mention that my hatred for Nate Keith just grew another degree. My poor great-grandmother! How lonely she must have been and how afraid that Nate would find out. Because if he had, he would've killed her for certain.

"I have a half-uncle who lives in Tennesee, too. Or used to. He's dead now. That's the three I know of," said Johnny.

"How do you know for sure?" I managed to say.

"Well, I guess I don't. Those are the three that my grandpa admitted to and my father told me about. Sorry to upset you," he said. "You know, my grandpa was a great man. He really was. He was larger than life and people were just drawn to him. I guess the temptation was too much for him. He ate a lot, drank a lot, spent a lot of money, and had a lot of fun with women. But you couldn't help but like him anyway."

I swiped at the tears. "Here I thought you'd be the one who'd be upset by my news."

"Not at all. It makes me feel better."

"That your mother was murdered?"

"That she didn't abandon us. Don't you see? This is what I always suspected. That somebody killed her. Not that she left," he said, shaking his head.

"But her bags were packed."

"Yes," he said. "Dad said that Mom was seeing somebody. She said she needed a break, to sort things out. She was leaving, but she was coming back."

"Then why did your father tell the authorities that she'd run off with a lover?"

"I guess by reason of deduction. He knew she had a lover, so I guess he thought she just decided against the 'time out' and just left. Not to mention that everybody loved my mother, so I don't hardly think murder would have been his first thought. When she didn't come home within a week, he assumed she'd just abandoned us all—but I knew better."

If Eddie Morgan knew about her past as Isabelle Mercer, then he knew it wasn't past her just to take off. He must have thought she was doing to him what she'd done before. It made sense that he wouldn't have been suspicious of anything else.

"How so?" I asked.

"I was four when she left. In every memory I have of her, she was singing to me and my sister or playing with us. I have not one memory that was negative. I just had a feeling of being loved by her. It's hard to forget that," he said.

I glanced around his living room. There were at least six houseplants sitting in pots and hanging from the ceiling. On the television was a photograph of his mother and father. "May I?" I asked.

"Sure."

I took the photograph down and studied it. It was a

family picture, not a publicity shot. And after looking at it for about a minute, I was completely convinced that Belle Morgan was Isabelle Mercer. "Did your father say anything at all about her past?"

He rubbed his chin absentmindedly. "He didn't talk about her much. Only when I asked. One time, I did ask him why I didn't have grandparents or aunts and uncles on my mom's side. He said she'd left them a long time ago. Left that life and never wanted to return. That's all he said."

"Who do you think killed her?" I asked.

He shrugged. "What does it say in the song?"

"The singer just says that she killed Belle because she'd seen Belle with another man, and evidently, the other man was somebody that the narrator was in love with, too. Something along those lines."

"Then you're looking for a scorned woman," Johnny said.

"Who was Belle having the affair with? If we knew that, we might be more likely to figure out who the woman was," Colin said, speaking for the first time. I was impressed by how quiet he'd been.

Johnny shrugged. "I don't know. The family traveled six months out of the year. It could have been anybody, anywhere."

"No," I said. "Think about it. It had to be somebody local, because whoever killed her was local. Otherwise, she wouldn't have buried the body nearby, under the bridge. Nor would she have had access to . . ."

"To what?" Johnny said.

"To the recording equipment," I said. "It had to be somebody who knew the Morgans, who lived nearby, maybe even somebody who sang backup for them occasionally. Because whoever she was, she just flipped the recording button on, played the guitar, and sang the confession. I mean, that couldn't happen with just anybody."

"So she had to be from one of the families around there," Colin said.

"Right," I said. My cell phone rang just then. I answered it.

"Torie, it's Glen Morgan. I understand you've made an interesting discovery," he said. He sounded a bit miffed, but I didn't really care at the moment.

"I can't talk to you now," I said. "I'll call you back."

"Why didn't you tell me the second you knew?" Glen said through static.

"Knew what?" I asked him.

"What happened to Aunt Belle!"

"Glen, I said I'll call you back." I hung up the phone and glanced apologetically around the room. "Sometimes I'm not so sure that cell phones are such a great invention. The idea that people you don't really want to talk to can reach you at any point and time . . . Who thought this was a good idea?"

Johnny smiled and then stood. "I hope that you'll keep me posted, if you find anything new."

That was my cue to leave. One that might not have happened so quickly if we hadn't been interrupted by Glen Morgan.

"My cousin is writing a book, I understand," Johnny said.

"Yes," I replied.

"Watch him," he said.

"Why?" I asked at the same time Colin did.

"He's ambitious. Ambition is oftentimes accompanied by an overwhelming lack of morals."

"Right," I said. "Oh, one more thing. Are you named after my grandpa?"

He smiled at me, and for a moment I thought he'd probably been a very handsome man in his time. "Yes, I'm named after Johnny Keith. He and my father were best friends. And for the record, my father, Eddie, and my grandpa Scott didn't speak for almost six years because of Johnny Keith."

"Why's that?"

"Because my father thought Johnny should get some money or credit for writing those songs. See what I mean about ambition? My grandfather was the most ambitious person I knew. And as much as I hate to admit it, if he got the chance, he screwed people over six ways to Sunday. But I still loved him."

"I understand," I said.

"At any rate, your grandpa was my dad's best friend. Well, at one time anyway. So they named me after him."

I smiled and offered my hand, which he took. "I adored my grandfather," I said.

"As you should have. I did, too. You know, I probably met you when you were a kid and we just don't remember it. I guess you were at your grandpa's eightieth birthday party, weren't you?"

"Yes."

"Well, I was there, too," he said. "Such a small world."

"Yes," I said. "Thank you for your time."

Colin and I left, and when we reached the car, he just automatically took the keys from me and switched sides. I got in and stared at the little brick ranch, now covered in a storybook frosting of snow.

"You all right?" he asked.

"I'm not sure."

"Why's that?"

"Well, because what if my *grandpa* was the person that Belle was having the affair with? I mean, aside from the fact that my image of my grandfather would be seriously altered forever . . ."

"Would that make a difference in how you feel about him?" he asked as he backed out of the driveway.

"No. I adored him. I still do. I still would."

"So then, what does it matter?"

"Well, what if Johnny Morgan is my grandpa's son?"

"You don't have any reason to think that at all. You don't even have any reason to think your grandpa was the one Belle was seeing," he said. "You're talking crazy. First you think Scott is your grandpa's real father and now you're saying your grandpa might be Johnny Morgan's father. My head's hurting just trying to wrap around the fathers and the sons and who did what to whom."

"The ax in the grave. It was my grandpa's."

"What, nobody else in Progress had the initials JRK?"

"I've seen his mark like that on other tools before," I said. "So that would mean Belle was killed on my grandpa's property."

"Speculation," he said. "Up until you started on this little paranoid side trip, you were doing good."

I stared at him, mouth open. "What is that supposed to mean?"

"I watched you in there. You handled yourself well. Asked the right questions," he said. "But this . . . You're being paranoid."

"My grandpa always put his initials on all of his tools. And the tail in the *R* always went way down and under the *K*. It's his mark. I know it. My grandma used to put her initials on all of her kitchenware, too. I'm telling you, it was his ax."

"Then I think I'd be more concerned with the fact that somebody in his family may have killed Belle. Or somebody with access to his tools. You've heard the song. It was clearly written by a woman. So I'd say if— and that's a big if—that ax is your grandpa's, then Belle was killed by somebody who had access to his tools."

"So, did your toenails curl when you gave me that compliment a minute ago?"

"They were starting to pucker," he said. "But I made it through."

"You know, Colin, sometimes I think there's hope for you yet."

"Funny, I was just thinking the same thing about you."

211

Nineteen

"Here's my new and improved Christmas list," Matthew said as he jumped into my bed and shoved a piece of paper in my face. I took the paper from his plump little hands and tried to focus on it. Since his spelling wasn't the greatest and he had trouble writing most of his letters, he'd decided to make his Christmas list in pictures. Well, that was just as well, since I could read pictures.

He jabbered on, explaining what each toy was and what part of the store I could find it in. This kid must seriously think I'm shopping disabled, I thought. After all these years as a mom, I could find a Spider-Man action figure, but it made him feel better to explain it all, so I just let him ramble. Besides, it was nice just to cuddle with him while he talked.

Then I heard a crash and a scream. "Ugh," I said.

"Yeah," Matthew said. "Rachel's been throwing things at Mary all morning."

"Has she hit anything?"

"No, she's a bad thrower," he said.

"What's Mary doing?"

"Ducking."

"Oh," I said. He continued to read and explain his entire Christmas list, and I let him. I preferred to have him treat me like I were senile or stupid than to have to get up and face the terror down the hall.

"So, Venom is not the same thing as Black Spidey. You got that?" he asked.

"Got it."

"You think Santa will understand all of this, or should I send him instructions, too?"

I loved it when my little kid used big words. When he was four, he discovered the word "actually," and he used it in nearly every sentence for six months. "I think Santa will do fine. You know, his elves are pretty hip, from what I understand."

"Good," he said. Then we heard another crash and more yelling. "I'm going outside."

"Put on your coat and your boots, and don't go in the woods!" I called after him.

"I know!"

"Hey, wait, you have to eat breakfast," I said. Then I just lay there, because I knew he wasn't going to acknowledge my last sentence, since if he ate, he wouldn't be able to get outside as fast.

Crash. Scream. *"I hate you, you wench!"*

Not that I could blame him. I dragged myself out of bed and wondered briefly where my husband was. I toddled down the hall, nearly tripping over a soccer ball and stepping right on a dinosaur. Triceratops no less, so one of the little horns went right into the arch of my foot. "Dammit," I said, under my breath.

Then I came to Mary's room, where all the excitement was happening. Mary had decided to take the offensive, it appeared, and was standing on top of her bed with an armful of books that she was flinging at

Rachel. Rachel, on the other hand, had put on her riding helmet and elbow pads for protection and was going through Mary's closet.

When they weren't fighting, they were really pretty cool kids. Mary's room was painted white, with big orange and turquoise circles, and there were posters of all sorts of anime and manga characters hanging crooked on every wall. In and among all of that Japanese chaos was a painting that my mother had painted for Mary of two little girls having a tea party—a *civilized* tea party, with unbroken china and dressed-up dolls and teddy bears around the table. My mother said the painting reminded her of Rachel and Mary. I'm not sure on what planet Rachel and Mary had ever acted that civilized, but they were no longer on it.

"I found my earrings!" Rachel said to me.

"Well, good, now we can stop all of this fussing," I said, rubbing my eyes and yawning.

"Mom, tell her to get out of my room!" Mary said.

"Rachel, get out of her room," I stated. As if that would matter.

"Tell her to quit taking my stuff!" Rachel countered.

"Mary, quit taking her stuff," I said, again summoning as much authority as I had the first time.

Rachel's head was buried deep in the closet, and she was tossing stuff out left and right. Every time she'd pull something else out of the depths of the closet, Mary would throw a book at her. More often than not, she missed. I was assuming Rachel's costume of riding gear was protection for those rare moments when Mary actually hit her target.

"Get out of my room!" Mary screamed. "I'm sick of seeing your fat butt up in the air."

"I found my earrings right here on her closet floor!" Rachel screamed—they were far beyond speaking in a normal tone of voice. That's the bad thing about screaming and yelling. Once you start, you have to keep getting louder and louder or your words just don't have as much emphasis as when you started. "After she said she didn't have them, so I thought I'd look and see what else of mine she has. So far, I've found my pink sweater—"

"Oh, like I'd be caught dead in pink," Mary said from her lofty position.

"Well, it was right here, Mary. Explain that! And I found the ring that Grandma gave me, and my library card! God only knows how many books she's checked out on my card and never returned."

"Oh, now, Rachel," I said. "You don't know that."

Just then she pulled out two—no, wait—three library books. "Yes? You were saying?" Rachel screeched.

"I checked those out on *my* card!" Mary screamed.

"I'd be careful what I said, Mary," I began. "I can easily check with the library to see who's telling the truth and who isn't."

"Get out of my room! Neither one of you belongs in my room!" The veins popped out in her forehead when she screamed at us, so I knew she meant business. I kept thinking her head was going to start spinning around and I'd find pea soup splattered all over the wall, but it hadn't happened yet. God must have been having mercy on me.

"Stop it!" I screamed. "Both of you, just stop!"

"Oh, and here's my pen set I got from Six Flags three years ago," Rachel said, pulling yet something else off the floor of Mary's closet. I swear Mary's closet was like Mary Poppins's handbag. Surely, Rachel had pulled everything out by now.

"I hate you!" Rachel screamed at Mary, and stormed past me. Mary stuck her tongue out at her sister as she went by and then hopped down off the bed.

"She has every right to be upset with you," I said.

Mary said nothing.

"Why do you take her things?" I asked.

"It's the only way I have to get back at her for all the stuff she does. Like the way she talks down to me and the way she thinks she's so much better at everything. She tells me how to dress, how to talk. She tells me *how I'm supposed to feel*! She drives me crazy all the time, Mom. And then I did all that research to help her get that stupid job, and she doesn't even give me any credit for it! Well, this drives her crazy. So this is what I do. Besides, she bit my pinkie when I was nine months old."

That last sentence was delivered with a half smile, and although it was true that Rachel had bitten Mary's pinkie when she was nine months old, I thought maybe, just maybe, we could move beyond that. As for the other things Mary listed, she wasn't wrong. "Mary, we all have idiosyncrasies that drive other people crazy, but that doesn't mean we resort to stealing other people's things."

She folded her arms and blew an exhausted breath so hard that her bangs flew up.

"Well, I think you both are pretty unlikable right now. Neither one of you even stops to think about what you're doing to the rest of the family," I said.

"Oh, sure, Mom. Think about yourself, why don't you?" she said with her hand on her hip.

"Well, clearly, nobody else is going to," I said and walked out of her room. Then without having eaten breakfast, I pulled on my sweats and my boots and went outside to play in the snow. I was entertaining the idea of just locking the two of them up in the basement and letting them duke it out. There might be some bloodshed, but at least the fighting would be over and life could resume its natural course.

I knew Rachel would move out sooner or later, but that was no consolation, since by that point, Matthew would be prepubescent and all of this would start all over again, only with him and Mary. I suppose knowing this ahead of time was the only thing that kept me from being really stupid, throwing caution to the wind, and actually being optimistic.

I wondered if they let women be monks?

I threw a few snowballs at Matthew and hauled the sled out for him. Then I went to the stables and made sure the water for the horses wasn't frozen. Rudy had already fed them, as I could see the oat bucket sitting next to one of the stalls.

I thought about everything that I'd learned the day before. As is the case most of the time, everything I had learned only brought new questions to mind. I kept hearing Colin's words echo in my head. He'd said that the person who killed Belle Morgan had had access to my grandpa's tools, and I remembered how Johnny Morgan had said that I was looking for a scorned woman. So how many women who'd had access to my grandpa's tools and the Morgans' music equipment would want Belle Morgan dead?

I mentally made a list of the obvious. There was Toot's wife, Nancy. George's wife and my grandma's cousin, Ava. Roscoe's wife, Hattie; Cletis Morgan's wife, Rosa, and Miriam Morgan Weaver— Clifton's mother. There was also Scott Morgan's wife. . . . I think her name was Florence. She was sort of the one overlooked in all of this. She was the mother to the children in the Morgan Family Players and the wife of the very philandering Scott Morgan.

So, these Morgan family women: Nancy, Ava, Hattie, Rosa, Florence, and Miriam, all would have had access to the Morgan music equipment, and since they were neighbors of my grandpa, I suppose they could have had access to his tools.

Oh, and I almost forgot about Emma Morgan, the daughter of Scott and Florence who was "touched." I wasn't exactly sure how mentally ill Emma was. I didn't know if she was capable of playing the guitar as beautifully as it had been played on that recording, but I supposed I couldn't leave her off the list.

Now, I thought, if I just knew what mystery man was involved, I might get a better idea of who the killer was. Not that it mattered, since they were all long dead, with the exception of Nancy. It wasn't as if this was a case that could be prosecuted.

I walked out to the corral and spooked Cutter. I didn't mean to, but he wasn't expecting me to come around the corner. I held my hand out and said, "Come here, boy. Didn't mean to scare you." He eventually did come, since I was usually the one with an apple or carrots for him. I rubbed his nose and listened to him breathe, watching as the warm, moist air billowed out of his nostrils. Pretty soon, the Percheron became jealous and wandered over. I petted her, too, although it was a higher stretch for me to reach her nose.

Okay, but what if the killer wasn't any of the Morgan family women at all? I asked myself. What if it was somebody in my family? My grandmother would have had access to those tools, as would my great-grandma. My grandpa's three sisters would have had access, too. The thought made me a tad bit sick to my stomach.

As would have twenty other women within a five-mile radius. Anybody visiting my grandparents could have picked up that ax and taken it along to use later, but how many women in my family had played the guitar? My grandma and great-grandma hadn't. Plus, I would have recognized my grandma's voice on that recording. It wasn't her. Two of my grandpa's sisters had played the guitar. I had pictures of them sitting in the front yard, strumming away while my grandpa played the fiddle.

I had to face the fact that without a confession, I would probably never know who had killed Belle Morgan. I didn't think the Progress police or sheriff would be reopening that investigation, either, considering all of the prosecutable suspects would be long dead. Even if I did figure out who it was, the woman—whoever she was—had gotten away with it.

I went inside and made a few phone calls. I made them as casually as I could, since it would be very startling to have a second or third cousin call you up and start inquiring about your mother's whereabouts in October 1936. And that was the great thing about being a genealogist or a historian. I could always use my occupation as an excuse for asking these types of questions, but I still had to be casual about it and try to work it into the conversation as though it was the natural thing to ask next.

Three hours later, I had learned that one of my grandpa's sisters was in Oklahoma during the fall of 1936. She'd lived there for three years before returning to Missouri. Another one had been about eight months pregnant. I could have figured that out myself if I'd gotten out my family charts and looked. I doubted that a woman in her third trimester would be wielding an ax and digging a very deep hole, one big enough to hold the body of Belle Morgan. In addition to that, she would have had to drag or somehow lift

Belle's dead and limp body onto a wagon. The other sister was the one who did not play the guitar, so I just ruled out all three of my grandpa's sisters. Unless it was my great-grandma, it was nobody from my grandpa's family.

Which meant it either had to be somebody from the Morgan family or a neighbor. If it was a neighbor, I'd never figure it out. It could have been any number of women.

My phone rang. It was Glen Morgan. He wanted answers. Well, I didn't feel like talking to him just then, so I didn't even bother answering the phone.

THE NEW KASSEL GAZETTE
The News You Might Miss
by Eleanore Murdoch

"Sleigh bells ring, are you listening?" Well, those cash registers are ringing as much as those sleigh bells, that's for sure. Bonnie at the Christmas All Year shop said she's had a record-breaking season so far, and we still have more shopping days left to go! I want everybody to take part in the Trim a Tree program. Even if you don't normally attend church, I want you to stop by one of the churches in town and leave a gift for a needy family. Father Bingham said it will do you good and he might forgive some of you your gambling debts that you owe him. Okay, he didn't say that, but I thought it would be good to throw that part in.

The Fabric of Life is sponsoring a program for children. Make a blanket, a quilt, or a pillow for a child and drop it off, and they'll give you one free yard of the fabric of your choice!

The Smells Good Café says for you all to come by and try their new gumbo recipe.

Anybody who heard the scuffle the other night behind the Knights of Columbus hall, not to worry. It was just Elmer finally getting his hands on the raccoon that nested under his porch. I think the raccoon won, but Elmer is happy to report that the raccoon has moved on to greener porches.

Oh, and Tobias is in need of new knickers, if anybody wants to volunteer to make those.

Until next time,
Eleanore

Twenty

A few days later, Sheriff Mort cornered me in the Kendall home while I was giving a tour. When giving tours of the Kendall House, I wore reproduction dresses in styles that ranged from about 1900 to 1930. The purple flapper-style dress was a lot of fun, since it had a matching hat that nearly covered one of my eyes and came with lots of jewelry. The earlier, World War

I-era dresses were my favorites, though, because I could wear the special patchwork aprons that Geena Campbell had made for all of us. I also had, just for fun, a long dress made entirely out of crazy patchwork. So it was like I was wearing a crazy quilt. That was the dress I was wearing when Mort arrived. It was long-sleeved and warm and embellished with lots of buttons, lace, and fancy stitchery. Geena had also made this dress.

Really, what other job in the world could I have possibly worn this dress to? That's what was so great about New Kassel.

At any rate, Mort did a double take and stopped me in the hall after the museum patrons had moved to the upstairs. I said to the guests, "Please wait for me at the top of the stairs. I have to explain the mural in one of the bedrooms before we go in." Then I turned to Mort. "What's up?"

"You're wearing a quilt," he said with a frightened expression on his face.

"So? How's this any different from a guy wearing camouflage? Huh?"

"Yours is girlie; camo is not."

"Your opinion," I said. "What is it you want?"

"You get right to the point, huh?" He handed me a file. "Here's the police report back from when Belle disappeared. There's a note at the bottom of the third page as to what was in her bags. Aside from that, the remains are Belle Morgan's for sure."

I leaned back on the doorjamb. I had known they

were hers, but it was still sad to actually hear the words. I looked down at the report. "All right, can I keep this?"

"No."

"Well, can you wait for me to complete this tour? I've got people waiting upstairs."

"All right," he said.

It took about twenty minutes for me to finish the tour. As usual, I had been very touched to see a few of the patrons overcome with emotion when they saw the World War I mural, drawn by the hand of a very disturbed veteran, Rupert Kendall. In every group, there was usually at least one person who swiped at tears. I had one historian who came to visit the mural once a month. As if it were going to change or something. When the Girl Scout troop had come last summer, they'd left flowers and a candle in front of it. It was truly amazing how much this had touched everybody, and it was even more amazing how it had almost been lost forever. It had been on these walls for over eighty years, telling Rupert's story, and nobody even realized it.

"Thank you all for coming," I said as the guests stepped out onto the porch.

Mort met me in the sitting room. "That's a nice quilt," he said, pointing toward a Mariner's Compass done in red and white. It was a hundred-year-old quilt, donated by a woman who lived in Farmington. The Mariner's Compass pattern is a circle made up of very narrow triangles of alternating colors, so it appears like a compass. This one had been done without the technique known as paper piecing, so I couldn't even imagine how the quilter had gotten all those points to meet. I smiled at the quilt. "Yes, it's pretty amazing."

He handed me the file and I flipped through it, opening to the page with the contents of Belle's bags. There had been nothing in the two bags except clothing, a hairbrush, hair pins, that type of thing. This was a dead end. I glanced at some of the other pages and learned that the authorities at the time had questioned everybody in the family. Even Emma, the disturbed sister, had been questioned. The report of her interview read like this:

"Miss Emma, do you know where your sister-in-law went?"
"No."
"Did she talk to you before she left?"
"Yes."
"What did she say?"
"Daddy gonna be mad."
"Why?"
"Chickens ain't been fed."
"Did Belle tell you to feed the chickens?"
"That rooster, he's a something. Think he owns the whole roost."
"Miss Emma, about Belle. When did you see her last?"
"Daddy gonna be mad."

The officer doing the interview made a note that they could not get anything out of Emma Morgan that made any sense whatsoever. The interview with Florence Morgan was just as one-sided, although not as cryptic:

"Mrs. Morgan, were you aware that your daughter-in-law was leaving?"
"Yes."
"Do you know where she was going?"
"No, said she needed to think."
"Was she upset the day she went to the mill?"
"No."
"Do you go on tour with the family?"
"No."
"So you wouldn't know if something or someone was bothering Belle on the road?"
"No."
"Do you think something bad has happened to her?"
"I don't know."
"Do you think she just left for good without saying good-bye?"
"I really can't say."

Wow, you had to love those talkative women. I glanced through an interview with Roscoe, who was a bit more open, though not by much.

"Roscoe Morgan, was your sister-in-law unhappy?"
"Yes."

"What about?"

"Her marriage."

"There were problems between her and Eddie?"

"No. Her and Eddie got along fine. My brother bent over backward for her."

"Then what was the problem?"

"She was in love with another man."

"Did she tell you this, or did Eddie?"

"I asked Eddie, and he told me. Then I asked Belle. She admitted it."

"Did she say who it was?"

"No."

"Do you have any suspicions?"

"Could be anybody."

"What about you, Roscoe? Were you in love with Belle Morgan? "

"Everybody was. Most beautiful woman I ever laid eyes on. "

"Are you admitting to being in love with Belle?"

"Sure. But never did nothing about it. I been faithful to Hattie."

"Roscoe, think about this carefully. Where were you the day Belle went to the mill?"

"Over in Simpson, helping the preacher man put a new steeple on his church."

At this point, the interviewer made a note that he had checked with Brother Olnik at the Baptist church, and Roscoe had indeed been at the church all day helping him with repairs.

The interview with the famous Scott Morgan was a little more colorful:

"Mr. Morgan, sir, did you know about Belle's love affair with another man?"

"No."

"No? It seems everybody else did."

"Well, I heard some rumors here and there, but I didn't really know for sure."

"Were you aware that she was leaving?"

"No."

"No? Your wife knew."

"Well, guess I'd heard something about it. Just thought she was going off on one of those vacations."

"So you have no idea who she was seeing?"

"No."

"Did you ever ask Eddie about it?"

"No."

"You didn't want to know who it was?"

"No, look, this was none of my affair. Eddie can take care of himself. If he can't, then I suppose he gets what's coming."

"What do you mean?"

"I mean, if his wife is gallivantin' around with some other man and Eddie don't do nothing about it, then he can't really complain when she leaves him."

"Mr. Morgan, that's pretty harsh. He's your son."

"I know, and he's always been a softy. I swear, any

woman with legs could sweet-talk Eddie out of his life savings. Always has been like that. Looks like he just finally got one that would actually do it."

"Do you think Belle took money from him?"

"No, she took his heart. Worth a lot more."

"So, clearly this means a change for the Morgan family. "

"What? You mean the music? It won't change none. They don't come to see just her. They don't buy our records to hear Belle. I can get another guitar player."

"So, this won't change things at all?"

"No. Now if it was Miriam that was gone, then I'd be worried. Nobody plays a fiddle like that gal."

I knew for a fact that a few months later Scott Morgan had changed his tune. Publicly, he was quoted as saying things like "I can't believe Belle would do this to us." Scott Morgan was right. He could have replaced Belle with another guitar player. She wasn't that outstanding. She didn't have a unique picking style like Lefty Frizzel or a voice like Rosetta Tharpe. She did blend beautifully with the rest of the singers in the band and she was a very good guitar player, but still, very replaceable. The people you couldn't have replaced in his band were Miriam, Toot, and Scott Morgan. Toot had an amazing sound on the harmonica, one I'd yet to hear anybody duplicate. My grandpa used to say it sounded as though Toot was wheezing into the harmonica. Miriam was just the most fantastic fiddle player I'd ever heard, and Scott was not only the front man and the main voice but wrote most of the music, too. As songwriting went, Eddie would have been sorely missed, too, but as far as musical talent went, Roscoe, Eddie, and Belle could have all been replaced with just as equally talented musicians.

So then why had the band fallen apart?

"Earth to Torie," Mort said. "Find anything useful?"

"Why is it when you're hot on the trail of something like this, there're always more and more questions before you get even the smallest of answers?"

"Nature of the beast," he said.

"Oh, speaking of beasts, here comes my stepfather," I said, glancing out the front window.

Colin didn't knock, just walked right in and made a beeline for me. "Hey, I looked in my book to check on this jewelry. . . . Good God in heaven, you're wearing a quilt," he said.

"Better a quilt than camo," Sheriff Mort interjected.

"Save your jokes," I said. "What have you got?"

"That necklace is definitely a Cunningham Brothers necklace. They made it in 1921. It's a locket. So I'd be interested to see what's inside. Anyway, sorry it took me so long, but I had to wait for Sheriff Marceau to fax me a picture of it so I could look it up."

"Great," Mort and I said together.

"Right, well," he said, rubbing his hands together. "I just wanted to pass that along."

"Thank you," Mort said. "I'll give Marceau a call and ask if they've opened the locket to see what's inside."

"Good," he said. "Well, I'm having lunch with Chuck. Talk to you later."

As Colin left the museum, I turned to Sheriff Mort. I thought long and hard about the words that came out of my mouth next. "Colin is miserable as mayor."

Mort scratched his neck with his finger, then leveled a gaze at me with those violet eyes. Why is it guys get things like long eyelashes, or naturally curly hair, or violet eyes? I mean, who has violet eyes? Other than Elizabeth Taylor, *nobody*! But I didn't have time to think about the injustices of Mother Nature.

"I gathered as much," he said.

"He would like to get back into law enforcement."

There was a really long pause—so long, I began to get uncomfortable. I figured if it went on any longer, I'd have to make some insipid comment about the weather.

"What exactly is it you'd like me to do?" he asked.

"Well, nothing, exactly."

"You wouldn't have mentioned it if you didn't want me to do something. I like my job. I'm contracted for—wait, are you planning on knocking me off?"

"No!" I said. "Don't be stupid."

"Then what?"

"Offer him a job as a deputy," I said.

"What? Are you serious? Do you really think he could handle being a deputy when he used to be the boss of all the guys he'd be working with? He'd be their equal, not their superior. Could he be a deputy when he used to be sheriff?"

"Here's the thing, Mort. He is absolutely miserable. I mean, he's starting to get philosophical, and that's just outright dangerous. Not to mention scary. He wants back in law enforcement; he said so himself. But he's not going to come and ask you for a job. I know he won't."

"Too proud?"

"And how. He might casually inquire about openings in the department, but he's not going to say he's interested. You'll have to offer him the position," I said. "Do you even have any openings?"

He shook his head in the negative. "Not right now. Maybe in a year or two. I've got one thinking about going back to school to be a CSI."

"Great. You could just say something to him like 'Hey, I might be getting an opening in the department. When your time is up as mayor, would you be interested? I could sure use a . . . seasoned veteran.' Or 'I could use a pair of trained eyes.' Yeah, that sounds good. No, the 'seasoned veteran' sounds better, but I'd be afraid that he'd think you meant he was old. Damn. I don't know which you should say, but you get the picture. Right?"

"I don't need a script to offer a man a job."

"Good," I said. "Could you do that? Because then he would at least feel like he had options."

"Sure, I can do that," Mort said, smiling.

"What?"

"Why do you care?"

"'Cause if he's miserable, then I bet he's driving my mother crazy."

He shook his head. "No, I think you're worried about him."

"Mort, when Colin gets philosophical, I get scared. Really scared. Just do this for me, please."

"I will."

Twenty-one

One of the great things about having a mother is that you can always go back to her house and eat dinner. No, seriously. I cannot explain how fantastic it is to eat dinner with my mother. Not just because she's a great cook, not just because she instinctively knows what food I'm in the mood for, but because I'm partaking of a meal with my mother. Nobody loves you like your mother, even if you don't get along. Which, I guess, could be a bad thing, if you were the type of person who had a lot to hide. But sitting at the dinner table, with the silverware clanking against the dishes and the conversations floating back and forth and the smell of chicken fried in a cast-iron skillet, and green beans made with bacon grease and Rhodes raw-dough bread baked to perfection . . . well, I know that someday there will come a time when I'll give almost anything to have these moments back.

A few days after my conversation with Mort, we

were having just such a dinner at my mom's house. Even the girls were behaving and actually laughing—with each other! I had to admit that I was a bit irked that they could behave for Grandma but not for me. At that moment, I hoped all of my children would grow up and have, like, six kids apiece and I'd get to return the favor.

"Christmas is only a little while away," my mother said. She was wearing her deep green sweater, and it made her cheeks glow. The kids all piped in with what they wanted for Christmas, and, of course, Rudy had to complain about all the hype and money spent at this time of year. I swore that he was turning into my father.

At any rate, I had just taken a bite of my green beans when the conversation finally got around to bowling.

"No, really, Rudy, you almost had a strike on that last frame," Colin said, chuckling. Rudy was agreeing wholeheartedly, because almost getting a strike in their bowling league was just as good as actually getting one. Last time I'd checked, Rudy was leading the league in nine pins knocked down, which said a whole lot about the other bowlers.

"My concentration was off," Rudy said. "Otherwise, I think I would have actually gotten the strike."

"Amazing," Rachel said in a condescending tone from behind her chicken leg.

"Oh, I see you're wearing that ring I gave you," my mother said to Rachel. "Haven't seen it in a while."

"Well, that would be because Mary stole it out of my room and hid it."

I kicked her under the table. "You just can't let it go, can you?"

"No, the whole world should know just how big of a brat she really is," Rachel declared.

"That's great, Rachel, but while you're spouting your mouth about how big a brat she is, you're just letting the whole world see how big a one you are, too," I said.

"I don't get it. She's the thief, and you call me a brat."

"Do you ever listen to yourself?" I said. "You never, ever, let anything slide or give anybody a break. I just want to know when you're going to live up to this perfection you expect everybody else to live up to."

"Whatever," she said and did the perfunctory eye rolling. "Whatever" is the word that most American teenagers would be lost without. Take it away, and they can't communicate.

"Having a sister is pretty tough, huh?" Colin said to Mary.

"You have no flipping idea," Mary replied.

But that was it. They returned to their formal angelic state, because they were in the presence of Grandma. I ate in silence for a while, enjoying every bite. "So, Torie, are Stephanie and her family coming for Christmas?" my mother asked.

"As far as I know," I said.

"And your father?"

"Yup."

Stephanie is the love child my father had with

another woman while my mother was married to him, but my mom's just amazing like that. Stephanie is always welcome at her house. The great thing is, Stephanie likes my mom and never turns down an invitation. I know it sounds like my mother is perfect, but she's not. I swear, she does have a few flaws. For example, she likes to tell everybody when they're doing things wrong, especially me, and she's pretty bad about rubbing it in when she's right.

"So, you guys will never guess what happened," Colin said.

"What?" Rudy asked.

"Mort asked me if I wanted to be a deputy," he said, beaming.

"You mean you wouldn't be mayor anymore?" Rachel asked.

"Well, I'd finish out my sentence first," he replied.

"You mean your term," my mother corrected.

"What? What did I say?" he asked, piling another heap of mashed potatoes onto his plate.

" 'Sentence,' " Rudy repeated and laughed.

"Oh, sorry, my term."

"So, you're going to do it, right?" I asked. "I mean, isn't this what you wanted?"

Colin gave me a peculiar expression then. As though a window in his mind had been wiped of the grime and he could get a clear picture now. I knew that he knew that I had asked Mort to offer him the job.

"I don't know," he said. "I told him I'd have to think about it."

"Why?" Mary asked.

"Colin's not sure how awkward it would be working with everybody again," my mother added. Clearly, he'd discussed this with her before dinner.

"I don't want to make Mort feel uncomfortable," he said.

"Oh, he'd love to have your help," Rachel said.

"We'll see. So, how's your job going?"

Rachel put her fork down to begin her big long description of life and work as a tour guide in a drafty old house. "Well, in the first week, I tripped over a tourist's foot and fell into the fireplace. Thank God there was no fire in it."

"I guess that depends on who you ask," Mary countered.

"I ran into another tourist's camera, which the woman dropped, but it landed on her son's head and so it didn't break. Her son has a huge bruise on top of his head now, but the camera is fine."

Colin laughed and Rudy just shook his head.

"I forgot my lines, like, a bajillion times, and I spilled Dr Pepper all over the front of my brand-new, historical dress, which is really pretty."

"Sounds like you earned your money," Mom said.

"Well, at least you weren't wearing a quilt. Have you seen that horrible thing your mother wears over at the other house?" Colin asked.

"Hey!" I said. "It's really pretty."

"Mom," Mary said to me. "Just don't even try to defend it, all right? It's lame."

My cell phone rang then and I checked the number. It was Glen Morgan. I had been avoiding his calls ever since we'd found Belle's body. I ignored this one, too, but after dinner, I cleaned up the dishes and then went out onto Mom's back porch to return Glen's call. I knew I couldn't keep avoiding him forever. Well, I could have, but that would have been rude, and I figured he would probably start showing up at my work or home. In fact, I was surprised he hadn't already. He seemed like the type of person who wouldn't let personal boundaries stop him from getting what he wanted. All right, so we were a lot alike, but it sounds creepier now as I'm describing him.

"Glen, it's Torie."

"I don't like the way you bailed on me," he said.

"It's complicated," I replied.

"I need to talk to you," he said. "Urgently."

"Someplace public," I said.

"What, you don't trust me? You think I'm going to hurt you?"

"I'd be an idiot not to be careful."

"Fine," he said, exasperated. "Meet me at a place called Smugala's. It's a pizza place on Lindbergh."

"I know where it is."

"When can you be there?"

I figured it would take me at least a half hour to forty-five minutes to drive up to St. Louis County from Wisteria, then another ten or fifteen to maneuver down that traffic trap known as South Lindbergh. There are several streets in St. Louis County that are like Lindbergh in the fact that they are full of traffic almost any time of the day, due to all of the businesses and restaurants and schools along them. Manchester, Watson, Gravois, Page, and Olive, just to name a few.

I looked out upon the sunset over my mother's fence, watching the birds flitter in and out of the two large holly trees that flanked both sides of the yard. It really was amazing how much time could pass while watching a bird do nothing more exciting than eat a meal. It was one of those beautiful winter evenings, where the sun painted the snow a brilliant orangy yellow and the barren branches of oak and elm trees scrawled their presence across the frosty sky. "Give me an hour and a half," I said.

"I'll be there," he replied.

He would probably be there early, if I knew Glen Morgan.

I went back inside and kissed Rudy. "Something's come up. I gotta go meet somebody."

"Who?"

"Oh, that guy with the recordings," I said.

"Who, Leo King?"

"No, he's the one putting recordings onto CDs for me and Dad, but thanks for reminding me, because I actually need to go see him, too. This is the guy who gave me the recordings initially."

"Oh, the one who said your great-grandpa wasn't your great-grandpa."

"Yup, that's the one."

"All right," he said. "Where are you going and when

will you be home?"

"Hopefully by ten or eleven. I'll be at Smugala's, that pizza place we've eaten at."

"All right," he said, a little irritated. Since it was a little, not a lot, I shook it off and told everybody good-bye. Colin didn't ask where I was going, but I was sure he'd ask Rudy once I was gone.

I took advantage of already being in Wisteria and drove by Leo King's studio. I just took a chance that he'd be there, and he was. He gave me a big broad smile when he saw me come in. "And how are we tonight?" he asked.

"We are fine," I said.

"I'm not quite finished with your dad's CDs, if that's why you came by," he said. He removed a bunch of stuff from his counter—some record books, a McDonald's cup, some empty CD cases—to make room for me. I set my handbag on the counter.

"Yeah, I just wanted to check. Also, I've got a copy of an old recording. It's been dubbed twice already. Can you clean it up?" I was referring to the copy that I had made of "The Blood Ballad," which I'd conveniently forgotten to mention to Sheriff Mort.

"Probably some, but it depends on what it was recorded on in the first place," he said and glanced at my purse. "Did you bring it?"

"No, but I did bring a few photographs to put on the case of the CDs you're making for my dad. They're of his dad and the Morgan Family Players." I shuffled through my purse until I found the enve-

240

lope and pulled it out. "I've been carrying it around for a few days now. Can you do that for me?"

"Yeah, sure," he said. "So, what are the specifics on this other recording?"

"Oh, well, it was recorded onto a CD; then I copied it onto a cassette tape on my boom box. Do people still use that term, 'boom box'?" I asked and chuckled.

"I think so, but hell, I'm so old now, I don't really care," he said. "Well, I can try to clean it up and put it on CD for you. Just bring it in."

"I will."

"Where's the original?"

I shrugged. "Not sure."

"Is this more of your grandpa's stuff?"

"Sorta. That same time frame," I said. "So, you plan on attending this year's Pickin' and Grinnin' Festival?"

"I do every year," he said and smiled. "Great, I'll bring that recording by soon."

"Sure thing," he said.

I then headed north to meet Glen Morgan.

Smugala's is a pizza joint on South Lindbergh, just south of Watson Road. It used to be located in Ronnie's Plaza, but it soon became obvious that with the amount of business Smugala's did, that space was too tiny, so the owner relocated. The new location isn't really new, as it is attached to a hotel with a swimming pool. So when you walk in the restaurant, you're greeted with this sort of weird mixture of chlorine, basil, oregano, and beer. Not that it matters, since they have great pizza—that St. Louis thin style—and I think everybody overlooks the bizarre mixture of smells. The place is filled with beverage signs and televisions hanging from the ceiling. There's a small game room off to the right. Smugala's is usually packed on the weekends.

When I entered, Glen Morgan was sitting at a small table by the window, watching for my arrival. That alone was sort of creepy, but I let it go. Maybe when he arrived, there had been no other tables.

I sat down quickly and tried to smile.

"Would you like something?" he inquired.

"No, I just ate."

"A drink?"

"Just a Dr Pepper."

He called the waitress over and added my Dr Pepper to his order. "You want to tell me what the hell is going on?" he asked.

"Where do you want me to start?"

"How did you know where to tell them to find Belle's body?"

"I received a recording in the mail."

"So?"

"Well, the recording was a confession of sorts. I figured out that Belle had been murdered and where the killer had put her body."

Pounding his fist on the table, he said, "And you never thought to call and tell me!"

"Whoa, look, if you're going to get angry, I'll just leave," I said.

"You know I'm working on a book about the family. This is *my* family!"

"When I received the recording, I was still under the impression that it might be my family, as well. That theory has since been laid to rest."

"How so?" he asked.

"What, you haven't talked to Phoebe?"

He sat back then and glared at me. His pizza arrived, along with a side order of french fries, and he began to eat. "I saw the letters," I continued. "Phoebe brought them to me. In those letters, my great-grandmother was speaking of a boy named Rufus Kiefer."

"How do you know?" he asked.

"Research. Not to mention that I spoke with your cousin Johnny Morgan, and he confirmed it."

"Johnny?"

"Really, Glen, if you're going to write a book, you should interview all of your surviving family. Johnny could have told you who Scott Morgan's illegitimate children were. Johnny Keith was not one of them, but apparently his sister, my great-aunt Rena, was. You were right about one thing: My great-grandmother did have an affair with your grandfather. Which is probably why she felt as though she could speak to him that openly in those letters. Scott Morgan refused to help pay for even the basic necessities for little Rufus Kiefer. My great-grandmother was appalled by his behavior."

He took a drink of his beer and then stared into his glass for a moment.

"That's just what Johnny has to say," I went on. "Look, his story and the research I'd already done back each other up. If you really want proof, how about you and my dad get some DNA tests done. I'll bet if you tested my great-aunt Rena's offspring, you'd find you match up to them, not us. It's a simple blood test."

"All right," he said. "It's a deal. We'll get DNA tests done."

"Fine," I said.

"I still can't believe you didn't get in touch with me when you got that recording," he said.

"It was a judgment call."

"So, when can I hear it? This is a Morgan Family Players recording I've never heard, in which someone confesses to killing my aunt Belle. I mean, this is huge. It's like a true-crime novel. After all these years, I've discovered what happened to her."

"Well, last time I checked, you hadn't done much of anything, except spread the rantings of my poor demented cousin. The recording was sent to me, not you, and I'm the one who figured out where Belle was."

"So, what, you want credit on the book? We can coauthor if you want. That's how big I think this thing is going to be." He wiped at the pizza sauce in the corner of his mouth with his napkin.

"No, I don't want to coauthor the blasted book, but you should document how it was discovered. And good luck getting a copy of the recording—it's evidence."

"For what? They're not really going to try to investigate Belle's murder, are they? I mean, there's no way to solve it. No way to punish whoever did it," he said.

"Not that crime. A different crime."

He swallowed his pizza then and stared at me. His eyes grew wide and he took a very large drink of his beer. "You got the recording from my cousin Clifton?"

"Yup," I said. "And I'm not sure about all the law enforcement in the state, but in my book, that would make you a prime suspect."

"That's preposterous."

I held my hands up in surrender. "It is what it is."

"But anybody could have killed Clifton. I mean, anybody who listened to that recording would know that it solved one of the more notorious disappearance cases in the early twentieth century."

"We'll see what the authorities think."

"That's crazy," he said, clearly worried.

"Well, I'll tell you what. I know the sheriff in New Kassel pretty well. And that's who is going to be hot on your trail, considering the murder of Clifton Weaver took place in his jurisdiction. So, you tell me what I want to know, and I'll be sure that the sheriff is fair with you."

"This is bullshit."

"Well, maybe," I said. "My association with you ends now."

I stood to leave, but he grabbed my arm. "No, wait," he said. "All right, what do you want to know?"

"Who was Belle having an affair with? That's the

245

key to everything. If I can find out who he was, I can really narrow down my list of suspects who might have killed her. As of right now, anybody in Progress could have killed her. Give me the name of her lover, and I'll bet it boils down to about five women."

He laughed and shook his head. "You have no idea what you're asking," he said.

"Why is it so hard? Do you know or don't you?"

"I know what my father told me. And a few of my cousins."

"Who?" I asked, swallowing hard, hoping like mad that he wouldn't say it was my grandpa.

"Scott Morgan."

I must have blinked three times at least. "Wait. You mean Belle was having an affair with her own father-in-law?"

"That's exactly what I mean."

Well, that sure as hell put a spin on things.

Twenty-two

After leaving Glen Morgan, I went straight to the Gaheimer House. Our meeting didn't take as long as I thought it would, so I had time to go to my office and check a few things before I went home.

Almost as much as my family, the Gaheimer House had been the center of my world for close to twenty years. This had been Sylvia's whole world, and I gladly shared it. The house itself might not have been magnificent, but for the time it was built, on the edge of the frontier, it really was something special. It wasn't the red brick and mortar or the flaking green paint on the trim of the windows that made it so special. Or even the hardwood floors and the wainscoting. It was all the stuff you didn't see: the years of love shared between Sylvia and Mr. Gaheimer, the house's involvement in the Underground Railroad, the countless number of homeless victims from the stock market crash who had sought refuge there during the Depression, and the overwhelming sense of "ground control" that it represented. Everybody knew the Gaheimer House was the center of New Kassel. The house was the repository of the histories of all the families that had come and gone in this town and the surrounding areas.

I forgot all of that sometimes and thought of it as just another piece of real estate that needed the foundation fixed, the trim painted, and the roofing tiles replaced, but it was much, much more than that.

In my office, I stared at the antique Rose of Sharon quilt that Glory Anne Kendall had made almost ninety years ago. I had debated whether or not to put it with the rest of the collection over at the Kendall home, but it had been a gift to Sylvia, and it had hung in my office forever. It got taken down every now and then and replaced with another antique quilt for a few weeks, while it was being cleaned, but I always made sure I put the Rose of Sharon back. It lent such a spark of cheerfulness to the otherwise cramped and cluttered room.

I booted up my computer and opened the file on the families of New Kassel.

Back in the seventies, during the nation's bicentennial, Sylvia had started collecting family group sheets and five-generation charts for all of the residents of New Kassel. Believe it or not, New Kassel was not the type of place that too many people moved to for jobs. My family happened to be one of the families that had moved here from someplace else, but such families represented about 10 percent of the population. Most families had been here since the 1920s, when New Kassel was a major stop on the rail line that ran along the Mississippi. When the train no longer stopped here, New Kassel had declined—that is, until Sylvia came along and turned it into an enchanting tourist attraction.

By gathering the five-generation charts and group sheets of the people who lived here in the seventies, Sylvia had been preserving the history of the town. Most of those people could trace their families here back to the mid-1800s, or at least to the turn of the twentieth century. So while my personal family charts wouldn't help anybody with the history of New Kassel, most of Sylvia's charts would. Not to mention that Sylvia had added a lot of her own research when working on this project.

I typed in the name Mercer and waited to see what came up. I clacked my fingers against the side of the computer while I waited for the information. Back in the seventies, before the age of genealogy software, genealogists recorded everything on charts. On a five-generation chart, a person puts his or her name in slot one, along with pertinent vital statistics, such as birth date and place, spouse, and so on. Then for generation two, he would give information for his parents; for generation three, his grandparents; for generation four, his great-grandparents; and last, for generation five, his great-great grandparents. When I first started tracing my family tree, I thought, Gee, I just want to get this five-generation chart completely full. Well, if you've done any research at all, you know you can't just stop there. If you know all the names of all of your ancestors for five generations, you should have thirty-one names on your completed chart.

A family group sheet is an individual's family. So, a group sheet for my grandparents would include all their vitals, plus information like their burial place, their occupation, et cetera. Then I would list all of their children, not just my direct line. If you do a group sheet on all of your direct ancestors, you can record who your ancestors' siblings were. Believe it or not, you can actually find out information on a direct ancestor by following the trail of one of that person's siblings. You never know who might have a family Bible, letters, or some other form of information.

When Isabelle Mercer's name came up, I wasn't surprised. Her family had lived in New Kassel during the first few decades of the twentieth century; that, I knew for sure. Unless Sylvia had submitted the information, somebody in the seventies or later had filled out a family chart for the Mercers. I glanced down at the name of the submitter. It was Frank Mercer. The chart was for the family of Huxley and Evelyn Mercer, whose children were Thomas, James, Isabelle, Lucille, and Grover. That meant Frank had to be a son or grandson of Thomas, James, or Grover. Frank Mercer's address was for Ona, a little bitty speck on the map just north of New Kassel. The town, situated on a bluff, had maybe sixty residents, a gas station, a church, and a little clock shop with cuckoo clocks sitting out on the front porch.

I picked up the phone to call him, then realized that even if he still lived there and still had the same number as the one listed on the chart, I shouldn't call right then, since it was at least eleven o'clock at night. Putting the phone back down, I pulled out some ancient volumes of biographies of the noted gentlemen of Granite County, Missouri. I love the way the women are never included in these old histories and biographies, except about three-fourths of the way through a biography, where it mentions whom the gentleman married. Then, more often than not, the woman is just named, and you get more information on her father than you do on her. It really irks me. It seems to me that women are treated as a footnote to history, when nothing could be further from the truth.

At any rate, I knew that Huxley Mercer would be in one of these volumes, since he'd been the mayor of New Kassel. Sure enough, there was even a photograph of him. The information included was typical of the biographies of that day. "Huxley Mercer was a noted and distinguished gentleman of great intellect and character. Educated locally in his youth, he later attended school in St. Louis. When he returned, he married Evelyn Geist and raised a very handsome and respectable family." It was full of the usual adjectives—*noted*, *distinguished*, and *respectable*, among others. I've yet to read a biography in one of these books that doesn't include those terms. It then went on to describe his religious and political preferences and his career as mayor, as well as giving a very brief history of his family. For example, it mentioned where his parents and grandparents were from and that they were part of the "esteemed Mercer family of Connecticut," as if that would mean anything to the average reader. It wasn't as if he were a Vanderbilt, for crying out loud.

I got lucky, though. At the time the biography was written, his daughter Isabelle was engaged to be married. They had to mention that, because she was engaged to a member of a "distinguished and esteemed" family in St. Louis. Her fiancé's name was Archibald Louis Patterson King III. A May wedding was planned. The ceremony was to be held in St. Louis, at the groom's residence on Westmoreland.

You don't realize how quiet a house is until somebody disturbs the quiet. I'd been happily reading along, and suddenly there was a loud knocking on the back door of the Gaheimer House. I jumped and let out a squeal, then felt silly. I got up to go answer the door, but and my cell phone rang at the same time. I skipped back into the office, picked my phone up, and flipped it open. "Hello?"

"Torie, where are you?" It was Rudy.

"I'm at the Gaheimer House, going over some charts. I was just about finished. Why? Am I that late?" I asked.

"No, no. You're not that late. Somebody just set off a smoke bomb in the stables."

"What?" I stopped in my tracks.

Another knock at the door.

"Yeah, it spooked the horses like crazy. And while we were all out trying to calm the horses down, somebody slipped in the house and ransacked your office."

The knock at the door grew louder and more insistent.

Chills scooted along my scalp. My hair moved involuntarily. "W-what do you mean?"

"Somebody was looking for something in your office!" he yelled.

"Okay, you don't have to scream." I stepped into the hallway and peered at the door in the kitchen.

"Well, you're not hearing me," he said.

"Are the kids all right?"

"They're fine."

"Is that a siren I hear?"

"Yes, the fire department is out here."

"Why?"

"The smoke bomb. Look, are you all right?"

Another knock at the door. This time, the curtains moved with the force of the knock.

"Can you stay on the line and call the police if you hear me scream?"

"What? What! Torie, God—"

I stepped toward the door and took a deep breath. Then at the last minute, I glanced around for some sort of protection. I grabbed the rolling pin off the wall and set my cell phone down on the counter. Grasping the end of the rolling pin, I yanked the door open and smacked Eleanore square in the forehead.

"Oh, for the love of God!" she screamed.

"Oh my God, oh my God, oh my God!" I said.

"You're crazy!" she screamed, holding her head. Her eyes were watering. "You're a menace. A plague!"

"I'm so sorry," I said. "Come in."

"I'm not stepping foot in any building that you're in ever again," she said, and raised her chin—just enough for me to see the huge goose egg that was forming in the middle of her forehead like a third eye.

"I really wish you would move to California . . . or Canada!" she said, seething.

"I said I was sorry. You know, you shouldn't sneak up on people."

"Sneak up! I was banging on the door!"

"Well, you shouldn't do that, either," I said.

She glared at me. "I just came by to give you the results of our national standings and the photographs of your kids in the horse show we had last fall."

"Our national standings for what?" I asked.

"For the birds that we saw on Olympic day."

"You mean we weren't the only town having a birding Olympics?"

"No, there were cities all over the country," she said as snottily as she could with a giant bump on her head.

"Oh."

"You really are a menace to society," she said and shoved a handful of papers and photographs at me.

"This couldn't have waited until morning?" I asked.

"I was excited. I saw your light on. It's not like we live in a big city. People can walk around here at night. We do it all the time."

I ran to the refrigerator, got out an ice pack, and handed it to her. "Well, you know, Eleanore, I was feeling pretty guilty about your forehead until you told me that you were out wandering around at eleven just to give me bird statistics!"

"You bludgeon me, and I'm the one to blame, is that it?"

"Well, something like that," I said.

"Stay away from me," she said and left with my ice pack.

"That's what I've been trying to do for twenty years!" I called after her.

I picked up the cell phone and said, "Hello? Are you still there?"

"Did you just maim Eleanore?" Rudy asked.

"Yeah, I thought she was the same person you just told me ransacked my office. Or a burglar."

"Does a burglar ordinarily knock?" he asked.

I was quiet a moment, contemplating that. "Well, it

wouldn't have happened if you hadn't just called and told me about somebody ransacking my house. You freaked me out."

"As well you should be freaked out. Can you come home now?"

"I'm on my way."

Twenty-three

As soon as I arrived home, Colin, Rudy, and Sheriff Mort were all thundering toward my car in the snow and the cold, their billowing away in puffy clouds. If it hadn't been for the fact that they were all upset—some more than others—I would have made some joke about how they reminded me of the zombies from some B horror movie. When I got out of the car, Rudy put his hands on his hips and said, "Thank goodness you're all right."

"Well, of course I'm all right. I wasn't here when everything happened. The question is, Are *you* all right? How are the kids?"

"I told you everybody's fine." Then he hugged me, but I could tell he was upset. It wasn't as if I had done anything to provoke this; he just needed to be angry with somebody in general. Quite often a spouse is the default punching bag.

"Why were you at your office this late?" Colin asked.

"I can be at my office as late as I want," I said. I'd say I was a bit defensive, but that would be an understatement.

"You should be more careful," Rudy and Colin both said at the same time.

"I can't believe you went off and met that cousin guy of yours without taking anybody with you," Colin chided.

"Wait just a doggone minute. I am a grown woman. I can go wherever I want. Hell, Colin, I've done far stupider things than this, and you know it," I said.

After a moment's pause, he said, "Well, that's true."

"See?" I said. I figured this was probably the only time that I'd be happy that Colin agreed that I'd ever been stupid. "There you go. In the grand scheme of things, this was barely stupid at all."

"All right, all right, I need to talk to Torie," Mort said. Rudy and Colin exchanged glances and then decided to leave me alone with Mort, although they took only about ten steps to the left and stood at the fence, watching the sheriff and me the whole time. Mort looked me straight in the eye and said, "What did you find out?"

"About what?" I asked.

"Somebody was after something," he said. "You have to have something for them to be looking for it."

"All right, I'm going to pretend for a moment that sentence made any sense whatsoever," I said.

"You know what I mean. What is it you have?"

"I don't know," I said. "Has anybody checked on my cousin Phoebe's whereabouts?"

"Why?" he asked.

"Well, whoever did this went to great lengths to

make sure he or she didn't actually hurt anybody. Not even the animals. Which makes me think it's somebody who knows me. Phoebe's crazy. She could think I have some information that I'm not sharing with her."

"I don't understand," he said.

"She's been working with Glen Morgan. Who knows what she's thinking?"

"What about Glen, anyway? He could have followed you, seen that you didn't go home, and then come out here to try to get whatever it is you have."

I shrugged. "It's a possibility."

"Is there anybody else I should know about?"

"Honestly, it could be anybody in the Morgan family. Somebody in that family doesn't want me to know either the truth behind the murder of Belle or the secret of who wrote some of the music. You know as well as I do that Clifton Weaver's killer was somebody in his family. It has to be one of the Morgans."

"So, where do we start?"

"With all the living cousins," I said. "I don't care how old they are, either. You don't rule anybody out just because they're old and feeble."

"And your cousin Phoebe," he said.

"Yeah, her, too. Although, seriously, Mort, I don't think she killed Clifton Weaver. She's out there and she can be petty, but she won't hurt any living things. She's a vegan."

"Right, I'm going to base my investigation on her eating preferences." He snickered.

"You know what I mean," I said.

"I know." He smiled then and glanced over at Rudy and Colin. Then he shook his head. "Call me if you find anything else out. I mean *anything*."

"I will."

"And you have no idea what the person was looking for."

A recording of "The Blood Ballad," I was fairly certain.

"No, not a clue."

Needless to say, sleep eluded me. So I got up and went to my office and decided to pore over everything I'd discovered in the past few weeks.

The copy of "The Blood Ballad" that I had made was safely tucked away in the locked desk drawer in the guest house at the back of the Kendall House. I had thought for a moment that since Glen Morgan was the only person who knew I had a copy of the song, the vandal at our house had to have been him. But then I realized that he could be working with any number of relatives or friends on this "investigation" of his, so he could have told any of them. And, seriously, if I'd been after the song, I would have assumed that the person who turned it over to the authorities had made a copy. So anybody trying to get their hands on this song could have just assumed I had a copy. So I was back to the fact that anybody could have set off that smoke bomb.

In truth, it could have been any one of several

people. Maybe there was a war going on in the Morgan family over who could get a book written faster. I realized there could be people involved that I knew nothing about.

Not to mention that whoever had the original would be in serious danger if anyone discovered they had it.

At 1:00 A.M., I plopped down at my desk, rubbed my eyes, and started going through papers. I moved aside the photographs and bird standings that Eleanore had given me earlier and then realized that I hadn't even looked at the pictures from the horse show. I glanced through them and found several of Matthew on Cutter. Basically, he'd gotten first place for riding around the ring without falling off.

The girls had competed in the egg race, where they'd had to hold an egg on a spoon while their horses wove in and out of plastic cones. The last one with an egg on a spoon won. You wouldn't think it would be that difficult a task, but it actually is. Cute pictures, I thought, and set them aside.

I found the photocopies of yearbook pictures that I'd made with Colin back when I first started investigating this case and we'd gone to Progress. I went through every face in the grade before Clifton Weaver, the grade Clifton Weaver was in, and the grade after him. In the grade after him was one of my uncles. I also found several of my second or third cousins scattered about in the different classes. Looking at a photo of the class the year before Clifton, I noticed somebody I wasn't expecting: Leo King. It didn't really surprise me, though. A lot of people from Progress move farther north to be closer to St. Louis, where there are better jobs.

I knew I was missing something, but I couldn't figure out what it was. I also knew that most likely I would never figure out who had killed Belle. It really could have been anybody. It could have been Scott Morgan's wife, Florence, or any woman who was in love with him, including my great-grandmother.

Sighing heavily, I glanced around my desk for some divine guidance, as if staring at the empty water bottle or the jar of antique buttons would suddenly help me figure it all out. Instead, I happened to get a really good look at the corner of one of the photographs from the horse show. I was fairly certain my mystery Percheron was in the photo.

Snatching the picture, I scoured it for a clue as to who owned the horse. The horse show had been sponsored by the Granite County Saddle Club and been held down on the fairgrounds in the southwestern part of the county. You couldn't get farther away from New Kassel and still be in the county. People from several counties all around had entered the show.

I got out my magnifying glass. I swore the horse in the photo was the Percheron out in my corral right then. It was in the distance behind Matthew. The owner, or the rider, was obscured by Cutter's hindquarters. I could barely make out the number on the saddle: 183.

All I needed to do was call up Bonnie Overkamp and

ask her who owned number 183, and our mystery horse would be solved. Bonnie owned the facilities where most of the horse shows around were held, and she always kept records of the shows. It would have to wait until morning, of course. It was far too late to call.

Twenty-four

The next morning, I called Bonnie Overkamp right away but just got her answering machine. I left a message and went about my business. On my list of things to do was Christmas shopping. Helen Wickland and I usually did at least one day of Christmas shopping together, because we needed each other in order to keep focused and sane while deep in the belly of the beast known as the mall. Neither of us liked big crowded places, and so neither considered it fun to make a trip to the mall in south county at Christmastime. And it wasn't as if I could just skip the mall, since my daughters had both requested items from Hot Topic, and there certainly wasn't a Hot Topic in New Kassel. If there had been, we'd have had little old ladies throwing rocks through the windows, I'm sure.

It took no less than twenty minutes just to get into the parking lot and find a space. The first thing we did was head to Auntie Anne's for a pretzel. Then we meandered our way down to the lower level, where Hot Topic was located. "I'm usually finished shopping by now," Helen said.

Helen and I go way back. The first time I walked

into her chocolate shop and ordered a pound of fudge, we clicked. Then I volunteered to churn fudge at one of the festivals, and our friendship was cemented. Believe me, you do a lot of bonding over stirring fudge for hours on end.

"No, you're not," I said. "You say that every year, but it's never true."

"Oh," she said, thinking about what I said for a moment. "You know, you're right."

"Me? I wait until the last minute, and I'm still usually a gift short come Christmas morning."

"You really are terrible," she said.

"I know."

We turned into the Hot Topic store and were greeted by a someone with five studs in his lip—no, wait, make that her lip—pink hair, and an eye patch. The Ramones were playing overhead, and Helen plugged up her ears with her fingers. "Hey, no, this is good music. Be happy they're not playing the scary stuff," I said.

"Oh. This is the good stuff?"

"Yes," I said.

"Okay, I'll try to remember that."

"Can I help you find something?" the girl with the eye patch asked.

"Yes," I said. I pulled out my list and read it off to her. "I need a My Chemical Romance T-shirt and a Kyo hat."

"Sure thing," she said.

Helen looked at me and said, "What the hell is a Kyo?"

"It's an anime character who evidently is an orange cat at the same time he's a teenager."

Helen appeared confused. "Do you find that the Japanese are a bit more . . ."

"You know, Helen, I don't question it. I just go with it," I said.

"And what's a romantic chemical?" she asked.

"A band," I said. "Let me do all the talking, okay?"

"Sure thing," she said.

"I still have to get *Naruto* wrist bands," I said to myself.

"Your children are so weird."

Four hours later, we had eaten cookies and pizza—neither of which was as good as what we could get in New Kassel—and we'd gotten separated twice. I realized then that cell phones definitely have their upside. Years ago, we would have just wandered around the mall lost; now I just picked up the phone and called her, and two minutes later we were back together.

The second time we got lost, we decided we'd been there long enough. Helen and I dragged ourselves from the mall, only to realize we'd come out on the wrong side. The car was way down by the buffalo wing place, and we were up by the bookstore. "I'm not walking back through there," she said. "I'd rather walk in the cold."

"Me, too," I said, and so we walked all the way around the mall in the cold, hauling what felt like 472 packages. And, of course, my cell phone rang. "Oh, Helen, can you get my phone? It's in my jacket pocket. . . . No, not that one, the other one. . . . That's right. Thanks."

"Hello?" Helen said. "Hang on."

Covering the mouthpiece with her hand, Helen said, "It's Bonnie Overkamp."

"Oh, well, put the phone up to my ear," I told her. "Hello? Bonnie?"

"Hi, Torie, what's up? We're not having any riding camps or classes for another six weeks," Bonnie said.

"No, that's not why I was calling. Back in the fall, when we had the horse show at the fairgrounds . . ."

"Yes," she said.

"I know this is going to sound strange, but can you tell me who the owner or the rider of horse number one eighty-three was?"

"Why?"

"Well, you may have heard that somebody dumped a Percheron at our place," I said.

"Oh, vaguely. Somebody mentioned that, but I thought they said you bought one."

"No, it just appeared at our house, and, well, there was a Percheron at the fall show that looks just like the one in our stables right now. Maybe they don't realize we have their horse," I said.

"I gotcha," she said. "No problem, if you can just hang on a second."

"Sure thing."

Helen and I finally made it to her car. She unlocked the trunk and took my packages, then handed the phone off to me. I helped her load up the car, waiting for Bonnie to return. "We should have bought some chocolate," Helen said.

"Why?" I asked, as if one ever needed to ask that question.

"For the wait," she said, and pointed to the line of cars waiting to exit the mall. "We could be here for eternity."

Bonnie came back on the line just as my call waiting clicked. I glanced at the caller ID and saw the number for Leo's music shop. In addition to having Leo record some of the music for my father, I had asked him to put a few things on DVD and CD so I could give them to my sister as a Christmas present. I assumed that's why he was calling. "Hang on, Bonnie. I've got a call on the other line."

"That's all right. I don't have those records upstairs, so it's going to take me a while to find them. I'll call you back when I get to them, okay?"

I just let the other call go into voice mail. "Sure, Bonnie. Look, I know you're probably really busy this time of year, but as soon as you can let me know, I'd appreciate it."

"I understand," she said. "It's not a problem."

"Okay, thanks."

Helen and I gave a collective sigh of relief when we passed the exit ramp on 55 for Meramec Bottom Road 55. That meant we were officially leaving the congestion of south county. Sure, parts of Jefferson County were congested, too, but not like the areas around the mall. With each mile south we traveled, we relaxed a little more, and finally we hit the Granite County marker.

"Helen, can we stop by Ona?"

"Why?" she asked. "You want to buy a cuckoo clock?"

"No, I want to speak to Frank Mercer."

"Who's that?"

I filled her in as best as I could while she made the appropriate turn for going to Ona. I didn't go into a lot of detail, but I told her about the recordings, Glen Morgan, the connection my family had with the Morgans, and the body of Belle Mercer Morgan appearing in Progress.

"You really do keep busy," she said.

"I would die of boredom otherwise," I replied, thinking of my stepfather. "You know, Colin hates being mayor."

"I know," Helen said, and put on her blinker. "Everybody knows. I mean, he's not slacking or anything. He's doing his job. It's just so uninspired."

"Yup," I said. Helen pulled into the gas station. "Okay, stop here. I'll ask if anybody knows where Frank lives."

Believe it or not, there are still places in America where you can hop out of the car and inquire about a local person's address. One time, at least ten years after my grandparents had died, I got lost driving around the hills surrounding Progress. I stopped to ask a woman for directions, and she wanted to know who I was and why I was wandering around "her roads." I

266

told her my grandparents had lived around there—which was at least ten miles from her house— and when I told her who they were, she suddenly smiled and gave me directions. In these rural communities, people know who their neighbors are. Or were, as the case may be.

I walked into the convenience store and asked the lady behind the counter if she knew where Frank Mercer lived. "Well, no, not exactly," she said. "Hey, Troy, come tell this lady how to get to Frank's."

"You go back out here, make a right, go up the first street that has a water pump in front of it. It goes back up on the hill, and his house is the first one on the right. Highest point in Granite County," Troy said.

"Thank you."

When I got back to the car, I relayed the directions to Helen, and within minutes we were pulling in his driveway. "I'm glad we brought your Jeep. That was a pretty steep hill."

"You don't say," Helen replied.

We got out of the car and noticed right away that there were two bloodhounds sitting on the front porch. The house was a stately white-and-black building with a wall of windows facing the Mississippi River and the state of Illinois. From Frank's driveway, you could see for miles. I glanced to the south and could see New Kassel in the distance. If I'd had a telescope, I most likely could have seen the Gaheimer House.

Frank Mercer had a well—most likely for decoration—sitting in the front yard. It was covered with Christmas lights. I glanced at Helen, who eyed the bloodhounds with quiet fear.

As soon as my hand touched the fence that enclosed the front yard, the dogs leapt to their feet and began barking.

"Gee, the guy in the gas station never mentioned anything about dogs," I said.

"You think they can jump the fence?" Helen asked.

"Nah," I said. Just then, they lunged for the fence, their heads coming as high as ours. We jumped back and squealed, and Helen made a mad dash for her Jeep. "Nice doggies," I said.

"Honk the horn," I called to Helen. I figured if Frank was home, he'd hear that for sure, but she didn't really get the chance to, because Frank opened the door and stepped out onto his front porch. He was younger than I thought he'd be. Frank looked about fifty-five, which meant that he had been in his twenties when he submitted the genealogical charts to Sylvia for the bicentennial. He wore a plaid shirt and jeans, and his thick hair was combed straight back.

"Can I help you?" he said.

"Hi, Mr. Mercer, I'm Torie O'Shea," I called out, trying to be heard above the dogs. "I'm the historian down in New Kassel."

He put his fingers to his lips and whistled. "Hansel, Gretel, go sit." The dogs instantly shut up and went to opposite corners of the yard.

"Come on in," he said.

I glanced toward Helen, who gave me a very firm shake of the head. She wasn't getting out of the Jeep. Smiling at Frank Mercer, I tried not to look in the direction of the dogs. I walked quickly to the porch and all but jumped inside when he opened the front door for me.

"Sorry about that," he said. "They don't know the difference between friend or foe until I tell them."

"Right," I said, wondering what in the world he needed to worry about in the first place.

"So, what did you need to talk to me about?" he asked, and motioned for me to go inside. He ushered me into the living room and we both sat down.

"I need to speak with you about your aunt, or maybe it's your great-aunt—Isabelle Mercer."

"What about her?"

"Obviously, you never knew her," I said.

"That's correct."

"I noticed you filled out a family group sheet back during the bicentennial, so I thought maybe you could give me some information. We think we've discovered what happened to her."

"Oh?" he said and leaned forward in his chair. I explained as much as I could as quickly as I could about how we came to find her under the bridge.

"She was wearing some jewelry. One piece was made in Wisteria. I've seen photographs of Isabelle Mercer and Belle Morgan. They were one and the same woman," I said.

"Doesn't surprise me."

"Why not?"

"I think my grandpa knew what happened to her," he said. "I mean, I don't think he knew she was murdered and buried under a bridge, but I think he knew that Belle Morgan was his Isabelle."

"Why?" I asked.

"Because one time I asked him about her. I guess I was about seventeen. I had to do a family tree project for Boy Scouts, or something like that. Maybe it was for school. Anyway, when I asked about her, the family clammed up. I got tired of messing with everybody and went straight to my grandpa. He answered all of my questions, and when I asked him what he thought really happened to her, he said, 'She found another family. Down in Progress. But I don't think she ever found happiness.' And that was it. So one day, Sylvia Pershing came around asking questions, and she alluded to the fact that Aunt Isabelle could have been the same woman as Belle Morgan. Then I realized my grandpa had known all along."

I thought about that for a moment. "But he never tried to contact her?"

He shook his head. "No."

"Why?"

"Evidently, there had been a huge fight at some point over the baby, and things were said that could never be taken back."

"The baby," I replied.

Frank smiled at me. "Isabelle's baby. You didn't know about it?"

"Know what? I don't know what you're talking about," I said.

"The reason her fancy fiancé called off the wedding was because she got pregnant by him."

"Wait," I said, holding up a hand. "Don't people usually get married because of a baby? You don't usually call off a wedding because of a baby. I'm confused."

"Well, her fiancé said that he could not marry a woman with a tainted reputation. And if she was pregnant, then she was tainted."

"Well, if he didn't want her tainted, then he should have kept his trousers on!" I said.

Frank laughed and nodded his head. "I agree wholeheartedly."

"Of all the nerve."

"You see why she was so distraught. All that time, she thought he loved her. And he did love her, as long as she didn't damage him. So he called off the wedding, and Aunt Isabelle was left pregnant and unmarried in the twenties."

"What happened?"

"Grandpa told her to go back to her fiancé and plead with him, which she refused to do. So Grandpa called his lawyers, and they sent her fiancé a letter saying that they would sue him and destroy his name if he did not marry Isabelle or support her and the child."

"Well, what happened?" I asked. Frank could not speak fast enough for me.

"Archie, her fiancé, replied in a nice letter that he could supply the names of at least three other men who would all claim they'd had their way with Isabelle, too, and that my grandfather could not prove he was the father of her baby."

"Oh my gosh," I said, and sat back in my chair.

"Aunt Isabelle said it wasn't true."

"But your grandfather didn't believe her," I said.

Frank nodded. "I know all of this because Grandpa confessed it to me. Said if he had believed Isabelle, she never would have left."

"Oh my gosh," I said again.

"And he was probably right," Frank added. "He always blamed himself. So much so that he felt the need to tell me. So that I'd know the truth."

"Did you tell any of this to Sylvia?"

"Ms. Pershing?" he asked. "Yes."

I thought about the chapter Sylvia had devoted to Isabelle Mercer in her book about unsolved mysteries. She had never mentioned any of this. Sylvia had decided to be discreet. Maybe in case Isabelle came back. There was no way Sylvia could have known that Belle Morgan was dead. So she didn't want to slander Isabelle any more than she had to.

I rubbed my eyes and sighed. "What happened to the baby?" I asked, realizing that neither one of Belle's two children was old enough to be the child of Isabelle and Archie. She did not come to the relationship with Eddie Morgan with a baby in tow.

Frank shrugged. "We don't know. Maybe she lost it. Now wouldn't that be horrible if all that big fuss was made and the baby never even lived."

Somehow, I didn't think that was the case. "Yeah, that would be a shame."

"So, she was murdered?"

I nodded. "Sadly enough."

"By whom?"

"I don't know for sure. I only know that it was a jealous woman. It seems Belle's choice in lovers didn't get much better as she went on. I mean, Eddie, her husband, was a good man, and I think she loved him, but evidently there was something missing."

"Either that or the other man was just really special," he said.

"Yeah, or that," I said. I couldn't help wishing I could bring Scott Morgan back from the dead so that I could jerk a knot in his tail. He deserved worse, and I was actually fantasizing doing much worse things to him, but jerking a knot in his tail would suffice.

"I can't thank you enough for sharing this with me," I said.

"I hope it helps."

"It helps a lot," I said. "You have a good day."

"And Merry Christmas to you," he said.

I hesitated at the door because both dogs perked up as my fingers touched the knob.

"They won't move with me standing here. Now, if you slapped me or something, you'd be lunch."

I held both of my hands up. "No, I'm not laying a hand on you."

He laughed, opened the door for me, and watched to

make sure that I got in the Jeep safely. Waving as I got to the car, I couldn't help but wonder what secrets lay in every house. I was willing to bet that in every home in America, somebody had a story to tell just like the one Frank Mercer had just told me.

Twenty-five

We had one more stop to make before going home for the day. Christmas shopping always made me feel like I'd just gone through boot camp in stilettos. I could not wait to go home and soak my feet and then shove the wrapping off onto Rachel, except for her presents, of course.

We pulled into Leo's music shop to pick up the DVDs and the CDs for my sister's Christmas present. Part of the reason that Rachel would be doing the wrapping was because I had a slide show to make on the computer for my sister, using these CDs, DVDs, and old photographs that I'd scanned. But I couldn't do any of it without the help of Leo's magic.

I walked in the shop, leaving Helen outside with the car running. Leo greeted me with his brilliant smile. "Glad you came by," he said.

"Me, too."

"I've got all of your stuff finished for Christmas."

"Leo, you're amazing."

"I try," he said. "Hey, I want to get together with your dad and do some jamming."

"I'm sure he'll be up for it," I said.

Leo pulled a big brown bag from under his counter and then rang up the bill for his services. As I gave him my credit card, my cell phone rang.

"Hello?"

"Torie, it's Bonnie. I've got that information for you. Number one-eighty-three was indeed a Percheron. It's owned by Leo King. His granddaughter was riding it that day."

"Leo?" I said.

"Yeah?" he replied.

"I, uh . . ."

The horse in my stable belonged to Leo King. That had to mean something. I couldn't remember exactly who it was, but somebody had suggested to me that the squatter in the woods behind my house had left his horse. Presumably because he could no longer afford to feed it.

What if the person who'd left his horse in my corral did so because he'd been interrupted? Leo might have ridden his horse out to my house because he could arrive without headlights, and if I heard a horse, I wouldn't think anything of it. Then maybe somebody came out and spooked him. Perhaps he didn't have time to grab his horse, so he left it behind, hoping we wouldn't recognize it as his. The other times Matthew had seen him out there, Leo might have been trying to figure out a way to get it back out of the corral without being seen. But why? Why would Leo King, of all people, be watching my house?

"I'm at Leo's," I said into the phone, hoping that Leo

wouldn't notice me falter in the conversation. "Well, thank you so much."

I clicked the phone off, slid it into my pocket, and tried to figure out what to do. I figured I could dial the sheriff 's office on my cell phone, but nobody would understand what was going on and they wouldn't know how to find me. I could call Helen! I thought. I didn't want to take a chance on dialing all seven digits of her phone number without looking and thus get the wrong number. I remembered I'd called her in the mall when we got separated. With the phone still in my pocket so that Leo couldn't see, I hit redial—a button I couldn't screw up.

My mind reeled as I tried to make a connection to Leo. Had I ever mentioned "The Blood Ballad" to him? No, and even if I had, what could he possibly want with it, aside from the fact that it was a piece of musical history? I had nothing else that he would be interested in.

Then I remembered. Isabelle Mercer's fiancé's name was Archibald something, something King III. King. Leo King. Could it be that easy? Had Isabelle given her illegitimate son his father's real last name? I almost laughed at the thought of it. If she had, she would have gotten the last word after all. What better way to slander Archie King than to give his baby his last name?

And then there was the fact that Leo King had gone to school with Clifton Weaver. So he knew the family.

"Leo," I said.

"Yeah, Torie?"

"Did you grow up around here?"

"I lived here when I was a boy; then we moved to Progress for a few years, then back here. Why?"

I shrugged. "Just curious. I thought your name sounded familiar, that's all."

He handed me back my credit card, and with a shaking hand, I signed the sales slip. Then I took my bag and mumbled a thank-you and headed for the door.

"So, what about that other recording?" he asked. "The old one you said had been taped a few times? When are you going to bring that in?"

Slowly, I turned and made eye contact. It might have been my imagination, but I could have sworn he was sweating. "Soon," I said.

"How soon?"

"Next week," I said, inching closer to the door.

"Well, I can't wait to hear it. Not every day you get to hear a song about—"

"A song about what?" I asked.

He didn't answer.

"Their names are on your birth certificate, aren't they?" I said.

Confusion swept his face, He was clearly unbalanced by my switch in the conversation.

"Your real parents. Who raised you? A cousin? A friend of the family? A member of the clergy? But on your birth certificate it states, plain as day, Isabelle Mercer and Archibald King, doesn't it?"

Leo pulled a gun from behind the counter. "I don't want to hurt you, Torie. I really don't. I've always liked you. But I want that recording."

"Is a recording worth killing over?" I asked, clutching my bag to my chest.

"It's a confession to the murder of my mother," he said. "This is my birthright. All of my life, I've just wanted to be able to claim what's mine."

"And what is that?"

"I am a part of the Morgan Family Players' legacy. In addition to that, I'm also entitled to the fortune from my father's family. But have I ever gotten any of that? No. I was raised in the orphanage here in Wisteria until I went to live with foster parents in Progress. Imagine my surprise when I got my birth certificate and learned of my true heritage. I was just miles from where it had all happened. And I was going to school every day with my half brother and sister! Do you know what that feels like?"

I shook my head because I didn't know, and it would be stupid to try to convince him otherwise.

"How did you know Isabelle Mercer was Belle Morgan?"

"Are you kidding?" he said, shaking. "Just look at her. Once I learned who my real mother was, I studied every photograph I could find of Isabelle Mercer. I even went to Sylvia Pershing, and she told me what she suspected, but by that point, Belle Morgan was gone, too. But that didn't stop me from learning all about her. And the music."

Come on Helen. Hear what's happening!

"I just want the recording, and I just want to set the record straight," he said.

"What record?"

"About what happened to my mother. I knew in my gut that she was murdered. Now you've got the proof, and I want it. You've got no right to it. I want to be the one to break the news to the world, not you. Not that pimply-faced Glen Morgan. It's my mother. I should be the one to write the book and set it all straight."

"Leo," I said, realizing that he had most likely killed Clifton Weaver to try to get "The Blood Ballad" from him, as well. If he could have gotten it from Clifton, then the only other person who would have known of its existence would have been the elderly relative who had given it to Clifton originally. All he'd have had to do would be to wait for the relative who'd had the recording all those years to die, and he'd have been scot-free. But it hadn't worked out that way. Clifton had already sent the recording to me. It was clear now that I was not the only one who'd heard it and understood what it meant.

"What are you going to do? You're going to have to kill me, because I know everything. That's the bad thing about when you start killing people. It just keeps on going. You have to keep killing more to hide the ones you've killed before. It's insane."

Just then, Helen's Jeep came roaring through the front window of the music store, crashing into the display of guitars and drum sets. I lunged for the ground, found a cymbal, and threw it at Leo. I guess all of those Frisbee games I played with the kids paid off, because I hit him square in the head with it and he went straight down, dropping the gun and calling out in pain. I scrambled to my feet, picked up the gun, and held it ever so cautiously above Leo's head.

"You okay?" I called out to Helen.

"I'm fine. Are you?" she said.

"Yes. No. Yes, all right, I'm fine. But how do you put the safety on this thing? I'm shaking so hard, I'm afraid I'm going to shoot him."

Twenty-six

Good King Wenceslas la, la, la, something, something pony, something . . .

I never could remember the words to that song. And just who the heck was King Wenceslas anyway? I'm a history major and can't tell you who he was, yet he gets forever remembered in a Christmas carol.

We were all gathered at my mother's house for Christmas. We'd already eaten dinner and we were about ready to open presents, when there was a knock at the door. I glanced about, wondering who it could be, since everybody, including my grandmother, was here. Well, I had a few aunts and uncles who might be dropping by, but they were unlikely to come until later.

To my surprise, standing in the doorway was Sheriff Mort with Glen Morgan.

"Merry Christmas," I said. "Are you under arrest?"

"No," Glen said. "I think we've discovered who killed Isabelle Mercer Morgan, and, well, I wasn't sure where your mother lived, and the sheriff knew, so he escorted me."

"Oh, do come in," I said.

They both came in and Glen asked if I had a CD player. My mother and Colin had one in the living room, so I showed him to it. He put the CD in and played "The Blood Ballad" one more time. The room was quiet with everyone in awe. It's not every day you hear a confession to a murder sung by the murderess. It was a bit of a downer, especially when it was played on the heels of "Good King Wenceslas."

"It's my grandmother," Glen said.

"What?" I gasped.

"Florence Morgan. I knew as soon as I heard the recording that that was my grandma's voice. To make sure, I took it to a couple of my cousins, and they all agreed. My grandma, I suppose, could take my grandfather's philanderings, but not when it came to his own daughter-in-law," he said.

"Oh, Glen, I'm really sorry."

He shrugged. "At least we know the truth. Half of the family isn't speaking to me, since this means our grandmother was a murderess. But it's the truth. And thanks for talking your sheriff into giving me the CD."

"You're welcome," I said. I can't say that I wasn't relieved that it was his grandmother who was the murderess and not my great-grandmother. I had been trying very hard not to judge what my family had done

281

before me. Whatever my great-grandma did or didn't do with Scott Morgan, I'm sure she ultimately had to answer for in some way or other. As far as my great-aunt being a Morgan, well, I'd decided to leave that alone, as well. If her children or grandchildren came and asked me for the truth, I'd tell them. But I wasn't going to go to them with any unpleasant surprises.

"Leo King admitted to killing Clifton Weaver," Mort said after a minute. "He said he really thought Clifton would tell him where the recording was, and he beat Clifton up trying to get him to talk. When Clifton wouldn't tell him anything, Leo hurt him pretty bad. Then Leo realized he couldn't leave Clifton like he was. Clif would go to the police, and Leo would go to jail for assault, so Leo killed him. Leo claims that he didn't realize how much damage he was doing to him—evidently, he used a bat—and was afraid that Clif was going to die anyway, so he put him out of his misery. The thing is, he was probably right. One of Clif's ribs punctured his lung. He probably would have died from that. Leo said he shoved Clif in his truck and took him to what he thought was a remote location, shot him, and then shoved him in a trunk. Well, you know what happened after that."

"Yeah," Mort said."

"So, did Leo just happen to have a trunk in the back of his truck?" I asked.

"He said he'd bought it at an estate sale a few days before, just hadn't taken it out of the truck, so he used it as a makeshift coffin. Anyway, after he fired the shots, he happened to see some sort of movement or light and realized that there were people—you and Eleanore—down below, and that's why he kept shooting. He said he wasn't trying to kill you guys; he just wanted you to leave so he could dump the body. But then he realized he'd fired shots, so he just had to dump the body as quickly as possible before somebody reported hearing them."

"Yes, but how did Leo find out about the recording in the first place?" I asked.

"He and Clifton knew each other, and they happened to run into each other somewhere, and Clifton mentioned that he'd discovered this recording. Clifton was scared for his life, because people in his family were very upset and didn't want this made public because it showed their grandmother in a bad light."

"His life was in danger all right," Glen added. "Just not from who he thought."

"Wow," I said. "That's really something. So why didn't Clif give it to Leo, if he was willing to give it to me?"

Mort glanced at Glen Morgan and back at me. "Clif wanted a nonbiased, nonrelated person to have the recording, and when he thought it was safe, he was going to have you do something with it."

"How do you know?" I asked.

"The relative who gave him the recording in the first place said the same thing. She has asked to remain anonymous. I'm assuming once Leo grabbed Clif and started asking him about the recording—with the help of a baseball bat—Clif knew he was in trouble. What was he going to do? Put you in danger by telling Leo that he'd sent the recording to you? He just shut up and took his beating."

"To save me," I said and shook my head.

"At any rate," Glen said, "I just wanted you to know who was on the recording and to thank you for all of your hard work. With this new recording and information, I've got a bidding war going on for the book. You sure you don't want to help me write it?"

"No, thank you," I said.

"I may need to get some info from you, though, on the Mercer family and all of that for the book."

"Anytime, just call," I said and held out my hand. He shook it and said his good-byes.

"Oh, Mort," Colin said, stopping the sheriff before he could leave. "I wanted to speak with you about that job."

"Oh yeah?" Mort said.

"I'm afraid I'm going to have to decline."

"Oh," Mort said, glancing at me with a confused expression. "But I thought . . ."

"I've decided to become a private investigator," Colin said.

"You what?" I all but screeched.

My mother's expression was a mixture of humor, dread, and exasperation.

"Yes, I'm going to look into it just after the first of the year," Colin said.

"Well, good," Mort said. "I wish you the best of luck."

I walked Sheriff Mort to the door. "Wait right here," he said. He went out to his car and brought back a white box. "This is for you."

"For me?"

"Consider it a Christmas gift."

"But . . ."

"You'll understand when you see it. It was my great-aunt's. She made them. She had no children, and so I thought it would be better off in your museum."

"Oh, well, thank you," I said. I opened the white box, moved the tissue paper, and found twenty quilt blocks that had been painstakingly appliquéd in a beautiful tulip pattern.

"I want to say she made them in the 1930s or '40s," he said.

"Well, thank you very much."

"Merry Christmas," he said.

"Merry Christmas."

I went back inside and decided it was time to give my sister her Christmas gift.

"Attention, everybody," I said. "Stephanie, we had a conversation a few weeks ago about how you wished you could spend one day with our grandparents at their house. Well, since Sears didn't have any time machines for sale this Christmas, this is the closest I could come."

Rudy hit the lights, and I started the slide show that I had put together. I had made a master CD of all the old recordings I had of my family on a Christmas like this, where Grandpa was talking about baseball and

Grandma was singing a carol in that high-pitched voice of hers that could shatter glass. In the background, one of my cousins ran through the house yelling, "She poked me in the butt!" While this recording played, I began the slide show of photographs of times spent at our grandparents' house.

To make things more realistic, I had enlisted the help of my family. Dad lighted up a pipe with tobacco like Grandpa had used. Rachel brought in a freshly baked cherry pie and carried it past Stephanie. Then Mary brought in an open jar of mincemeat and one of strawberry preserves—my grandmother's specialties. Rudy rocked in the rocking chair to add to the sound effects. More music started, recordings of our dad and his brothers. I loved these recordings made in the front yard or the house because you could hear the brothers talk back and forth when a song was finished or cuss if they messed up the song. Then Grandpa started playing his fiddle. He played some little ditty and then he said, "That's how they used to play it when I was a young'un."

Then my childhood voice came on and whispered, "Merry Christmas and to all a good night!" A photograph of Grandma and Grandpa waving from their front porch was the last image in the slide show.

When the lights came up, Stephanie was in tears. "Torie, I . . ."

"It's as close as I could get," I said.

"This is the greatest gift I've ever been given," she said, swiping at the tears on her face.

"I'm glad you like it," I said.

I looked over her shoulder at the picture of my grandparents frozen on the screen. It was obvious from the lyrics of "The Blood Ballad" that Florence Morgan had spent the rest of her life running from the face of the dead, but I hoped the faces of my grandparents would stay with me forever.

Center Point Publishing
600 Brooks Road ● PO Box 1
Thorndike ME 04986-0001 USA

(207) 568-3717

US & Canada:
1 800 929-9108
www.centerpointlargeprint.com